CW01663480

PAGAN REVENGE

Sam Taw

This is a work of fiction. Names, characters, organisations, places, events, and incidents are either products of the author's imagination or are used fictitiously.

Cover art supplied by Carantoc Publishing Ltd
First edition, 2020
ISBN 978-1-9163059-2-2
Carantoc Publishing Ltd.
www.carantocpublishing.com

Please note that this novel was created by a British author. Except for Cornish words, slang and dialogue, spelling and grammar are corrected to **British English**. There are also scenes which may offend more sensitive readers. It is not deemed suitable for children.

To my incredible family.
My love for them is beyond description.

CHAPTER ONE

The encampment was vast. From what I could see, their rawhide shelters almost covered the valley floor. Some of the more permanent structures were constructed with woven hurdles and thatched with cut peat turf. Those were the huts for the important family elders. Great fire pits roasted whole goats, with rows of rabbit and hares suspended above. Their smith's clanging hammers jarred my senses, and filled me with dread.

At the far end of the camp, I could just make out the lines of young warriors practising their skill with axe and blade. Beyond them, the women strung new bows and cut lengths of wood for arrow shafts. Every clan within their tribe busied themselves with stern expressions and a determination that sent a chill right through me.

It was as though the entire Durotriges Tribe had emptied their lands to settle along the border. This was no temporary camp on their way to another destination. This was a community built for one purpose, to revenge the death of their beloved Ruvane and wife of the Chieftain, Wenna.

Tallack and I lay on our bellies at the peak of the escarpment. Below us lay the largest of the tents. Outside its entrance was a platform of rough-hewn wood, with three tall chairs in its centre.

"I had no idea that their tribe was this large." Tallack grumbled.

"They have our Priest Clan to swell their numbers, don't forget." I scrambled along the edge, hiding on the leeward side of rocky outcrops and boulders to get a clearer view.

Tallack was close behind. "Glad to see the back of those kyjyans. Nothing but hemp addled troublemakers."

I tried not to roll my eyes, but he was testing my resolve. "They're still warriors, with vengeance in their hearts and sharp blades in their hands. We could have handled that whole affair better." I used the term, we, in its loosest possible sense, for we both knew at what I was driving. Tallack and his twin brother had declared the leader of the Priest Sect guilty of fouling our water, with a swift and brutal punishment.

Beheading the old man sent a ripple of discord through their clan. Banishing them to the moors with their half-brother to lead them, was a mistake. It needed thought and consideration, but my dear nephews are young and inexperienced. Sharing the role of Metern to the Dumnonii came too soon in their lives. Their father had little time to ready them for such responsibility.

"Should have let Blydh kill that back-stabbing kyjyan, Paega as well as his grandfather." Tallack spat on the floor. It was as though even speaking his half-brother's name left a nasty taste in his mouth.

"What's done is done. Can't change the past." I squinted in the low sunlight, assessing the numbers of fighting men among the community of old, women folk and children. Paega was hard to miss, waving the long silvery sword about that once belonged to me. Seeing him with it brought back memories of my slave, Jago. I'd asked him to hide it in an abandoned mine shaft at the Bentewyn mining settlement.

There was only one explanation for how it came to be in the hands of Paega. He must have followed my slave boy and stolen it away as soon as Jago was clear of the tunnel. Jago would never have betrayed me. He was true and courageous. He hated Paega as much as Tallack, particularly as he treated slaves with such hostility and contempt.

"I have to say, they've got a pretty neat set up here; all the smiths and livestock downstream of the fletchers and carpenters, the families upstream where the sweet water flows." Tallack pondered out loud. "It's such an efficient system."

"Well, while your admiring them, perhaps you'll take note of their stockpile of weapons. They're not here for the scenery." I couldn't help but be sharp with him. "You think that dullard of a Chieftain organised all this? That's your lover down there calling all the shots." I gestured towards the young woman sitting at the side of the tallest chair.

Brea's fine tunic and expensive jewels showed her lofty status within the tribe. She must have taken advantage of the Duro Chief's grief and swooped in to offer comfort and succour. No other explanation fit for how she came to be in such a prominent position so soon after Tallack refused to bind with her. Tallack said nothing. His thoughtless actions had brought about so much sorrow and pain.

I let the matter drop. My own decisions have been similarly poor of late, and the urge to make restitution gnaws at my innards daily, but how can I tell the Chief a secret which I know could ignite his temper and result in his hatred of me? I blocked it from my mind. We had more urgent business with which to tackle.

"We must hurry back to the camp on the River Exe and warn the others. The Duros have at least three warriors for every one of ours." I glanced at my nephew. He didn't look worried in the slightest that their neighbours and enemies were gearing up for slaughter, and that they were better equipped and more prepared than his own tribe could ever be. Was this the hubris of youth, or sheer ignorance of battle on such a huge scale? His lack of reaction was deeply concerning. How could I make him see the dire situation we now faced?

Tallack scurried back towards our horses, tethered in a sheltered dell. "We should poison their water supply and kill off as many as possible while we're here."

I scoffed, treading on a high rock to heave myself onto the pony. "How do you propose we do that?"

"Same way that the priests did on ours at the mining camp, shove a load of rotting carcasses in the flow upstream."

"Don't be daft. Where would we get rotten meat from? Besides anything else, not even Paega is dumb enough to fall for that. He'd recognise the signs. And before you ask, no, I don't have a poison strong enough to taint the brook. Forget it." I mounted my steed and arranged my bundles around me. My medicine kit and knife wrap were all that I had left in the world, other than a couple of ratty old furs.

Without thinking, I glanced about for Jago. It was a habit of making sure he was near me before setting off.

For that single moment, I'd completely forgotten that he'd perished on the fateful trip to the healing stones at the top of the world. A wave of pain and anger swept through me. I wanted nothing more than to be left alone on some tor in the middle of the moor to cry out my anguish.

"If not poison, we should find a way to dam the supply. With no water, they'd be forced to move on." The young Chieftain smiled. One of those mischievous grins that made it impossible to be annoyed with him. He always knew how to get around me, even when I was feeling my most belligerent.

"Fine, since we have to ride that way anyhow. Let's just hope that it doesn't encourage them to shift even closer to our compound." I kicked my heels into the horse's flanks and clicked my tongue to hurry the animal along.

We rode side by side at a brisk canter, over the arid peaks and boggy valley floors of the moorland, until we could no longer spy the shelters from the Durotriges camp. Taking great care to avoid the patrols of scouts posted as lookouts on advantageous peaks, we picked our route along the water course, until Tallack could see a suitable way to divert the stream.

From a high tor at the edge of the moor, he spotted an opportunity. "There." Tallack pointed to a tight meander in the shallow waters below running through a narrow gap in the valley. "If we stack those rocks up to form a dam, it will sink into the banks either side and form a new pond."

I thought about his suggestion. "There is just one small flaw in that plan. The waters below this point are fed by lots of marshlands and peat bogs anyway. They will still get some water to the camp, but it'd be dirtier."

"Better than doing nothing at all. Come on, Aunt Mel. Why are you arguing with me on this?"

I knew that he'd been tolerant of my glum mood for the entire trip back from the Skotek Isles, but I couldn't shake myself from mourning the loss of someone so dear to me. Tallack was the joint Chieftain of our tribe, and as such, commanded my respect. He and his father before him, allowed me such privileges on account of my useful skills as a healer. I'd like to think it was also because I'd had earned a lifetime of wisdom and esteem from all the tribal elders. Discord between us had always been short lived and met with patience and forgiveness.

Seldom did he treat me as though I was of lowly status, demanding that I observe the titles and hierarchy. To both he and his brother, Blydh, I was simply Aunt Mel. To the rest of our people, they came to call me Fur Benyn, or wise woman in our tongue.

This day, I was in no mood for conflict. I led my horse down into the valley after him, and stayed mounted while he hefted the stones about the river bed. The early spring warmth of the afternoon sun did nothing to take the chill from the water. Tallack's hands reddened and his joints locked up in the icy stream. Twice he bashed his fingers between the rocks, before muttering curse words and blowing on them to restore the blood flow.

Stifling a cackle, I knew that I ought to get off my horse and help him, but watching his clumsy efforts was more fun. Guilt was beginning to get the better of me, when I heard the heavy hooves of many horses, thundering towards us. Tallack was still knee deep in the gully, hoisting another rock into place. I whistled, gaining his attention. He shrugged.

"By Cernonnus, boy, can't you hear that?" I hissed at him.

"Almost done. One last stone should do it." He waded back to the side of the stream and reached down to clasp his fingers around another rock.

"Leave it. They'll be on us in moments. Move!" Dragging his horse closer by its reins, I urged the headstrong Metern of the Dumnonii out of the frigid water before we were discovered. The noise grew louder. A hunting party were bearing down on us at a gallop.

The first I saw of them was the chalky dust kicked up by their horses along the top of the ridge in the distance. Luck was with us. We had just enough time to dash into the cover of the trees at the side of the vale. Hiding among the thicket of scant shrubs and small trees, we did all we could to silence and steady the ponies, in the hope that the hunters wouldn't notice the new dam in the stream and descend into the valley to investigate.

The Durotriges are skilled with horses like no other tribe. Folk say that their children learn to ride before they can walk. Their territories support enormous herds of wild horses roaming the plains. Unlike we Dumnonii, they have no need to breed their stock. They can ride out at any time to round up a stallion with all his females ready to break into work. That's unless they stray into the much larger territory of the Belgae. If that happens, they risk the wrath of another enormous and powerful tribe if they decide to retrieve them.

The closer the hunters came to our copse, the more I had to fight against praying to our gods. Since the ordeals at the top of the world, I struggle to believe they even exist. I can't think why they would be so cruel to us mortals unless it was solely for their entertainment.

As the party of hunters drew level with our position on the valley floor, one near to the back of the crowd pulled on the reins of his horse.

The hunter came to a full stop, churning up the thin soils under his horse's hooves. His head was shaved at both sides, leaving a long thick tail bunched from the top of his head. To me, it looked no different from the arse of his pony. Perhaps that was his aim. As comical as he looked to us, it was clearly not shared by those in his party. He possessed a high degree of authority over his men, for they too noticed his decision to remain still. They turned their horses with some difficulty on the ridge top and trotted back to his position.

I stared for as long as my old eyes could cope without watering, but I couldn't figure out what they were watching. Was it the slight movements of our horses within the shelter of the bushes, or something else that had caught their attention?

"I think we need to prepare ourselves for the worse, Aunt." Tallack whispered, unsheathing his short sword from its scabbard hung from his pony. He moved to the edge of the copse and crouched down as the riders dismounted and sneaked a little way down the hillside. There was no way Tallack could fend off such a large group of seasoned warriors. I prepared myself to surrender or to accept the end of my long and tiring life, when I saw two of the men nocking arrows into their bow strings.

They aimed further down the valley from us and let loose. As their bolts found their targets, I realised that they'd spotted a family of hares. Two lay dead before them. I pulled Tallack back into the cover of our trees and directed his gaze to their catch.

"They haven't seen the dam, keep your head and we'll escape without any trouble." I muttered. Sure enough, the hunters collected the hares and strung them to the rest of their catch. Pleased with themselves, they galloped off towards camp, leaving us dizzy with relief.

"Nothing like a near miss to get your heart racing, ay Aunt?"

I blew out my cheeks. "Can we head home without any more of your crazy stunts to put us in jeopardy?"

Tallack chuckled and helped me up onto my horse. We raced off as fast as we dared into the next gorge in a southerly direction. Despite the lengthening days, light began to fail before we could get near to the compound at the River Exe.

We made camp for the night, safely within our own territory and well beyond the moors. Tallack traded a small quantity of tin for a couple of eels from the fishermen where the River Creedy twists itself about the bends of the River Exe. They're not my favourite food, too many bones for my liking, but after all the watery porridge and scrawny game, it made a nice change.

Tallack built up the fire and watered the horses, while I mixed up a bit of flat bread to cook ready for the morning. It was all the flour I had left, but I figured we could afford to use it up, being so close to home. Neither of us had much conversation left that night. I sensed that Tallack was just as apprehensive as I, now that we'd had time for everything to sink in.

He finally understood the peril our people faced, with the tremendous horde of Durotriges on our border, led by a wild and vengeful Chieftain, and advised by the most traitorous woman from our family. She may be Ordoviches Tribe by birth, but we welcomed Brea into our tribe as one of us. Well, most of us did.

Being so close to the site of our old Chieftain compound made me anxious. I could hardly sleep, despite the warm fire and the full belly. I had held on to the secret about Brea for too long. Only she and my slave knew the nature of her treachery. The more I ruminated on it, the more I realised that I had to come clean. Both of the young warriors needed to know the truth, no matter how they might react, or what punishment they may exact upon me.

At daybreak, we ate the hard flat-bread and bundled our furs back onto the ponies. We were on the homestretch of our long journey and Tallack was keen to see his kin. I dawdled, knowing what lay ahead of me. My meal lay heavy in my gut as it churned to give me discomfort.

We followed the course of the river, cutting across the meanders to save time. I tried on several occasions to stop and harvest the early spring growth for my medicines, but Tallack wouldn't indulge me. He began to suspect that I was causing the delays on purpose.

There seemed little point in angering him further, especially in light of what I had yet to tell him and his brother. As we passed through the last bend in the forest, I was shocked to find that our new compound which Blydh had pledged to rebuild with his warriors after the raiding party of Duros had burned it down, was barely complete.

It had no gates, nor watch towers. The tall fence was not yet half finished and there were few huts with roofs or walls. It looked little more than a travelling camp. From my nephew's expression, I could see that he was seething with anger. What had Blydh done with his time since we parted?

I could see that Tallack was spoiling for a huge row with his brother. That would make them even less receptive to my news. What punishment would I have to endure for withholding the name of their father's killer?

CHAPTER TWO

We trotted into the compound without anyone noticing. It was bad enough that there were no proper defence structures to keep our people safe, but to have no one on guard was far worse. As much as I wanted to get my secret off my chest, now was not the best time. Tallack kicked his horse and cantered through the boggy ground towards a small cluster of shelters. I watched him jump from his pony as it skidded to a halt. He poked his head through the closest of the tent flaps. His wild roar of anger brought many of the warriors out into the open to see who was causing the commotion.

"Where is my brother? Blydh, show yourself." He bellowed, moving to the next tent in his search.

Blydh wandered up from the bank of the stream carrying the bloody haunch of a deer. "Ho there!" He grinned, speeding into a run. "Well met, dear kin. You took your time."

Tallack fumed. His fists tightened at his side; his fast panting whistled through his nose as I caught up with him. "What do you call this?" He raised his arms at the state of the unfinished compound, the massive midden piles and the disorganised state of his lazy warriors.

Some lay drunk outside their tents. Others lay on their bunks smoking hemp pipes.

"What? We have made good progress, don't you think?" Blydh dropped the meat and his knife, ready to embrace his brother.

"This is not progress. This is a kyjyan mess. Why are your men lounging about doing nothing? Where are the watchmen, the smithies, the kyjyan fences? You didn't even have scouts out warning you of our arrival."

"They're out hunting. There aren't many of us to do all the work." Blydh said, crestfallen. He approached me and touched his forehead to mine. "It's good to see you, Aunt. I was beginning to think you'd abandoned us. When Tallack's crew returned with the copper supplies, I was sure you'd been eaten by wolves or captured by the Skotek tribes at the top of the world. Come and tell us about your adventures."

I stayed quiet. The boys had to work this dispute out between them. It was not for me to get in the middle.

Tallack rounded on his brother. "Where are my men? Why didn't you command them to help you build?"

"They unloaded the copper and returned to your ships. They told me that you'd ordered them to make repairs over the winter." Blydh's temper altered. As far as he was concerned, he'd kept faithful to his brother's orders.

"I did no such thing. Have someone fetch them. They'll be flogged for this deceit."

I hoped that Tallack would simmer down in the time it took to fetch his crewmen from the banks of the river near to the estuary. We needed to keep everyone on side if we were to defend ourselves against the Duro attack. Having his men whipped would only turn them against us.

Tallack tried to cool his anger, but his tone of voice remained harsh. "You have been here for many moons since riding from the mines at Bentewyn. Why is the compound not finished? Have you any idea the size of the Duro force gathered at our borders?" He hissed the words across clenched teeth. I stepped back, fearing it may come to blows.

"The Duros won't attack until spring is full here. The catkins are barely out, brother, there's plenty of time to prepare." Blydh retrieved his blade and leg of venison, intent on continuing his butchery.

Tallack was too full of angst to form his words. He looked to me to convince Blydh of the urgency required in making battle plans. As loath as I was to speak, I knew that my words still carried weight.

"Nephew…" I called to Blydh. He turned back to face me. "Your brother speaks the truth. We have ridden south across the moors along our borderland. The Duros have amassed a mighty army of warriors, who as we speak are forging new weapons and training for the war ahead. It is not hard to see that they intend on slaughtering us all, and taking over our entire territory, mines and all." I scrutinised Blydh's expression. He had grown soft over the winter. His face had lost its lean appearance, the muscles in his arms and legs were weak and unused. His brow pinched in a frown as he listened.

"You have made an admirable start on rebuilding our home, but we must concentrate the entire tribe's efforts on reinforcing our defences and stockpiling our food." It was as gentle a scolding as I could manage. He was, after all, one of our leaders. It would not do for him to lose face. I ambled closer to him and rested my head on the side of his shoulder.

Without thinking, he put his arm about me and squeezed. "I'm glad you're back, Aunt. We've needed the voice of reason around here." Blydh steered me away from his ranting brother. "Come and see the hut I've had built for you and mother. I even had a crib made for the little one."

I didn't have the heart to tell him that a compound under attack, or siege even, was no place for Cryda and their tiny little sister. She hadn't even been given a name. The entire situation required careful handling, and I was too tired to argue. I let my nephew take me to a fine new hut, with the fire stones laid neatly in the centre and a hurdle enclosure outside housing three goats. He'd thought of everything.

"Where is your hut, Blydh?" I looked up at his vacant eyes. There was a hollowness about him, as though he cared little about the duties laid at his feet.

"I have my tent. It's all I need."

I patted his chest as we entered the shelter. "This is a real home, Blydh. Your mother and I will be very happy here. Thank you." His face lit up as though he'd been given a collar made of pure gold.

Pleased with himself, he swept aside the skins covering the doorway. "I'll send one of my warriors with a stack of wood for your fire."

He almost made it outside, when I felt compelled to call after him. "You will make things right with Tallack, won't you? He can't lead this war without you."

Blydh stood still for a moment, considering my words, then left me alone. The hut was much larger than my old home. There was space for everything, even a bunk to tend the sick and injured. He really had thought of everything. A part of me was grateful that I could languish in my grief in such luxury, while another part wished he'd used the time and the wood to build a perimeter wall around the compound.

Tallack continued shouting his orders at Blydh's men and causing more rancour between them. I should have picked my old bones up and smoothed over their disagreements, but I didn't. The size and emptiness of the hut just reminded me of all that I'd lost. Herbs can be collected anew, seeds sewn, pots moulded and baked, tinctures and balms mixed, and skins cured, but no one could bring back my Jago. I took my furs from my pony and set him loose to graze by the riverbank, then returned to the new bunk to sleep.

It was dusk when I awoke. Without a piss pot, I had to venture out into the cold to relieve myself. The sky was clear and the grass was already freezing close to my door. Just as Blydh had promised, there was a stack of wood against the side of my hut, beneath the overhanging eaves of the thatch.

I could see that most of the men were sitting around a huge blaze, roasting the deer and swapping stories together. I took that to mean that the twins had put aside their differences and that work would begin in earnest on constructing the defences in the morning. It didn't take me long to build a fire and climb back into bed.

When the moon was high in the sky, Tallack entered my hut and shook me awake. "Aunt Mel… are you unwell? Why didn't you come to eat with us? I saved you a nice hunk of venison with roasted bull rush roots."

I pulled my furs up over my head. "Not hungry."

"But you haven't eaten since that tasteless flat bread. Are you sick?"

"Sick of life, that's all. Go be with your friends. Your crew will be keen to see you."

"You shouldn't say things like that. Cernonnus might hear you and carry you away in the night to the Underworld." Tallack warned. It was something I used to tell him as a child whenever he said something unkind about his siblings and friends. He was trying to make me laugh, but nothing would melt my gloom.

"Maybe it's time he did take me away. I've had a good life. These days are for the young to shape."

"What utter kawgh! I need you to snap out of this, Aunt Mel. You're the only one who can get through to Blydh. You know what's coming for us. Please, Aunt Mel." He leaned in closer and whispered through my furs. "You have to guide us, even when we think we know better, like you did for our father."

I lay still under my furs. It hadn't occurred to me that Aebba's sons would notice my tiny nudges and course corrections whenever he was being stupid. His wives had little impact on his drunken ideas and foolish quests. I thought I'd been more discreet than that. Was he trying to shame me into helping him or liberally applying salve to my ego? He almost had me roused into action, until he mentioned the cause of my malady.

"Look, if it will make you feel better, I'll ride out tomorrow and buy you a new slave. Two if it pleases you, but you have to pull yourself out of this misery. We'll need your healing skills as much as your wisdom." When I failed to move, he grabbed the edge of the furs and uncovered me. I gave him my blackest scowl and let my bones fall limp as he tried to pull me up out of bed.

"Grrr! Have it your way, but starving yourself is a terrible way to die." He clomped across the rushes on the hard-packed floor and left.

Come morning, I heaved myself up and peered outside. The entire compound was filled with frozen mists against the orange glow of a low sun. It gave the whole valley a magical feel to it, as though some mystical creature might swoop down and pluck me off my feet while I crouched in the long grasses. As I staggered back towards my bed, I could hear the bustle of men at work, sawing, chopping and yelling at each other in the fog. Tallack must have stirred the warriors into work. Both he and Blydh would have to manage without me one day. I cannot live forever.

Lifting the door skins back with an armful of logs for the fire, I saw a brace of ducks hanging under my eaves. Someone had left them there for my supper. I cast my eye about camp, but saw no one other than my own shadow. The kindness was wasted on me. I had no appetite. With the logs piled high on the fire, I drank a little stale water from my travelling bladder and returned to my bed.

All morning I napped between the disturbance of horses trotting past my hut, of axes falling on tree trunks and of hammers clanging in the new forge. Cursing my nephews for their tardy start to rebuild our community, I stuffed what cloth I had in my ears and tried to will myself back to sleep. Nothing seemed to shut out the noise. In a bitter mood, I dressed myself and sat by the fire sulking.

I could hear rustling and coughing outside my hut, but assumed that it was more of Blydh's men shifting willow withies and posts for construction, until I heard a young voice call out.

"Pardon us, Fur Benyn. May we enter?" It was a girl's voice.

I sighed. "Are you sick or injured?"

"No, Fur Benyn, neither." A boy this time, but high pitched as though his voice had not yet broken.

"Then get off with you. Go on, scram!" It went quiet for a few moments. I expected to hear them moving away. Instead I heard them muttering to each other next to the doorway.

When I lurched at the door flap and drew it back, I immediately felt wretched. These filthy children were no more than skin and bone, their clothes in tatters and barely enough to cover them, let alone save them from the cold. I took in a slow breath of air.

"Where have you come from?" I asked, cautiously examining them for signs of ague.

"Our owner from the large homestead on the other side of the river gave us to Chief Tallack in tribute. He sent us to you." The boy said, casting his eyes down at his feet. The girl was less cowed by my gruff manner.

"What are your names?" I looked at the girl first, narrowing my eyes. My she was a wilful one. I could just tell by looking at her.

"Finola." She stared right back at me.

I had to stop myself from grinning. "That's not a Dumnoni name. Where are you from?"

"Stolen away from my mammy in Iwerdon."

"Hmm." I glared at the boy. "And you? What do they call you?"

"If it pleases you, Fur Benyn, you can call me Jago."

That was all I could take. "Oh no. Scat, be off with you both. Tell Chief Tallack that I don't want you."

The boy fell to his knees in a fit of tears. "Please, don't send us away. We'll be beaten. You can call us whatever suits you. We'll do all your washing, hunt for your supper, anything, please." The streaks of tears left clean patches on his grubby face.

It was a pitiful sight. The girl folded her arms across her chest. She was not bothered in the slightest at the prospect of a beating. No doubt she had suffered far worse in her time. Most slaves did. Softening a little to the child's plight, I dragged him to his feet by the scruff of his tunic and told him to dry his eyes. With my wooden pattens covering my feet, I marched them through the mud to the bank of the tributary that brings our water. Here I found a number of row boats tied to a jetty, and a young crewman whom I knew vaguely.

"Treeve, isn't it?"

The lad jumped up from the boat and straightened his backbone, though he barely stood taller than I. "It is Fur Benyn. Is there anything you need?"

"Only the whereabouts of Chief Tallack." I growled.

The young sailor pointed to a tent further along the bank. I nodded my thanks and prodded the slaves in the same general direction. When we were outside the shelter, I bellowed my nephew's name at the top of my voice. He came running outside as though his arse was on fire.

"What? What is it? Are the Duros raiding us?"

"Not yet, but you might wish they had by the time I'm done with you." I shoved the slaves towards him. "You can't just replace one slave with another and expect my grief to disappear." I began to walk away.

"But I thought you'd be happy with my gifts. They will take care of you until you feel better."

"I'm not ill, my Chief." I said the last bit in such a spiteful way, he looked hurt. "And mind you don't beat them or I'll know about it. It's not their fault that their Chiefs are kyjyan idiots." No one followed or rebuked me. I had little hope left in me anyhow. My heart was broken. I thought then that they may as well do their worst. I got a couple of cart lengths away and then I turned and shouted. "When you find your brother, bring him to my hut. I have something important to tell you both." Trudging to my shelter, I started to have doubts about my plan to tell all. What if they decided that my punishment was a slow and agonising death rather than a quick beheading? The boys were keen on making an example of their enemies, not least the woman they drowned at the low tide mark after I had falsely accused her of murdering their father. Had I sealed a similar fate for myself, or worse?

I paced about my hut and built up the fire to keep busy and take my mind off what I had to do. Unrolling my knives, I was about to collect the ducks to prepare them for a meal when Blydh and Tallack arrived. Their glowers were not surprising, given the way I had treated them both. Rather than coming straight to the point, I found myself blathering about their gifts and apologising. It turned out that I didn't want to die after all.

"I am sorry for my dreadful mood and the way I have behaved. I am grateful for the hut and the wood, the slaves and the ducks, it's all far more than I deserve." I took a deep breath to steady myself.

"What ducks?" Tallack looked at Blydh who shrugged. "What critical thing did you need to tell us both?"

There it was. A direct question that I couldn't avoid. It was now or never. "Your father's second wife, the Lady Eseld did not murder him. I made a terrible mistake. Brea poisoned his stew and cast all suspicions her way. Like the old fool that I am, I was taken in by her schemes and planted evidence." The Chieftains stood by my fire, each with their mouths gaping in disbelief. When Blydh's brow wrinkled up with a seething fury. I knew that I'd lost their favour.

"Go ahead." I stated. "I deserve it, but I beg you to make it quick." I closed my eyes and jutted out my chin, expecting to hear him unsheathe his blade.

CHAPTER THREE

The longer I waited there with my eyes tight shut and my knees trembling in fear, the more I was convinced that they would make me suffer. When I heard my bunk creak, I opened one eyelid and peeked out. Both of my nephews sat on the edge of my bed. Neither had their swords in hand. Confused, I looked at both of them to judge their state of mind.

Tallack seemed to be near to tears. Blydh smouldered with a burning hatred, but whether that was for me or aimed at Brea, I knew not. Afraid to break the spell and send them into a spiral of killing, I didn't move.

In the low fire light, Tallack twisted to face his brother. "Father is not in the Summerlands with our ancestors. He roams the Between Worlds still."

Blydh nodded slowly. "We killed the wrong wife."

"At least you didn't sleep with his murderer." Tallack rubbed his forehead, gently shaking his head. "What have we done?"

This, I was not expecting. They appeared to be taking the entire blame on themselves. Daring not to move, I waited. There was still time for them to take out their malice on the stupid old lady who believed the lies of our arch enemy.

My mistake cost more than their father's entry into the Summerlands, it sent his killer into the arms of the Durotriges. With her guidance, they would have the location of every one of our settlements, all their weaknesses and treasures. In holding my tongue for so long, I had set loose a stone-cold killer.

"Why did you not tell us, Aunt?" Tallack enquired.

"Jago and I saw Brea drop a hair clip he'd made for the slave cook, Gwyn." I began.

"The one who made delicious squirrel stew?" Tallack asked.

I nodded. "Brea murdered her to stop her from telling me that she'd seen Brea dropping berries into the stew pot. We only found this out after you had carried out Eseld's punishment on the beach. She made it clear that if Jago or I said anything, we would be next." The relief of unburdening my secret to them was immense, but short lived. Now that they had the facts, I was sure that Blydh would dispatch me with a single glancing blow of his short sword. My mouth dried and I was dizzy with panting.

Tallack pulled a quizzical face. "So, when you fell from the cliff side and almost died, that was Brea too?"

"She stamped at the loose soil beneath my feet and down I went. She tried to poison me as well, if you recall." The trembling inside reached my arms until my hand shook violently in fear. I was a wretched bag of bones, but it was only fair that I take my punishment as any other from the tribe. Staring down at my feet, I was ashamed to meet their gaze. Blydh may have softened of late, but in his heart, he takes the mantle of my brother, Cador the Cruel. They spoke quietly in front of me, but as though I was not present.

Blydh still fumed. "We should whip her in front of the tribe."

"She's an old woman! That'd kill her."

"She has to be punished, or the tribe will think us weak." Blydh growled.

"None of the tribe know about Brea, only us. Aunt Mel will never do anything so foolish as to keep information from us again, would you?" He turned to me, raising his voice.

I shook my head. "No, never. I promise."

"And we can make her tend the sick and wounded as her penance. Let's face it, she did try to warn me about Brea's duplicity after the fall, but I dismissed Aunt Mel as raving from all the poppy resin she'd taken." Tallack said. I saw in those glistening eyes that he pitied me. He and I had been through so much together. He understood and forgave me.

"She'd heal the injured anyway. It's what she does. That's no way to make her suffer." Blydh's coldness returned. It made me shudder.

"She's suffered enough, believe me. Anyway, we need her. My Chiefly decision is to keep this knowledge between us, and stop wasting time on trivial squabbles when we have a battle to prepare for." Tallack stood up and embraced me.

Blydh stayed sitting on the bunk. "It's not my decision, and I am just as much Chieftain as you."

"Please, brother. In her position, I'm not sure I would have done anything different." Tallack squeezed me so tight, I could scarcely breathe. Nonetheless, I was comforted by his strong arms about me. I freely admit that I shed more than a tear or two.

There was an awkward silence between the twins. It chilled the air about us, until Tallack changed the topic of conversation. He and I alone knew the extent of the Durotriges force. Blydh needed to know what we were up against.

Tallack released me and faced Blydh. “How long will it take for your men to complete the perimeter walls?”

“Now that your idle crew are working alongside mine, it should be finished within a couple of days.”

Prudence would have encouraged me to keep my mouth shut. Unfortunately, I have never had an abundance of that. “It won’t be enough.” I whispered.

Tallack rested his fists on his hips and frowned. “What was that?”

“My apologies, Nephew, I mean not to interfere in your preparations, but I have seen all this before in my father’s day. The walls are, of course essential, but they would not stand up to a prolonged attack with fireballs.” I couldn’t look either of them in the face, their collective power was humbling.

The two Chiefs considered my statement for a moment. A quick glance in Blydh’s direction and I saw his expression of annoyance, but he didn’t tell me to be quiet. As much as I infuriated him, he could not doubt a whole lifetime of experience such as mine.

Tallack encouraged me to speak up. “What do you suggest, Aunt?”

Emboldened by Tallack’s support, I kicked the rushes to one side, exposing the compacted mud beneath us. Taking a chisel from my knife wrap, I scored the path of the river tributary and sketched out the position of where the gates used to be before they were burned in the raid. My suggestion to them, was to move the gates further out, giving the compound a larger space to accommodate more warriors inside.

"But that would take another quarter moon or more of hard labour." Blydh snarled. "We don't need so much room. The warriors have their tents, they can double up or more if necessary."

Tallack interrupted him. "I think what Aunt Mel is saying, is that we need to train up more warriors. We must send out parties to gather up the boys and workers from the homesteads right across our territory."

Blydh's face slackened to neutral. I couldn't tell what was running through his head, but I had to make our vulnerabilities absolutely clear.

"Not just the boys," I said, glancing between them. "We must train the women too."

Tallack laughed.

Blydh scoffed. "Now I know you are addled. Have you been smoking stink weed?"

"You have grown up during the peaceful reign of Aebba. He grew fat and complacent because every other clan needed our tin and wanted to trade. He forged new allies in binding ceremonies and with privileged deals for our metal. Your warriors patrolled the borderlands and had a ruthless reputation. That was not the case in your grandfather's day. When Cador reigned, every man, woman and child in a tribe were given an axe as soon as they were large enough to wield one. These are no longer peaceful times. All must fight, if we are to prevail against the Duros."

The twins locked stares. They knew I was right, but the thought of arming women as weak and cosseted as their little sister didn't sit well with either of them. I needed to push the suggestion further.

"Tallack, you remember how we were attacked that night in the woodlands on Cornovii land?"

"I do. It was a blood bath."

"And yet Idina of the Catuve-Llaunii took most of our enemies down with her archery skill. At the very least, teach the women to make their own weapons and shoot."

Tallack sat next to his brother on the bunk. Both listened without further interruption, as I mapped out training grounds, covered battlements and a large ditch to surround the wall, filled from our diverted stream. Everything I could recall from my youth, I relayed to my nephews in readiness for the worst.

It surprised me how receptive they were to my ideas, but then they were hardly new. My knowledge was passed down from my ancestors like in any family. Mine just happened to be leaders of a mighty tribe of the South-West. While they talked over my scratches in the mud, I went in search of food. The ducks at my door were now plucked, gutted and hanging by their feet on one side of the eaves. On the opposite side, split logs and kindling for the fire. Who was supplying my needs like this? I ventured forth in the hope that I could trade for a little bread.

The mud through the central thoroughfare was horrendous. Blydh cared not for what he considered to be inessential compound things, like boardwalks. To him they took too much time and materials to construct and were not needed for battle. How could I make him see that having them was crucial?

Without boards on which to tread, people strayed onto grassier areas to avoid being bogged down. Within a moon's cycle, the entire compound would be a giant mud pit. All about me I saw chaos and confusion. I began to think that we would never be ready in time to fend off attack.

There were few women in camp from whom I could trade for bread or flour. Those I asked, told me that they were down to their last bag of grain and could not spare any, even for a large quantity of tin. This was not good news. This camp was not just lacking defence, but also food. If we were to endure a potential siege, we'd be eating rats within the first quarter moon.

We were too few to make headway on all that needed to be done, and of those of us who were left, many were young and inexperienced. I took a detour to see how the smithies were getting along. Only one man hammered now, another worked the bellows while the rest stripped wood for handles. There were no more than ten bronze swords and axes ready for use. Even at a distance, I could see that they had few resources to make enough to supply the new recruits. This camp had no direction at all.

By the time I arrived back at my shelter, Tallack was sitting crossed legged on the rushes, jabbing at the mud with one of my knives. I peered over his shoulder, looking at the crosses he'd marked out beyond my moat. "What are they?"

"Ramparts and embedded spikes to impale their horses." Tallack said.

Blydh seemed especially agitated. "There's no time for all these elaborate plans. All we need is trained men. I'll ride out with a team of my warriors and gather up whoever we can find. That's the one thing I agree with so far."

"No, the defences are crucial. We must protect our people. The Duros have the numbers and speed. All we have in our favour is a defensive position. We need ramparts and battlements as well as the ditch." Tallack's voice rose in pitch and volume. Had they been arguing the whole time I was out searching for food?

Frightened of losing their favour, I kept quiet and busied myself with the ducks. The fire rekindled in no time. While the boys debated their various stand points, I roasted the birds and passed them a jug of goat's milk. Both refused, expecting me to conjure ale from thin air. There was so much work to be done. I had almost no herbs left, no jars or pots and not a shred of cattle gut for stitches. The whole enterprise was overwhelming.

Their disagreements were taking an unpleasant turn once more. Tallack favoured building my defences, while Blydh stood firm on creating a sizable army to train. I couldn't see a way to compromise. Turning the roasting ducks, a half turn on the spit, I took my tin purse and went to find someone who might trade for ale. Taking a longer, drier route, I made for the row boats at the jetty.

Young Treeve welcomed me, commenting on my drab tunic as though it belonged to a Phoenician Prince. For the life of me, I couldn't figure out his motives. He's an odd little fellow. He offered me a large pike for trade, but with two ducks cooking nicely, it would start to rot before it could be cured. Anyway, I had no salt with which to preserve the thing. I was beginning to wish I'd stayed at the Bentewyn mines. Having to start all over again from nothing was exhausting.

Eventually, the lad pointed me to a shelter where he said I could trade for a jug of ale.

I approached and called out next to the door flap. "Ho there! I come to trade ale for tin, if you've a mind to?"

You could have knocked me down with a feather when Renowden appeared from under the skins. "Fur Benyn. It's good to see you."

"And you too, Ren. How come you're back so soon? I thought you were on Faolan of the Novantae's ship, sailing around Land's End."

"Aye, that I was. They made port at Bentewyn to trade for tin and supplies. I rode on like the wind from there. They shouldn't be far behind me. Day or two at most."

"I came to trade. The Chiefs are arguing in my hut. I figured that ale would ease their tempers."

"Both Chiefs, you say? Tallack and Blydh are there?" He seemed greatly perturbed.

"They are. What of it?"

"I must speak with them urgently. There is much to say." He ducked back into his shelter and returned with a jug of ale. I offered him tin in exchange but he would not take it from me. We hurried back to my hut through the boggy ground. Twice my pattens were pulled from my feet, slowing our progress to a grinding halt.

Thank Cerridwen that he was there to help me free my shoes and lean on while I put them back on my feet. If only Blydh had worked his men harder over the winter, the camp would be further along, and we'd all be less anxious.

"What has got you all in a state, Ren? I've never seen you anxious before."

"Begging your pardon, Fur Benyn, but it's best if we wait until we're with the Chiefs. I'll explain everything then. Weighed down in kawgh and filth, we scraped what we could from our feet and leggings and entered the hut. Both the chiefs were standing nose to nose in a heated discussion. I'd seen these spats before but none were this fierce. It looked to me that it would end in blows.

Taking the jug from Renowden, I did my best to barge the two warriors apart. "Excuse me, Nephews. I need to reach the cups over there. Good old Ren has brought you ale and some important news."

The Chiefs stepped back allowing me passage to the back of the hut. Each of them greeted Renowden in our customary way, grabbing one another's forearms securely and nodding.

"Well met, Ren. You made incredible time. How on earth did you get here so fast? Where are Faolan and his son?" Tallack said, surprised to see his old crewman.

"Rode like the wind from Bentewyn, swapped my horses for tin thrice on the way, to bring you the news. Faolan stayed longer to trade, they'll pick up the tide when they've restocked."

I served them cups of ale, watching them stepping over the mud map of the compound to sit by the fire.

"Come on then, man. What's so important that you've knackered up horses to get here so quick?"

Renowden took a great gulp of his ale and looked at each of the Chiefs. "We tried to stick within sight of the coast from our northern border to Land's End, but you know what the currents are like in that stretch of water…"

Tallack nodded. "I do. Can be nigh on impossible to fight the northerly slipstream."

"Well, we were tacking as best we could against the wind, when night fell. I suggested that we put in to land and start afresh at daybreak, but Faolan wouldn't hear of it. Insisted we sailed on through. Anyhow, come dawn, I could tell that we'd been blown off course. We were headed for the Iwerdon coast." He took in more ale and a deep breath. "That was when we saw the Ivernii ships."

Blydh wrinkled his nose. "So what? Probably fishing or delivering their copper for trade to the mountain people."

"They weren't fishing, nor were they low in the water like they carried metal in their hulls." Ren stared Blydh right in the eye without flinching. "They were practising boarding other vessels at sea and manoeuvring in defensive lines."

Tallack's eyes widened to the size of dishes. "You think they are readying for attack?"

"I do, Chief. That's exactly what I think."

CHAPTER FOUR

There was stunned silence for a while. The men absorbed Renowden's news with a surprising degree of calm.

Tallack picked up the stick from the floor and rooted about in the fire ashes. "So, we have a fleet of angry Ivernii headed for our southern coast and a gigantic horde of trained warriors ready to kill us all on land."

"That about sizes it up, yes." Blydh said. He finished his ale and handed me the cup. "There's no time to waste. I'm taking my men to round up as many people to fight as we can find."

Tallack stood up to block him. "We need your men to build the defences."

Ren looked to me to break the deadlock.

"Split the tasks. Tallack stays with his crew to build, Blydh take as few as you can manage with to get more folk to train. Men and Women, remember." For once, neither of them argued. I received a curt nod, before they rallied to their tasks. Ren stayed with me a little longer. When the boys had gone, I poured him more ale.

"How many ships are we talking about here, Ren?"

"More than we've got, although they're nowhere near as large or well built."

"You think we can take them on without too many losses?"

Ren shook his head. "If what you say about the Duro's on the border is right, most of the crewmen will be needed on land to fight. We can't hope to be in two places at once."

The man had a point. I sat next to him by the fire and plucked a roasted leg of duck to give to him. "Is there a solution?"

He took the meat and smiled. It was juicy and tender. I sliced a hunk off the breast for myself.

He swallowed his mouthful. "I was wondering if we can form an alliance with the Novantae. Faolan had more than one ship, and they were all large and sturdy crafts. His men are also fearsome warriors."

It was a sound idea, but for the fact that his people and their fleet were at the top of the world. When I mentioned that, he reminded me that we had sailed from the west of Skotek to the northern coast of Dumnoni lands in record time. It would be quicker to sail north to fetch his men, than it would to train up the youngsters from the local homesteads.

"I see what you're saying, and it would be an excellent idea, but for one fact. We have nothing to offer Faolan in return. Why would he risk his people and his ships to help protect our lands? From his perspective, he could simply wait until the Duros or Ivernii took over our tin mines and trade with them instead."

Renowden nibbled the last fragments of meat from the bones and licked his lips. "We've nothing to lose in asking."

"Might be better if you mentioned it to Tallack. I think the boys have had enough of their interfering old aunt for one day."

He squinted down at the map of the compound, twisting his head this way and that. "What are the crosses there?" He pointed with the stick that Tallack had used.

"Those are covered watchtowers."

"And the line here?"

"The tributary to the Exe."

He scratched his beard and pulled a face.

"What?" I asked. I knew Renowden to be far wiser than he ever let on. Tallack trusted him above all others of his crew. His mature years made him the ideal navigator on Tallack's voyages along our trade routes. He knew every bit of our coastline as well as the back of his hand.

"It's just, if we move the entire camp to the other side of the tributary, it would form an island with the main river on the other side."

I peered down at my map and then trawled through my memories to where he could mean. There was an entire section of land walled off by the diverging streams. It was criss-crossed with smaller water courses too. For the life of me, I couldn't think why the compound was not sited there in the first place.

"But they have already begun patching up the walls, not to mention this hut and a couple of others."

"So? It's not as though they'll have to cut down new trees to make the fence, well maybe a few. They can unearth the old trunks that did not succumb to the fire and use them again. I'm guessing these scratches are ditches? Imagine the time saved by not having to dig those."

I thought long and hard about his plan. Every obstacle I threw at him, Renowden had a solution. It made perfect sense. With the number of people we hoped to bring into the compound for defence, we'd need a larger space anyway. Even the materials of the hut we sat in could, to a certain extent, be used a second time.

"We should go and find Tallack." I said, standing to leave.

Renowden poured another cup of ale and handed it to me. "Give him a little while to settle back in, Fur Benyn. I dare say he'll want some time with one or two of his men." One of his eyebrows rose and there was a twinkle in his eye. He knew how my nephew's tastes strayed beyond that of women.

I rolled my eyes. "Do I know him?"

"Treeve." He chuckled.

"Is he likely to cause problems?" Tallack had a knack of stirring up trouble with his wayward loins.

Renowden shrugged again. "He seems like a nice enough lad, but you can never be too sure."

I returned to my seat and tucked into the ale and duck. It was the best thing I'd had in a long time. "I'll catch the Chief later, if you like. He'll be in a better mood by then."

As we ate and drank, we heard Blydh's warriors leaving for the homesteads. Their tradition of whooping and hollering as they left and arrived in camp, always struck me as odd. Underneath it all, Blydh was a quiet young man. Not one for glory and praise.

His brother, on the other hand, was quite the opposite. Get Tallack telling a tale or two and he would sing like a nightingale all night. It was the first time I had truly relaxed in some time. In Renowden's company, I had no need to explain my sullen mood. He knew all too well of my loss, but he had sense enough not to discuss it with me. For that I was grateful.

At length, when we'd eaten our fill, I pulled on my cloak and pattens and together we went for a stroll around the edges of the island. Crossing at the eastern side, where the shallow tributary flattens into a gravel bank, Renowden paced out where he thought a gate would be best placed, flanked either side by watchtowers. We walked on passed low shrubs and small trees which were hemmed in by yet another small rivulet.

"This water here is crystal clean. Come spawning season, we'll have salmon jumping right into your hands first thing when you wake up." He said, gesturing to where he thought I should relocate my hut. "I reckon the new long hut should be in the middle though, don't you? That way, you wouldn't have the drunken louts and warriors waking you at all times of the night." On we walked to the northern point of the island, where the main river branches. "You see how the men could clear the trees from over there, giving the watchmen a clearer view of oncoming raiders?" He said.

"It's deep though, Ren. What if the Ivernii took their vessels up here during the night and climbed our walls?"

"Good point, Fur Benyn. Then how about we put gates and towers up this end as well, but with a bridge on weighted ropes and pulleys? One tug and the bridge would stand up on its end. We could have a second one on the eastern side too."

"They could still sail up here in the dark."

"Not if we drive pointed logs into the river bed to rest just under the water level. If they sail this length, they'd be sunk in no time, giving the watchmen time to raise the alarm."

All the way around the island, we picked out problems and put our minds to solving them, so that by the time we'd reached the southernmost point, where the two water courses merged again, we had the entire compound and adjacent training grounds all figured out. With hope growing in my heart, we crossed back over the gravel beds and walked towards the jetty. Blydh had not gone with his men. He stood shouting at the sailors, directing and ordering them to leave their boats and join the remainder of his men working on the defences.

Renowden looked at me and I him. This would not be an easy discussion to begin. Before we even approached Blydh, Renowden pointed out a runner crossing the clearing from downstream. He knew the boy from Faolan's ship. He came with a request to send the row boats into the estuary to fetch them.

With all the row boats sent downstream, Blydh seemed to brighten. Just when I expected him to rage against more time wasted, he did the opposite. Curiouser still, he pulled off his cloak and tunic, leggings and boots and began washing himself in the stream. Renowden and I stepped closer.

"What nonsense is this? Are you addled with ale, Chief?" I asked, using his title for the benefit of Ren.

"I stink, Aunt. It's sweaty work building stuff."

We watched for a short while, thinking that it had to be part of some prank. When he failed to shift from the water, I judged him to be almost happy. There was no better time for us to speak with him about Renowden's idea.

Taking a cautious approach, I started. "You know, Renowden here has had the most brilliant idea that could save your men days of work."

Blydh sat in the freezing stream rubbing under his arms with soapwort from the banks. "Uhuh." He seemed open to the idea as bit by bit we explained in further detail, making sure to accentuate the benefits and play down the fact that his men had spent time during the winter repairing our old compound wall. When we said all that we intended to, Blydh climbed from the stream and began walking towards his shelter.

"Well, Nephew? What say you?"

"Fine, do it, but I'm putting you pair in charge of the whole development, the working parties, the food, everything. I have warriors to train." He didn't even look backwards as he hurried off shouting, "And you can persuade my brother too, stubborn kyjyan."

That was all it took. He disappeared into his tent and left everything to us. "Well, Ren, seems like you've been promoted to second in command, or third, if you count both Chiefs." Poor man looked like he'd had all the stuffing knocked out of him. "Have you had any sleep since your return from Bentewyn?"

He shook his head.

"And you rode non-stop all the way on three different horses?"

He nodded.

"Then go back to my hut and get your head down. Let me worry about Tallack and the working parties." He didn't argue with me. In fact, he looked relieved.

Down at the jetty, I asked one of the sailors who hadn't taken the boats to the estuary where to find my nephew. He snickered behind his hand and then pointed to a tent not far from Blydh's. I was almost loath to disturb him, knowing how he might be spending his time, but there was work to be done and he had responsibilities. Dragging my heels, I made it across the clearing to his tent and coughed loudly.

"Tallack. I need to speak with you urgently. Please can you come out here?"

There were a few giggles and the sound of things being knocked over and then just his head popped out from the tent flaps. “Yes, Aunt, can’t this wait?”

“No, it can’t. Put your clothes back on and walk with me.” I must have used my officious tone with him, since he disappeared for no more than a moment, and returned wearing his leggings and carrying his tunic over his arm. I led him back across the gravel bank to the island and explained Renowden’s plan, followed by a detailed description of our run in with Blydh in the stream.

When I got to that part in my story, Tallack accused me of exaggeration. No amount of assurance would make him believe me, until he caught sight of his brother leaving his tent sporting a massive smile.

Our interest piqued, we followed him as he sped along to the jetty wearing a clean tunic and leggings. He stood on the riverbank, shielding his eyes from the bright rays of the setting sun. The row boats were on their way back, carrying a great many more people than we expected. Tallack and I joined him in greeting our visitors. Among the party was a young lady I knew well. Kerensa was the daughter of Kenver, the leader of the Alchemy Clan at Bentewyn.

Before the row boat was even tied off, she launched herself onto the jetty and into Blydh’s arms. Now the cleanliness and smiles made sense.

“How long has that been going on for?” I asked Tallack.

“I didn’t know it had begun.” He smirked at his brother and watched him throw his arms about the young woman before kissing her.

“How would Blydh have known that she was aboard?” I asked.

Tallack shrugged. “Maybe they agreed that she’d follow him at the first opportunity.”

Blydh and Kerensa remained on the river bank long enough to welcome our guests and family before they scuttled off to be alone.

Luckily, Tallack was there to take over the formalities. He clasped Faolan’s forearm and slapped his back, the pair of them almost in a dance together. Ealar was next, Faolan’s youngest son. To him, Tallack embraced as a child, which from where I was standing, was not received well.

The twin’s mother, Cryda began whining the moment she set foot on dry land. “Here, Meliora, take the babe will you. She’s done nothing but grumble and puke all the way here.” Cryda dumped the infant in my arms and warned her son of the milk sick down her front. Anyone else would have been put out, but despite all our past differences, I’d missed her. The child was rosy cheeked and healthy, gods be praised.

Derwa and her husband from the mountains, both looked green. I approached her to rest my forehead against her, but she stopped me with a raised hand.

“I wouldn’t if I were you, Aunt Mel.” She swallowed, dipping her chin to her chest. “I don’t suppose you have anything to settle my stomach, do you?”

“Sea sickness, or are you with child?” I asked her, lifting her baby sister up with a smirk.

Her Ordoviches husband, Glaw, scoffed. “Only by an act of the gods could she ever be with child.” He strode off towards a crowd of men drinking ale, leaving me with my niece.

“Don’t mind him. He’s sore because I told him that I won’t share his bed ‘cause he stinks.”

There was little use in chiding her. The match was a disaster from start to finish. It was only a matter of time before it came to blows. Which of them would survive was anyone's guess.

The old Skotek wolf, Faolan scanned the activity in and around camp. "You have much to do here I see, and few shelters. I should bring more of my men ashore to lend a hand."

Tallack was taken by the idea, thanking the Chief of the Novantae for his offer of assistance. I bit my lip, wondering if this was the best use of their time. Stuck between the formalities of greeting a tribal elder and sticking my nose in where it was not wanted, I chose the latter.

Tugging on my nephew's tunic sleeve, I muttered into his ear. "I'd appreciate a moment alone with you Chief, it won't take long." Offloading the babe to Derwa, I pulled Tallack aside and briefly told him of Renowden's suggestion to forge formal ties of allegiance with Faolan and the Novantae, to help us win the war.

"I can't see him agreeing to risk his men and ships out of friendship. We already have a trade alliance of gold for tin. What more could we offer him?" Tallack said, keeping his voice low.

"You could give him your fine Phoenician ship in payment, or more tin if we can spare it." I rasped back. My desperation was justified. With the Durotriges outnumbering us, and the Ivernii fleet at our backs, we needed all the help we could get.

Tallack looked as though I'd offered him up for sacrifice. "That's my ship you're talking about. It's the finest and fastest in the whole land. Not for an entire fleet filled with gold would I part with that. It's more precious to our tribe than mere metal."

"What else do you propose? We cannot fight the Ivernii and the Duros alone. We are too few."

Tallack had no answer for me. He stood for a moment thinking, glancing about at the wood cutters and hurdle weavers scattered about the place. With a mild shake to the head, he could see that I was right. Whatever thought landed in his mind, it stirred him into action.

Returning to the welcoming party, Tallack invited Faolan and his son, Ealar, to join him in a cup of ale. They walked towards Blydh's tent where a large fire roared outside and logs were piled in a rough circle for his warriors to sit and share a pipe or two. This was a place for men to chew over the problems of the day. I knew that it was frowned upon for women to join them, but I went anyway. I had to hear what was said.

Tallack sent young Treeve to fetch cups and ale, and then dragged his brother out of his tent to join in the discussions. I stood behind Tallack, hoping that none would pay attention to my presence. Treeve poured all the men their drinks, and one for himself, before squeezing his rump down between Tallack and Blydh on a large log.

Faolan raised his bushy brows at the youngster's impertinence, but it went unnoticed by my nephews. That was their first mistake. I prodded Treeve in the back, encouraging him to leave the circle. He swatted me away as though I was a fly.

Tallack took charge of the negotiations, knowing the wise old Skotek Chief from our time in the north. He explained our situation, pointing out that if the Durotriges should take control over our lands and mines, they would most likely punish our allies with heavy levies and taxes on tin trades. I winced at his admission. This was not the way to secure his favour. It was more likely to make him side with the Duros against us.

Tallack's inexperience would be our downfall. Blydh remained suspiciously quiet. From his expression, I realised that he did not trust our Skotek friend. We were more vulnerable than ever. If Faolan and Ealar decided to take control from within the camp, they need only unsheathe their swords and they could take the heads of both my nephews in a single swipe.

Faolan gulped down the ale and rested his cup on his knee. "This is a good brew." He licked his lips and considered the young Chieftains before him. "If I understand you correctly, you want me to fetch my boats all the way from the top of the world, with as many of my warriors as they can carry to fight your war for you?"

"With us, not for us." Blydh corrected.

"And what would you ask of us in return for your assistance?" Tallack ventured. He'd put us in an untenable position. We were begging for help. The old man could take what he wanted and we'd be powerless to stop him.

CHAPTER FIVE

Faolan spat into the fire and stood up. He looked at me and then at his son. Ealar had seen fewer summers than my nephews, but he was tough and lean. The Skotek winters were harsh and their feuds with neighbouring tribes kept them battle ready and their blades keen. I shot my most imploring look to the wily Chief, hoping that he would favour allegiance over rancour.

At length, he said, "I want three things from you in exchange."

We were not out of the woods, but this was a good sign. I breathed out my relief.

"Go on." Blydh growled.

"I want a full hull of tin ingots and a two to one deal going forwards, tin to gold."

That was a vast quantity of tin, far more than we could hope to secure in a full cycle of mining and processing. The twins exchanged glances. Tallack urged him to speak his next demand.

Faolan smirked with superiority. "I saw your foreign ship in the estuary. Your crew told me that you made a bargain with a Phoenician trader. They said it was the fastest boat on the seas." We all knew what was coming next. "Make a gift of it to me."

Tallack spluttered, rising from the log snarling with fury.

Blydh grabbed his brother by the shoulders, dragging him back to his seat. “And your third request?”

Finally, the boys were beginning to realise the uneven position they faced. This was a negotiation. They had to think fast and counter.

“I have a daughter, Sorcha.” Faolan nodded to Tallack. “I think you’ll agree that she is a beauty, and a prize in any man’s eyes?” He expected Tallack to reinforce this with a compliment. I nudged him discreetly from behind.

“She is that, Faolan. A stunning woman whose skills with blade and bow is like no other.” Tallack crooned, choosing to highlight her warrior skills over her pink, wind-chapped appearance and wild red locks.

“Blydh is to bind with my Sorcha and she will become the Ruvane of the Dumnonii. No other wives Tallack might take will displace her position.” Faolan announced, grabbing up the ale jug and drinking straight from the spout.

“Why not Tallack?” Blydh said.

Faolan grinned. “What use is he in giving me grandsons. I may be old, but I’m not blind.” He tipped his head towards Treeve and then rolled his eyes.

A small cry came from Blydh’s tent behind us. Kerensa had been listening to every word said. Treeve grinned to himself, shuffling closer to Tallack on the log.

They were lofty demands and no mistake. If the twins agreed to all of Faolan’s wishes, the Dumnoni tribe would have nothing left for our own people or defences. Our mining communities would be little more than slaves to the Novantae.

Blydh looked to be retreating into his own thoughts. He was not used to settling disputes with words. The lad was a fighter through and through. Tallack was still seething from the thought of losing his ship. Unable to voice his objections without causing offence, he looked at me to find a solution.

"We thank you for your offer, Chief Faolan. Please accept our hospitality, while our Meterns discuss your terms." I cuffed Treeve around the ear, instructing him to fetch more ale and meats for our guests, and then grabbed at the collars of both my nephews.

They followed me across the gravel bank at the shallowest point of the tributary and onto the island beyond. Here, we perched on the logs felled to make the walls of our new compound.

Tallack launched his attack first. "He can't have my ship and that's final." It struck me as odd that he was more concerned about losing his boat than the slur on his abilities to father heirs to the tribe. Faolan was suggesting that my nephew's partiality for men, made him a lesser Chief and warrior. That seemed to pass him by entirely. I didn't raise it again.

"Nothing has been decided, Nephew. This is merely his opening offer; demand a huge amount to barter down to a smaller compromise. How about we agree to cover the cost and materials of building him a similar sized ship when the war is over?" At first, Blydh huffed and puffed, trying to think of alternatives. When neither came up with a better plan, both the men nodded at my suggestion. It was looking into their pitiful eyes that I realised how ill equipped they were to deal with such large promises. I had to steer them further.

"As for the amount of tin he asked for… it simply can't be done. You could give him the option of a half share in all the tin produced from the mine on the north coast for a limited time, but he must fetch it himself. That mine is not so plentiful as the Bentewyn settlement, but he won't know that. We can say it was chosen for its ease of access to the Iwerdon Sea. Start with a quarter share, if he'll take it and work up to half, but for no more than five cycles or he's robbing us blind." When they grunted their understanding at this, I got up to leave, thinking the rest was settled.

"I won't bind with his daughter." Blydh announced. "I intend making Kerensa the next Ruvane."

I stopped in my tracks and took a massive breath. There was no way around this demand. Faolan had already refused Tallack, and their only other unwed sister was a babe in arms. We had no other relatives to offer. "You must argue that between yourselves." I said, throwing my arms into the air. I'd done all I could to help them. The rest was up to them alone.

My head spun with all that needed to be done. Before I was across the stream, I yelled back at them. "Make sure you give them our best shelter while they're our guests. They'll expect to receive the same courtesy that they showed us." I knew that would mean giving up my own quarters, but it was a small price to pay considering all the kindness Faolan and his family had shown me.

I wandered back to my shelter to pick up my things and to ask Renowden to find somewhere else to sleep, but discovered it overrun by Cryda and her baby. It bawled its little eyes out on my bunk. Renowden was nowhere to be seen.

Scooping up the child, I jogged her in my arms. "Cryda, you should not have come. This place is not safe. The Duros are preparing for attack. Could be any day now."

"Tsk, hush. I go where my boys go. They will protect me." She unhooked the brooch holding the fabric of her cloak together and made herself comfortable on my bed.

"They will be shoulder deep in our enemies' innards. They can't fight and take care of you at the same time. There are men to train and lead." My words fell on deaf ears.

In her head, she was making plans on where to place her treasured belongings. I knew that my peace was shattered the moment she set foot on dry land. Cryda twirled in the luxury of space. "Yes, this will do nicely for the child and me." She turned to look in my direction. "Is your hut close by, Meliora? I shall need your help in minding her."

I was too stunned to speak. It had taken less time than to boil an egg for her to revert to her old lofty ways and assert her authority over the tribe. She was no longer the Ruvane, yet to all who looked upon her, she commanded the will of all our people. If Blydh got his own way, Kerensa would out rank her by becoming the next Ruvane in her place. That would knock the smile off her face. I'd lost my home yet again and acquired the lowly job of taking care of her offspring.

Wrapping the babe with my cloak, I wandered back outside to find the slave girl, Finola, who was offered to me by my nephew. She was weaving hurdles with the lad who trembled at my wrath. "You girl. I have a task for you and mind you do it well." I explained her new role, handed her the child and pushed her into the hut with Cryda. There was no way I was going to become Cryda's serf again. There was far too much to do.

It was when I went to check up on the working party of men in the forest, that I remembered that the hut Cryda now called home, would be dismantled during the move to the island. Blydh had charged Renowden and me to organise everything, including the sites allocated for shelters and huts. That was when I made the decision to ensure that Cryda was as distant from my own hut as possible on the island compound. Until then, I would have to seek shelter elsewhere.

Mounting my horse, I rode to the forest north of the camp and picked out three of Blydh's warriors whom I knew to be sharp shooters with the bow. If we were to show these Skotek men southern hospitality, we would need to arrange a feast. Their instructions were simple. Come back with the largest creature you can find. Failing that, bring many small birds and animals in its stead.

Next, I rode to Tallack's crewmen, ordering them to dig a large fire pit and set out the fishing nets. There were not many slaves left following the raid during the summer moons. Those that were not killed or captured, freed themselves and fled. Our buried hordes of treasure were uncovered and swiped by my traitorous niece. Unfortunately, she had the sense to send it back to Durotriges lands before her brothers caught up with her. It left our tribe struggling to trade for more slaves, food stores and copper to make bronze weapons.

With the added pressure of Faolan's demands, we would need to be more careful with our resources going forward. Our most urgent requirement was for wood and rope. If we were to put Renowden's plan into place, everyone would need to lend a helping hand. That started with clearing the forest to the north of the island so that we'd have fair warning of attack.

Blydh's men had already spent much of the day chopping logs and floating them downstream around the island. Tallack's crew were shirking by the row boats at the jetty. I rode back to them and gave them a choice. Either they gathered and made as much hemp rope as the local homesteaders could part with, or they took over the clearing of the woodland. Most chose the easier rope making tasks, though neither were easy or lacking in skill. With everyone I could find industrious in their labours, I went in search of Renowden.

He was in the same tent as before, snoring his head off among the stored ale jugs and dried meats. This was Blydh's storage tent, meant to keep his warriors fed while they trained.

Tripping in the darkness, I woke him rudely when I stepped on his foot. His forgiveness was instant and sincere. I sat on the floor by his side and caught him up with events. I could not keep this camp running without his help.

Before the sun set, the feast preparations were well underway, with a gnarly boar roasting over charcoal pits, with ducks, rabbits and a few squirrels either side for variety. In lieu of a Chieftain's long hut, we extended the fire outside Blydh's tent and erected temporary shelters with hurdles and pine brush for Faolan's men. I say we, but Blydh and Tallack's men did the work under Ren's instruction.

The fresh scent of the crushed pine needles masked the stink of the sweaty men. That was a welcome relief. Better still was the sweet pork, which crackled and fizzed as its lard rendered into the hot coals. More than anything, I wanted to sneak away and rest my poor weary bones, but the tasty meats were too enticing to miss.

By Cernonnus, it was by far the best thing I'd tasted in twenty or more summers. With pork grease running down our chins and wrists, we all ate handfuls of the stuff and drank ale until we could hardly move. For once, the weather was kind to us all, clearing the skies of rain clouds until every light from the Summerlands twinkled with the spirits of our ancestors.

Cryda was the first to raise the subject of Aebba's passing into the realm reserved for Chieftains and noble warriors. I hadn't the heart to tell her that he couldn't possibly be watching over us, since his killer still roamed the borderlands, his death unavenged. Aebba would be trapped in the Between Worlds, since his poisoning last spring. The twins glared at me from across the huge fire, reminding me of my shame. I had still a debt to repay, even if it killed me.

I sat with Renowden for most of the feast, discussing plans to secure food supplies and tapping the spring water should the battle be reduced to siege warfare. He had quite a few ideas about building pens to breed rabbits and ducks in the woodland areas at the sides of the island. Despite the exhaustion, I was buoyed in spirit for the first time since my Jago was taken from me at the top of the world. It wasn't as though I had forgotten him, or stopped missing him, it was that hard work and attention to my tasks had distracted me from my grief.

Cryda took much of the attention at the feast. Faolan was enchanted by her and the babe, insisting that she sat at his side so he could listen to her tales of Aebba's past conquests. The twins seemed grateful to her. They knew that time was pressing them from all sides. They had to begin final negotiations with Faolan, but were loathed to reached terms.

Derwa stayed close to Kerensa, giggling and whispering together about the Bentewyn settlement and all that they'd left behind there. From the way they glowered and sniggered, I got the distinct impression that Derwa had formed an unhealthy attachment outside her marriage to Glaw. It wouldn't be the first time she had strayed. Glaw didn't appear to be bothered either way. He sat with his back to Derwa, carving a hunk of wood with a small knife. I watched him for some time, trying to figure him out.

Why had this heir to the mountain people of Northern Kembra, succumbed to his stubborn wife's wishes? He had ample opportunity to drag her back to his homeland and insist that she performed her wedded duties as any man had. What did he have to gain by staying in Dumnonii lands, where he was made to feel less than welcome?

Glaw took small sips of ale, never lost control of himself and ate modestly. As far as I could tell, he was a nice fellow with an easy temperament who was abundantly kind to Derwa. She had little to nothing to complain about, other than the fact that she did not choose him as a husband. Her binding paved the way for a truce between the disgruntled Ordoviches and our tribe after a bungled agreement went awry.

As I watched Glaw, he pocketed the wooden block he'd been working on, and took out a rock with glistening patches of green on one side. He turned it in his hands, letting the flickering lights from the flames dance about its surface. Glaw looked transfixed by the glimmering effect. When he saw me watching, his face fell into a pout and he tucked the rock away out of sight. He is a puzzle to be sure.

The warriors and crewmen sat further away from us around a fire of their own. They feasted on venison and fish, with more ale than they ought to have been given. Come morning, they would be difficult to rouse into work.

At length, when the fires had burnt low and everyone had eaten their fill, Blydh rose to his feet. "The time has come for a decision. Faolan, brother, will you join me in my shelter for discussions?" All who looked on went silent, for word had spread about Faolan's demands.

The men stepped over the log seats and disappeared with their ale into the tent. Kerensa hurried after them, but Treeve caught hold of her arm as she passed him.

"Get off me." She snarled.

"You're not permitted inside. You aren't the Ruvane." He hissed spitefully.

"And never will be if you don't let go of me. I have just as much right to be there to hear my fate as they." She snatched her arm back and ran off to the tent. Treeve stood watching her. Kerensa ducked under the door skins and entered.

"Well if they allow her in, then I should be there too." Treeve said, sticking his nose in the air and strutting after her.

My gut churned at this development. Nothing good can come of their situation, especially for poor Kerensa. Mind you, Treeve should never have elevated himself to such a lofty position in the tribe either. Cryda sat with her mouth open at their gall. She waited less than a moment, before she too was on her feet and rushing to Blydh's tent. What a crush it must have been, all those bodies in such a confined space. I expected it to come to blows.

Renowden and I listened as well as we could, the raised voices were muffled and confused. I think many people were talking, or shouting at once. The longer it went on, the more convinced I was that Faolan would withdraw his offer of support under any circumstances. Just when I was gearing up to enter the fray, Kerensa reappeared from beneath the door flaps in floods of tears. She ran off into the night sobbing out her pain. I guess that answers the question of Sorcha's binding with Blydh, but to what else had they agreed?

CHAPTER SIX

When Faolan came out of the tent, I was itching to ask what had been decided. He walked over to his son, Ealar and patted his head as though he was an infant.

"Well, Pa?" The lad asked.

"You'll sail home and fetch your sister and the rest of the fleet come morning. Tell the men to make ready."

That was all I could discover. It was dawn before I found out the rest. Despite my warning, the old wolf had bullied them into half the tin from our northern mine for ten cycles, with Ealar managing the split and living in the community there. That would most likely result in the Novantae taking far more than a half share.

Tallack and I stood on the jetty watching the provisions being loaded onto the row boats to take to the ship in the estuary. He fumed quietly over the hard line the wise old Chief had taken. I can't say that I blame him. In his situation, risking his men and fleet for another man's war was folly. They had to make it worth his while.

What surprised me most was that Tallack took no offence at Faolan's insistence that Blydh should bind with his daughter in place of him. He bore no malice for the man at all. Perhaps his tribe are set against men like

Tallack, whereas for us it represents a mere inconvenience to the succession of Chieftains. If it were not for Blydh, I dare say Cryda would have more to say on the matter.

Over the course of almost a full moon cycle, the new compound took shape. The walls and towers were raised first, followed by the movable crossings at the north end and eastern side of the island. Both were Renowden's designs. He'd witnessed something similar in his travels with Aebba.

When the spiked posts were embedded in the water channels and where the streams dipped under the fences, Blydh lost interest in the developments. Every morning, he would gather his men and leave the compound to train with axe and spear in the clearing beyond.

Tallack and he argued on a daily basis, each time their anger bubbled over into fury. Their close relationship was breaking down in front of my eyes, and I couldn't see a way to fix them. Where Tallack was convinced that our hopes lay in sound preparations and self-sufficiency in the compound, Blydh believed that gathering new men and training them for battle was key.

Renowden ran between the two, and more often than not, received contradictory orders from each. Before long, the warriors and crewmen didn't know whether they were coming or going. In an attempt to regain some kind of order about camp, I tried to divide their command, stating that both approaches were equally important, but the lion's share of compound development was achieved by Tallack's men, while the training and hunting fell to Blydh's warriors. With a little give and take, everyone settled into some form of routine.

One morning Blydh's scouts returned with a fresh batch of homestead workers to train. They were a strange bunch. A couple of skinny little boys, a vicious unruly girl of about fifteen summers and one lad as big as a cart horse. I wished Blydh luck in training them and took my pony out to collect ingredients for my tinctures.

It was a cool morning, but sunny and dry for a change. I filled my bags with nettle and plantain, mallow, and a little yew and willow bark. My stores of herbs and medicines were at last beginning to fill out. I'd even sectioned off a parcel of land near to my new hut to plant the seeds I'd traded for last summer.

Life could be considered great, if it was not for the constant threat of the Durotriges on our borders. By now, they had to know that we were aware of them. I suspected that they were pinning their hopes on the surprise attack from the Ivernii, who had the ability to cripple our fleet. Our warriors were exhausted, and there was still much to be done to secure our safety from attack. We were less vulnerable than we had been, but Faolan's men and ships still had not returned from North-West Skotek.

Our new recruits were too green to be of use in battle. That was obvious, when I returned from my foraging expedition and walked across the training grounds. Using blunt sticks in place of spears and short swords, I stifled a chuckle at their ineptitude. Tallack and Blydh stood at the edge of the field in another heated debate over Chieftain orders. Blydh's men yelled their instructions to the recruits and clouted them around the backs of their heads when they failed to comply.

The bad-tempered girl did not want to be there. At first, she tolerated the smacks and lunges from her fellow trainees, dodging the worst of their blows and remaining still and uncooperative for the rest of the time. The skinny boys were no threat to her. Even I could see that she had the ability to flatten them if that was her desire, but she folded her arms and glowered instead.

If I had to guess, I'd say that she was taken from her home by Blydh's warriors without an opportunity to object. Why should she fight for us, when she could stay with her family? It was a common enough gripe among the recruits, but without their help, our lands would be overrun with Durotriges, and she and her family would be enslaved, or worse.

The big lad was defending himself against the ineffectual swipes from his puny sparring partner. His laugh was deep and booming and infectious. Within moments, I was chuckling too. It was all a game to him.

Although I had more chores to be getting on with, I stopped to watch the antics of this huge lummox trying to catch the agile youngsters ducking and diving around his lumbering limbs. He guffawed, swinging his arms about. Then, dropping the stick to the floor, he swept one of the boys up in his arms and hugged him tight.

All the recruits nearby laughed, clapping their hands together, until one of Blydh's warriors barked at them. The head hunter thundered towards them, furious at their attitude towards training. On his way past, the vicious girl lifted his axe from his belt. He was a good few strides away from her before he noticed what she'd taken.

With a petulant glower, she drew the axe back over her shoulder, aiming between his eyes. She screamed a mournful howl and then let go of the weapon. It hurtled through the air, spinning head over handle on a direct flight towards the warrior's face. Seeing the blade hurtling closer he fell to his knees, allowing the axe to whirl over the top. It flew directly at me.

They say you can see your ancestors when your time is up. A long line of family and friends waiting to take you into the Underworld. I am no warrior, nor Chieftain. There was no space for the likes of me in the Summerlands. When that hatchet came for me, I froze. I saw nothing, no warm memories or feelings of support from those long since passed, just the sheer panic of what was to come.

It was less than an arm's length from my face, when the great bear of a recruit reached out and punched it away. It clanged to the ground at my side, missing both me and my horse by a whisker. We all stood motionless for a few moments, taking in all that had happened.

The warrior rose from his knees and ran after the ill-tempered girl to exact his punishment. My spooked horse cantered off with my bags of herbs and the large boy stood by me dripping with blood. His knuckles were ripped to shreds but he was more concerned over my wellbeing than his injury. I examined his cuts and took him through the west gates towards the awning at the side of my hut.

He let me boss him about and tend his wounds, while he sat placidly on a stool watching folk going about their business in the compound. By the time I'd finished patching him up, Tallack had arrived to check up on me, having heard what had happened.

"Thank the gods that you are unhurt." Tallack gushed, though I got the feeling that was more to do with losing a healer rather than his aunt. "What's your name, boy?" That made me grin, for the massive lad looked to be about the same age as he.

"They call me Kewri, Chief."

Tallack and I exchanged glances. It was certainly an appropriate nickname, although not a terribly clever one, for Kewri in our tongue is another word for giant.

"What's your given name?" I asked him, smearing my famed plantain paste over the catgut stitches.

The lad shrugged. "Been Kewri long as I can remember."

It was certainly a name I'd never forget. I patted his shoulder and thanked him again for his quick reactions and courage.

"You should be rewarded. What can I give you, tin, a sword or a stout horse? What will it be?" Tallack said, waiting for him to consider his options.

Kewri pulled a face, as though thinking hurt his head. "I'd like a nice dry place to sleep, if that's in your power to give."

Tallack burst out laughing. "Not a bronze blade, or metal nuggets, just somewhere comfy to lay your head? I think we can manage that, can't we Aunt?"

"Eh? What are you saying?"

"You won't take on my slaves to help you, and we can't have our only healer and my favourite aunt in danger, so meet your personal guard, Kewri."

"Not a chance. I don't need a guard. That axe was not aimed at me. Find him a warm bed, certainly, but not under my roof." I'd finished dealing with the lad's injuries, he was all set to return to the training ground. "No offence, Kewri. I'm sure you're a nice man and all, but I like my privacy and space." I rolled up my things and scurried away inside my hut, leaving the pair of them outside.

Next to the fire in my shelter was a skinned rabbit. It was one of many such unexplained offerings to appear in and around my hut in days. I had no idea who was leaving food for me, but I was grateful nonetheless. I raked the coals and stuck a little goat's butter into the cavity, before resting the spit over the fire. It would cook itself while I went to retrieve my horse.

As I ducked under the door lintel, I could see the enormous feet of Kewri sticking out from my hurdle shelter. "You still here, boy? I thought I told you that I didn't need your services. Go on back to the training ground." I carried on walking.

Kewri hurried after me. "Can't. Chief Tallack ordered me to stay with you."

"You'd be better off training with the others." I tried to out run him, but his one stride to my two made it hard for me to get away.

"They'd be better off with me here." He wasn't even out of breath. I was gasping and had to stop to fill my lungs. Bending over holding my knees, I stared up at him. This giant of a boy, with hands the size of stew bowls, had just saved my life without a second thought. What possible reason would he have for avoiding warriors? It wasn't as though he feared pain, he hadn't murmured a bit over his gashed hand.

"Why won't you train with the others? You'd be a fearsome warrior, the best they'd ever seen. You are hero material."

He twisted his mouth to one side and shook his head. "I ain't no hero, Fur Benyn. Never will be." He wandered off towards the eastern fringes of the island where the wooded copse still provided cover for the few creatures that had not yet been eaten. I thought it to be an end to our discussion, but as I headed back home, he caught up with me leading my horse stacked high with herbs.

I watched as he tied the reins to the overhang of the hurdle shelter and lifted off my bags. Without asking, he carried my things into the hut and returned to the stool outside. Offering my thanks, yet again, I returned to the cooking rabbit and gave it a turn. Other than a mild creaking sound of the stool he sat on; I could barely tell that he was still out there.

The rabbit roasted long before I'd finished storing my herbs. It smelled incredible, making my gut groan with hunger. Taking it off the spit, I cut it in half and added it to a hunk of bread in a bowl. I went outside to give it to my saviour. His face lit up like I'd given him gold dust. "Don't think this means you're staying. Eat up and head back to the recruits."

His smile was as catching as his laugh. There was that twinkle in his eye again. This one was going to be hard to shake off. I kept my eye on him as best I could for the rest of the day. He moved only once from his stool, to wash my bowl in the stream, before walking into the wooded area. I thought he might have given up and wandered away, but he returned with an armful of fresh leaves to give to the goats.

At sundown, Cryda came to my hut. "Who's he?" She mouthed wandering in and collapsing on my bunk.

"One of Blydh's new warriors. I patched him up. He'll be gone by tomorrow."

She lost interest immediately. "The Long Hut is finished. The boy's want to have a big celebration in there this evening. You'll come, won't you? I plan to announce the babe's name tonight." She twirled a section of her golden hair around her finger. I noticed that she did that lot when she was trying to persuade men to do her bidding. It didn't work on me.

"I don't think I will, Cryda. I'm tired, it's been a long day."

"But you have to come. I want you to be a part of the naming ritual." She pulled her sad face, the corners of her mouth tipped down like she was about to cry. Did she really think that would tug at my heart?

"You should have named that little mite back in the winter. She'll be walking and talking before she has a name to call her own." I tied my last bundle of herbs together and climbed up onto the bunk to attach it to the roof struts.

Cryda watched me struggle for a time. I could see it amused her that I was too short to reach the last available space left to hang the mallow to dry. "You should get your warrior to do it for you." She grinned.

That made me even more determined to fend for myself. "I can manage." It almost wrenched my back, but I eventually got the bunch tied off. She was still laughing, rolling about on my furs. Maybe I had isolated myself for too long. After the loss of Jago, it was my way of coping. Being on my own meant I didn't have to listen when they made light of his death. If I heard, *but he was just a slave* once, I heard it a dozen times.

I could see that she wouldn't leave until I had agreed to go. "Fine. I'll come and eat all your food, but I won't stay long." That shifted her. After she had left, I went down to the stream and rinsed myself off, before refilling the goat's water supply. Kewri hadn't budged. I changed into my best tunic and clean shoes and hovered over my furs, trying to decide how cold it might be inside the Long Hut. In the end, I left them behind, choosing to use the cold as an excuse to leave early.

Lighting a torch from my fire, I left my hut and began the muddy walk across the grass to the Long Hut. Kewri jumped up from his seat and trailed after me.

"I think I'm safe crossing the compound, lad. Go back to your recruit tents."

"I got orders, Fur Benyn." Was all he'd say. Now I had another issue to contend with. New recruits were not permitted in the long hut. It had limited space inside. With both Tallack and Blydh's best warriors among us, the place would be packed to the roof. How could I leave the great lummox outside in the cold? There again, if I took him inside with me, he might get punished for his insolence. This was turning into a rotten day indeed.

My curiosity to see how the boys had arranged the inside of the Long hut was all that kept me going. I grabbed Kewri by the sleeve and pushed past Blydh's warriors through the entrance. "He's with me." I grumbled at their sour faces at seeing the giant.

Our old Chieftain hut had a long table at the back of the room, with Aebba the Wild's tall seat at its centre. To his right, sat his first wife and Ruvane of our tribe, Cryda, while to his left was the chair for his first-born son. Paega lost the right to inherit the Chieftain's chair when the twins challenged his right to rule. How would they arrange the elevated table now that their amicable arrangement was so strained?

CHAPTER SEVEN

Set far above all other tables at the end of the new Long Hut were two tall chairs. Each were made from thick lengths of wood and topped with a carving of a wolf's head on the right seat and a bear on the other. Between the two, was a smaller chair normally reserved for the Ruvane. Now I could see why there were so many raised voices as we entered. Kerensa and Treeve stood nose to nose in a fierce argument. Neither would back down, until it became more physical.

I could see that Tallack thought it amusing at first, his little man friend asserting his authority over the daughter of a mining leader, but Blydh most certainly did not. A fire burned in his eyes that spelled trouble. As if that were not enough to contend with, Faolan rose from his seat to the right of Blydh's to douse the dispute with grease.

"Neither of you should be permitted the Ruvane's chair. For Cernonnus' sake, look at you man. You're actually proud to be considered a woman?" Faolan prodded Treeve in the back. "Grow some balls, boy! That seat is for my Sorcha, when she gets here and no other."

That only served to inflame Tallack all the more. "Hey, that's enough. You don't get to decide how our Chieftain hut is run. Your daughter is not Ruvane yet." He shoved the Skotek Chief aside, making way for Treeve to step up to the chair.

"No way, brother." Blydh bellowed. "I won't have that poor excuse for a man at my side. Take him away."

Kerensa saw her chance. "I could very well be carrying the next Metern of the Dumnonii. I should be Ruvane."

It descended into pushing and shoving in short order. It was when I heard the sound of blades scraping against their scabbards, that something had to be done.

"Kewri, come along. I will need your help with this." I hurried up to the top table and shrieked at the top of my voice. "Stop this now!" Gesturing to Kewri he moved closer to the squabbling crowd and towered over them all. "Take the chair away. Until a Ruvane is officially bound to one of our Meterns, there will be no one at their sides other than guests. Kewri walked around the back of the raised platform and lifted the smaller of the three chairs down to the floor.

Other than a few grumbles and a good deal of huffing, the quarrelsome bunch slunk away, leaving Tallack and Blydh to their lonely seats overlooking us all. From their narrow-eyed glares at one another, I could see that it wasn't the end of the dispute. All I had achieved was a delay. This does not bode well for the coming conflict. If they cannot decide something as simple as a seating hierarchy, we stand no chance in battle.

Kewri sat on a bench at the far end of the room by the door, keeping his beady eye on me. Having put myself in the centre of all the fuss, it fell to me to dictate the proper order of things. Faolan returned to the visitor's seats to one side of Blydh. The second row of tables was supposed to accommodate the closest family and wives of the Metern. "Cryda, you, Derwa and the babe sit there, with Glaw the Ordo next to you."

Glaw sat down next to Derwa and took a turn at minding the baby. "I wish you wouldn't call me that, Fur Benyn. It makes me sound like an enemy of the people rather than family."

I apologised to the man from the mountains, but he was indeed an Ordo. He was heir to their tribe, and really ought to have returned to Northern Kembra a long time ago. Next, I had to find room in such a tight space for the troubling lovers. Pulling the line of benches apart, I isolated a small table in front of the relative's benches. "Treeve, you sit this side. Kerensa at the other end, and I shall sit between you until you learn to behave yourselves."

Only Faolan dared to laugh at this. He was much older than all others in the hut, bar me, and he could see the funny side to treating these tribal leaders as though they were naughty children. In truth, they were. Aebba's passing had left a void of experience in our tribe which I struggled to fill. Despite the unpleasantness all around, the slaves filed in and delivered platters of meats and breads, and the first fresh cooked vegetables and leaves of the season.

They were welcome indeed. We have been extraordinarily fortunate with hunts over the winter, but meat and bread without a few leaves to help clean the bowels leads to bad tempered warriors. I ate my fill and made sure that those around me had their fair share too, including Kewri. He might turn out to be more useful than I thought after all.

The one to keep an eye on is Kerensa. Her exclamation revealed the extent of her ambition. It is in her mind to force Blydh to bind with her so that she can bear him a son, thus assuring her place among the top table for all time. If she is swept aside in favour of Faolan's daughter, as the bargain insists, Kerensa will not melt quietly into the background. Her very presence suggests that her father approves of her union with Blydh. We cannot afford to offend the leader of the Alchemists, those in charge of all our mining assets in the south.

Treeve's reaction was also a surprise. To openly and flagrantly claim to be the equivalent of Tallack's Ruvane, is almost blasphemous. The crewmen of the Sea Warrior Clan will not take kindly to that kind of claim. He will make Tallack a laughing stock before he's through. I sat patting my full belly, content to return to my bed for the night, when Cryda spoke out.

She stood up and banged her cup on the table in front of her. "My sons, Faolan, respected elders and warriors. I have an important announcement." She waited until all were quiet and turned to hear her. "I have at last decided on a name for the last child of Aebba the Wild, and I would like for Meliora to perform the naming ritual, here in the new Long Hut at the next new moon."

There were cries of 'What name did you choose?" and "Another feast, may the Gods be praised," among the shouts and cheers. I remained silent. Where were my gods when Jago had his throat opened before my eyes?

"Well, Meliora. Are you excited to perform the rites? You have been on at me for more moons than I can count about her name." Cryda said to an eager crowd. They all hushed, awaiting my response.

I remained in my seat with my back to the top and second tables. "Name her by all means, the poor mite deserves one, but don't drag me into godly rituals and rites. I hold no faith anymore." The collective intake of breath did not scare me. If gods do exist, they are cruel and unjust.

It was Tallack of all people who took me to task over my outpouring. "You'll take that back, Aunt, and you will perform my sister's due rites. It is the eldest woman of the tribe's responsibility to welcome new life and that falls to you. I won't have you forsaking the gods and provoking their wrath at this critical time." He didn't sound like Tallack. It was as though he'd aged greatly during the building of the island compound, and it had soured his sweet nature. All the elders and warriors glowered at me over the top of their ale cups. This wasn't the time to argue with the Meterns for a second time in one night.

"Fine. I'll do what you command, but don't expect me to believe in any of it." More gasps, clicking of tongues and general murmurs of discord bounced about the room. "What name have you picked for the child?" It was then I knew that my bitterness and enmity for the gods, was ruining what should be a joyous occasion for Cryda and the Chiefs. At that moment, I hated myself more than Cernonnus and his goddesses.

"I thought that Delen might be a fitting name, considering her little ears are just like tiny petals." Cryda said it so softly, I knew that I had ruined the moment for her. Now it fell to me to make amends. Even if I did not believe in the gods, everyone did, and it wouldn't do to upset the Chiefs any further.

"That is perfect for her, Cryda. Aebba would be proud. I'm sure she'll be a formidable warrior when she's grown." Watching Cryda's reactions, I knew I'd done it again, said something thoughtless. Her face screwed up like she was in pain and tears trembled on the lids of her eyes.

"I don't want her to be a fighter. She was born to become a Ruvane of a great tribe someday." Cryda pulled herself together, sniffing back the unwanted emotion. "It's settled then. Her name day will be in a quarter moon from now."

I hadn't the heart to argue with her. It struck me as insane that this woman would happily sell her only daughter to the son and heir of another tribe, just so that she could become a Ruvane. What kind of mother would prefer beaten submission to a Chieftain, than a warrior maiden capable of defending herself? This tribe has become weak during Aebba's reign, and is set to continue while the twins do little to change things.

I smiled and nodded at those on the top table and left as soon as I could without offence. It was only when I got to the door that I remembered Kewri. What was I going to do with him?

"Have you a bed among the other recruits?" I asked him as we walked across the grass to my hut.

"No. We all just squeeze onto a pile of straw near to the cattle enclosure. It has a roof, so it's not all bad."

This huge lad had asked for one thing above all else when he saved my life and it had not been granted to him. Instead of a comfy warm bed, he'd been given the task of protecting me. We waddled through the filth, lighting our way with a torch taken from Blydh's guards. When we reached my door, he returned to his stool outside.

"I shall regret this, I'm sure, but come inside, Kewri. It's already cold enough to freeze parts of the stream."

That cheery smile spread across his smooth face. "Bring some logs with you too. We'll bank up the fire and have a little ale while I make up a bed for you."

I'd never seen him move so fast. Before I could roll out my best furs on the bunk built for the sick and wounded, he had the flames crackling away and filling the whole hut with warmth. That night, I slept so soundly, I almost forgot my grief. Having another beating heart under the same roof gives such comfort, and with Kewri's size and strength, protection too.

When I awoke, the porridge was simmering, the goats were milked and fed and Kewri had gathered a great stack of willow withies to make more hurdles.

"What shall we be doing today, Fur Benyn?" He asked, tying a cord about the thin branches and leaning them against the goat fence.

"I need to trade for some more pots and jars first, then we'll go out into the wood to see if we are blessed with new shoots and leaves yet." It mattered little if we came back empty handed. I just wanted a reason to be away from camp until Cryda and her boys had calmed down. I found that Kewri was pleasant company. He didn't prattle on, like so many of the young recruits about camp. He let me attend to my business in silence, and only interrupted to ask if he could help me with difficulties reaching or lifting whatever I needed.

We ate a small amount of cheese and day-old bread, collected as much moss as we could shove into a bag, and sliced off a reasonable quantity of birch bark to render for arrow gum. Kewri led my pony, laden with bulky bags through the undergrowth, heading south for the island. I let him get ahead and darted back into the undergrowth for a handful of bramble leaves.

When I looked up from my labours, I saw a brilliant white stag. This is the second of such sightings, although the buck I saw on Catuve-Llauni lands was defending his herd. This white hart was alone, and unafraid. We regarded one another for a few moments, him with curiosity, me with awe. He was almost as large as my pony, with sizable antlers not yet shed for spring. Folks often say that seeing a white deer marks a great change in fortune, whether for the better or worse. Was this a warning? I had renounced the gods brazenly and publicly. Was this Cernonnus come to give me a stark reminder of his existence?

I recalled the way Tallack had laughed at me when I spoke about the last stag to cross my path. Then and there, I decided to keep my sighting to myself. Not even Kewri would know about my brush with the God of the Wild Forest and of Death. Perhaps I had been too hasty in casting my beliefs aside.

On our return to camp, Renowden was just knotting the final rope in his lifting bridge. It was a marvellous invention, allowing us to cross the deepest stretches of the River Exe into the north end of the island.

As I suspected, the community was in a frenzy of preparations for the babes naming rituals. Cryda always did love to be the centre of attention. She paraded the child up and down the compound, hurling her orders and requests and invitations at anyone in her path. For all her nonsense, you'd never believe that we were supposed to be training the warriors and making battle preparations.

I dawdled until she was too far away to bother me and then hurried to my hut. Kewri made short work of the plants and bark we'd collected, and then set about weaving new hurdles to extend the porch outside. From the number of stakes in the ground, he was planning on an entirely new hut.

Yet another skinned and gutted rabbit hung from the eaves outside my door. As grateful as I was to have such an abundance of food set at my feet, I grew uneasy as to where they came from. No one had come forward to claim gratitude, nor were any hints dropped pointing to the culprit. I lay awake that night, pondering on this miraculous stream of food, wondering if the gods were testing me. Shutting out my fears, I tried to sleep but this growing unease had me shifting restlessly until dawn.

When most of the tribes were still under their bed furs, I heard the lonely scout gallop into the compound. Wrapping my cloak about me, I sped across the frozen turf to the Long Hut to hear the news. Blydh's warriors on the night watch woke him and Tallack, directing them to the weary scout with a bloody graze to his shoulder. Cryda must have been awake with the babe, for she arrived too with the little one bouncing on her arm.

"Well man, what news?" Blydh barked at him.

The poor warrior gulped at water and then ale, puffing between swallows from the exertion. "The Duros have moved camp. They are but half a day's walk to the east at the River Sid border."

It should not have come as a surprise to us, but it did. We had grown used to their presence on the moors north of us while they trained and prepared. It was inevitable that they would strike from a closer position. What was clear, was they were ready for attack, and we were not. Tallack and Blydh sat on the edge of the top table considering our next move.

Tallack spoke first. "We must double the watch and gather more food for siege tactics. Renowden completed the second lifting bridge last night, so he can concentrate on getting the ships ready. Dathi of the Ivernii will be lurking out there with his men just off the coast, you can be sure of that. We'll have to sail out and meet those Iwerdon scum with the few vessels we've got." He stood up and wiped his brow with the heel of his hand. "Where the kyjya is Faolan's son with those extra ships?"

Blydh said nothing. He stared at the floor for a while as his brother paced about the Long Hut trying to sound as though he was in control. Tallack walked closer to me and asked if I could perform the naming ceremony of his sister sooner. He wanted to direct all efforts into making spiked ramparts and collecting rocks to rain down on the Duros heads.

Blydh had finished his preponderances. "We won't need rocks, or ships or ramparts."

Tallack spun about to confront him. "Are you out of your kyjyan mind? We'll need much more than that to defeat them."

I felt a shiver ripple down my back. This was the beginning of the end, I thought. This is where everything falls apart. The bonds of siblings sharing a womb can only stretch for so long. I closed my eyes, almost expecting to hear the ties of brotherhood snap.

"No, we won't. I'm going to sneak into their camp and slice Brea and her new Chieftain's throats. Let's see them attack with no one left to lead them."

CHAPTER EIGHT

Tallack glared at his brother with a sneer of incredulity. "You really have lost your mind. That is a suicide mission and you know it. They'll have perimeter guards in their hundreds, not to mention the boundary defences. There is absolutely no chance of you accessing the Chief's tent, let alone cutting his throat."

"Father managed it on one of his raids. I am just as good a warrior as he was and I have more weapons." Blydh was always confident in his abilities, but this was beyond folly. The Durotriges camp was enormous and well organised. There were no gaps in their defences to exploit. I waited at the far end of the group for common sense to prevail.

Sneaking a peek at Cryda, I hoped she would take the hint and talk him around. She didn't. Her exhausted, glazed expression told me that she was barely thinking straight, let alone of the dangers her first born faced. I had to rely on Tallack to make him see the stupidity in such an action.

"Father had experienced men who'd seen a great deal of battle. They knew all the tricks of infiltrating enemy camps." Tallack said.

"You're suggesting my men are not worthy warriors. I'm sure they will be keen to hear what their Chief thinks of them. Almost all have raided with me for at least two summers, some many more, and all have taken their fair share of heads." Blydh squared up to his brother. "I can end this all in one night, then we will take their region and horses for ourselves. The Dumnonii will become the largest and most powerful tribe in the land."

Lofty aspirations indeed, for one so young. He assumed that the warriors who once followed and loved his half-sister Wenna, would forgive him for having her killed. Even if Blydh could breach their defences and kill their leader, none of the Duros were likely to fall into line behind him. I had already worn out their tolerance for my advice. If I was seen to favour Tallack's word over Blydh's, it might make the situation between them far worse.

It was when Tallack laughed at Blydh's claims, that the atmosphere took a darker turn. The disagreements from the past three quarters of a moon, spilled over into hatred. Blydh lashed out first, connecting his fist via a jab to Tallack's face. Bloodied and in shock, Tallack retaliated with a head butt. Now both their fine noses were broken. Undeterred, Blydh grabbed his sibling and forced his head down beneath his arm, driving his spare fist into Tallack's ear.

This was no honourable fight. This was the result of years of childhood resentment, spilling out in an unbridled squabble. Tallack was stuck, his neck clamped at Blydh's hip. There were only two choices left to him, a punch to the soft entrails near the back, or the even softer parts between his brother's legs. With no further consideration given, Tallack forced his arm skyward, driving his fist into Blydh's balls. The scream made me shudder. Howling in pain, Blydh let go of Tallack. That was when Cryda came to her senses and stepped in to stop them.

Grabbing both by the ear, she separated her children, putting her own body between them. "Stop this madness!" She yelled. "It's bad enough that we have an enemy horde on our doorstep, without you two bickering as well. You will not ruin your sister's name day." Without letting go of her wriggling sons, she swung them around to face me. "Meliora. The naming will take place before the sun is down today. Make sure everything is ready." Finally, she released the Meterns of our tribe. "You two will behave yourself. You'll be there as her chosen guardians and play your part."

Cryda was always one for spectacular scenes, but she took a massive risk in belittling the Chiefs in their own Long Hut, mother or not. It was fortunate that only one warrior was present to witness the humiliation, and he knew not to risk revealing what he'd seen to any other.

Something told me that we hadn't heard the last of Blydh's crazy idea, but there was such a lot to do, we all hoped that he would take the time to reconsider. Cryda hurried away, content that she had successfully diffused the situation, while I returned to my hut for a bite of porridge before the hard work commenced.

While Cryda spent her time washing and dressing her babe and collecting what few flowers could be found in the surrounding meadows, I had Kewri move and stack the tables and benches from the centre of the Long Hut so that I could draw out the circle with salt. This was one of the few rituals of our tribe that did not require a sacrifice. Well, other than animals for food.

A naming rite was always the domain of the eldest woman of the tribe, who took great pains to remind the young folk that life was precious and worth celebrating. With all the ways that our children could be taken from us, disease, hunger, battle, raiding parties, accident and others besides, having a family member grow up to become a valued member of each clan was a remarkable feat. I couldn't let Cryda down, especially since I had stayed silent for so long over her husband's killer.

After we had cleared away the rushes from the floor, I was ready to mark out the four winds. With a length of twine and two sticks, I dug one end into the ground at the mid-point of the Long Hut, unwound the string to the edge of the wall and scored a circle with the second stick attached.

When I was content with the size of the ring, I repeated my movements, this time pouring crushed salt from a jug into the groove. I used up my entire stock, plus some of Tallack's salt too, but it was necessary to ensure that no bad spirits could find their way into the babe while the gateway was open to the Underworld.

Since there was so little time to finish my preparations, I sent the two slaves Tallack had tried to give me on errands to fetch all I needed. They returned with ivy leaves for the Eastern Winds and milk and bread for the West. These were placed just within the circle along its edge. With the slave cooks doing their best to create a feast from the leftover meat of the last gathering, there were just two more items to obtain.

Leaving the most awkward until last, I trundled along to Tallack's shelter and called out at his door. As I suspected, he wasn't alone. The bothersome boy, Treeve poked his head out, demanding to know what I wanted with my nephew.

I clipped him around the ear. "None of your business. Now get out of my way." He grumbled at me as I pushed past him, covering up his manly parts with his hands. "You think I've not seen a man's pintel before?" I laughed. "Mind you, none so dinky as that one. Shift yourself, child."

Tallack's mood had not improved. His jaw muscles flexed with his clenching teeth. "What can I do for you, Aunt?" His manner suggested that he wanted to be rid of me as soon as possible. That was to my benefit in some respects, although I was surprised that he wasted so much time rolling in his furs with Treeve when the Duro's were so close to their invasion.

"Your sister's ritual. Can you assure the protection of the moon?" The ceremony was known to all in the tribe. He knew what was required of him. He also knew that I had reserved the most precious request for his brother. I felt that I had to explain my reasoning, to prevent any perceived favour on my part. "If you'd prefer to handle the protection of the sun…? Only I thought if I asked that of Blydh, he might see that he is too important to his sister's upbringing to risk a raid into the Duro camp."

Tallack said nothing. He just offered me a fixed stare, succeeding in making me uncomfortable.

"Look, it's up to you which part you want to play in her life" I shrugged, "only you must decide now since the time is fast approaching."

That seemed to do the trick. "Fine, Aunt. I will assure the moon." He rose from his furs, unashamed of his nakedness and pulled on his leggings. His partner started to whine. "Family comes first." Tallack snapped, shooting Treeve with a venomous scowl. "Always."

Tallack may not have liked my idea, but he was man enough to see my point. I left him to organise his part in the ceremony while I tracked down my angry nephew. Blydh was not in his shelter, nor was he on the training ground beyond the walls. I tried the archery targets and asked the recruits, but none claimed to have seen him.

When I finally caught up with Blydh, he was just leaving Renowden's tent near to the Sea Warrior's shelters at the east gate. His mannerisms were twitchy and his eyes darted from Renowden's door skins, to the gate and back to me.

"Ho there, Blydh. I need a word about your sister's ritual."

"Can it wait, Aunt, I have somewhere I need to be?" He tightened his belt as though some additional weight in his scabbard pulled down his leggings.

"No, it can't. The light already grows dim and your mother said it must be conducted at dusk."

He took a huge breath and sighed, throwing a hip to one side.

I took that to mean I needed to be quick in my request. "I have asked your brother to assure the moon's protection, will you assure the sun?"

He stopped his petulance and frowned. "You give the honour to me over Tallack?"

I watched him weaken in his resolve. It was having the effect I wanted; a reminder of his importance to the tribe and particularly for someone as vulnerable as his little sister.

"I'll do as you ask, Aunt Mel. She is family after all." Those words were music to me. He had no idea that he was of the same mind as his brother. With everything set in motion, I went to the stream to wash and took a pail of water to heat on the Long Hut fire.

When the sun began to set, tribal elders, selected warriors, and my family came in and crammed around the edges of the circle to await Cryda's arrival. Everyone except Blydh looked smart, wearing their best clothing and shoes for the occasion. I should have known the lad was up to something then.

A few stomachs growled their impatience as the smells of the roasting meats wafted in from the pits outside. With all the torches lit and the sun fading fast, Cryda and her twin boys stood in the doorway.

I welcomed them inside and directed them to their places within the salt circle. Taking the babe into my arms, I walked to the bowl of warm water laid on a table in the centre. Cryda had wrapped her in a soft length of woollen fabric, dyed blue like her eyes. The elders chuckled as the child grumbled and fussed at being exposed for a warm wash, but quietened again when I dressed her in a pretty tunic and laid her down on a crib lined with sheepskin.

Kewri stood at the northern point, ripping a loaf into pieces and handing the chunks to the elders as he paced around the circle. A bowl of warm milk was passed from hand to hand, each person dipping their bread and swallowing it down.

Derwa stepped forwards, her husband behind her. She stood for the North Winds, sheltering her half-sister from the cold and assuring her of food and nourishment. Cryda stepped up to the East, carrying the long tendrils of ivy to wrap in a braid about the crib.

The Eastern Winds bring foul beasts and unpredictable weather. Ivy is the most potent protection the earth can offer against such evil. Tallack moved to the west. He held in his hand, a tiny bangle of silver. He leaned over the crib, and laid a gentle kiss on her forehead. The last position was for Blydh. He produced a golden sun disc, its surface patterned with delicate markings in the shape of the four winds. This he held in front of him, for all to see. We were ready to begin.

I turned to Derwa at the northern point. "Who speaks for Cerridwen, mother and crone, keeper of the cauldron of knowledge?"

Derwa stepped forwards and placed the remaining milk and bread next to the crib. "I assure the protection of the mother; may she always have food and love." She kissed the babe's hands, and then dipped her fingers into the milk and dripped a few drops into her mouth. Many of the elders made affirmative noises and cooed at the happy child from outside the circle.

I turned to Tallack at the western limit. "Who speaks for Aranrhod, Goddess of Fertility, Rebirth, Fate and Time?"

"I assure the protection of the moon, may this circle of silver give you fertility and good fortunes through the seasons, rest throughout the night, and all the blessings of calm seas." Tallack slipped the bangle over the babe's wrist and smiled at her. She treated him to a giggle and splutter in return. With a single pace backwards, he clasped hands with Derwa, linking the north and west quarters of the circle.

Next was Cryda's turn. I faced her and nodded. "Who speaks for Cernonnus, God of All Things Wild and of Death and the Underworld?"

Cryda hesitated, it was a dangerous moment, allowing one so powerful to open a pathway from our ancestors to our newest member of the tribe. Her nervousness was mirrored by some of the elders' wives, who could relate to her anxiety. "I assure her protection and a place within our family and our tribe. We welcome her now and always. May she hear our wisdom, speak from the heart and summon our strength and courage to guide her." Cryda stepped up to the ivy braid and unwound a small section to allow the spirits of our loved ones to see her. This she did for just a moment, fearing that the protection from this potent plant might be breached, before closing the braid once more.

"That's long enough." I whispered to her. "We must close the pathway to the Underworld quickly."

Nodding in agreement, Cryda stepped back and held Derwa's other hand, linking three of the quarters together. Blydh held the key to that closure. The power of our sun god. I looked at him and he swelled with pride. This was the task normally assigned to his father.

"Who speaks for the Mighty Lugh, Keeper of Love and Light?"

Blydh did not wait for me to signal a start. He moved with haste to the crib and placed the sun disc next to her head. "I assure the protection of the sun, may this golden disc chase away all darkness and evil that may lurk, may she master many skills, always be warm, and be as fierce a warrior as her father. I close the gateway to the Underworld, in the name of Lugh."

All had gone without a hitch, and I had begun to relax to my task. "The four of you are guardians of this child. Give her name now, so that the gods may call upon her."

Blydh held his brother and mother's hands closing the four quarters of the circle.

Together they chanted, "We name this child, Delen of the Dumnonii."

Every elder, warrior and slave replied. "Welcome to our tribe, Delen of the Dumnonii." Then, one by one, the elders stepped into the salt circle and rested their hands on one of the guardians. Those at the back touched the shoulders of those in front, until the entire circle was filled with Delen's tribe. All were her family; all would love and protect her.

There was a moment of rapturous applause and foot stamping, before the laughter and gift giving commenced. My job was done. I picked Delen up from her crib and cradled her in my arms. Jogging her up and down, I walked closer to Blydh. "Did you want a cuddle with your new charge?"

Blydh scooped up a cup of ale from a passing slave and drank the lot down. "I'd love to, Aunt, but I can't right now. I have somewhere to be." He called out to his warriors, one of whom whistled to another outside. Within moments, a group of horses appeared at the doorway to the Long Hut, decked out with provisions and enough weapons to last a lifetime. He kissed his mother's cheek, threw his cloak about his shoulders and ran outside to his pony.

I tried to follow, but with Delen in my arms, I could not run. "Tallack you must stop him; he cannot go off like this."

"How do you expect me to do that, Aunt? His mind is made up."

"But the Duros will kill him on sight." I sank down on to a bench, clinging hold of the child. "All my scheming had come to nought."

CHAPTER NINE

For a short while, my desperation overcame me. I sat imagining all the horrendous things that the Durotriges and Brea might do to my nephew if they caught him alive. With such vengeance in their hearts, there was no telling what devious torture they would inflict on his body and mind. There was every chance that Blydh and his men were riding headlong into a trap. I closed my eyes and recalled my youth.

Blydh had so much in common with my brother, Cador the Cruel. He would often pile into battle without thinking things through first, or searching for an alternative to fighting. He'd return from raids with gashes the length of his torso and far fewer men than he set out with. Back then, he kept me close by to stitch him up so that he could begin another campaign.

Blydh would be half a day's walk away from help. Even if he kept enough blood inside him to mount his horse, the ride back to camp would be the end of him. I couldn't just sit by and do nothing. Passing the child to her mother, I helped myself to a couple of roasted duck legs, a thick slice of pork, and a small loaf and excused myself from the party.

Tallack called after me. "You can't leave now, Aunt, the merriment has yet to begin."

"I'm going after your brother. Someone has to pick up the pieces when it all goes to kawgh."

He flicked his wrist at Kewri to go with me. I'd forgotten all about my shadow. He was proving a useful addition to my household, and given his size and strength, I would need him if I was to stop Blydh.

Standing on tip-toe, clutching the food, I yelled over the elders' heads. "I need to borrow a couple of things, Nephew. I'll bring them back." Without waiting for his permission, I hurried from the hut with Kewri scurrying after me.

While I fetched my healing kit, knives, and packed the food, I sent him to collect my horse and find one able to withstand his hulking mass at a canter. There was no time to lose. If we could get within spitting distance of the border, I could be on hand to patch Blydh and his warriors up, should they make it out of the Duro camp alive.

It was tough going in the dark. My sight is not what it was in my youth. The only other option was to take the Chieftain's cart and horses and stick to the longer trails, but that would have slowed us down. I figured that if my pony could not see the track clearly, neither would Blydh's. It was cold too. The hoarfrost branched out in spikey white fronds from trees and bushes, casting eerie shadows in the waning moonlight. There would be no fires to thaw us out at the end of our journey either.

Kewri was a surprisingly good horseman, considering his bulk. He'd chosen one of Tallack's large set horses usually reserved for pulling the wagon. It might not have been as fleet as some of the other ponies in the enclosure, but its back was broad and its muscles stout.

What it lacked in speed it made up for with stride. Together we navigated the frozen ruts in the track and pushed hard to narrow the distance between us and the warriors.

From what I'd learned from the scout delivering news about the Duro's new position, I guessed them to be close to the River Sid. That would give them access to the coast and their ally's ships further south, plus a plentiful supply of fresh water past the tidal wash. The moon was already creeping over the compound walls when we left. It was higher still as we passed the last of the homesteads nearer to the borderlands. Most families had moved from the area since Blydh and his Head Hunter Clan had ceased their border patrols. Duro raiding parties were too fond of taking their women and cattle and burning their shelters to the ground.

We galloped across flat fields and picked our way through marshier areas with care, until I could feel that we were closing in on Blydh's men. The River Sid had been the boundary between our tribes since Aebba first became Metern to the Dumnonii after Cador's reign. On our side, we allowed the forest to grow lush, giving our warriors plenty of cover and access to good hunting on their patrols. Now it hid the Duro's camp. There was no way of telling their precise whereabouts. With the need to coordinate with the Ivernii in their boats, I guessed that they were not too far inland.

The natural slope of the valley flattened to a wide flood plain, with good fishing and closer to the shoreline, excellent salt pans. As a defensive position, they had the upper hand. Their scouts and watchmen would spot Blydh and his men crossing the river and galloping towards them from some distance. They would most likely take an arrow to the heart before making it half-way across. The more I thought about it, the more I fretted.

When we entered the dense forest of the western slope of the valley, I knew that we had to be close. The thick undergrowth of unused trails slowed us down to a trot. Not that the horses were complaining. We knew we had driven them hard, their flanks foamed with sweat and their breath froze as a fog. My hips ached and I had a raging thirst, but we couldn't afford to stop.

It was when we saw the glow of the Duro's camp fires through the trees, that we knew we had arrived. Blydh had to be close by. Kewri and I dismounted, leading the ponies through the woodland as quietly as we could manage.

We walked upstream for a short time, keeping within the cover of the shrubs and watching out for Duro scouts. In the dim moonlight, I could just make out a crossing, built from two felled trees and planking between them. With a mound of soil and gravel either side, it looked to me as though it was sufficient to pull a cart across.

These people meant business. They had guards stationed each side, with long bows, axes and short swords. Their ramparts were extensive, lined up without gaps along the edge of their outer shelters. Even a temporary camp like this was well organised and stacked with defensive structures.

There was just one weakness that I could discern. The largest of their tents, which I took to be the Chief's, was right at the edge of the marked-out area. Normally, I'd expect to see that right in the heart of the shelters, protected by all those around. They were densely packed too, as though they were short of space.

Where was Blydh? It was possible that he had led his men further north to cross at a narrower point. That way he could sneak around any weaker defences on the eastern fringes. All we could do was watch and wait. If we crept any closer, our whinnying horses would give us away. If we left the ponies in the woodland and climbed down into the frigid water, our splashes would be heard.

Tying the horses up out of sight, I crouched by the riverbank and wrapped my cloak about my legs. My teeth chattered and my calves cramped but I dared not move in case I missed my nephew. Kewri moved a couple of flat rocks for us to sit on and passed me some of the food from my bags. He had no trouble in wolfing down his share of the duck, but I could only manage a few bites. It stuck in my throat I was so shaken from fear.

I started to regret announcing that I no longer believed in the gods. At little Delen's ceremony, I just went through the motions to please everyone. I never for one moment thought that Cernonnus might unleash demonic spirits into our Long Hut to capture her soul.

We continued to watch late into the night, when their torches burnt out and their fires were nothing but embers. That was when the last of the revellers and drunkards dozed in the closest shelter, or returned to their largest Chieftain tent to sleep. I figured that the guards were on a rota, swapping when the length of a particular tallow candle had fully extinguished. We didn't get the chance to find out.

Kewri nudged me in the ribs. "Over there, Fur Benyn." He pointed towards the southern end of their camp. Blydh and his men had crossed lower downstream and were now crawling across the frozen grass towards their ramparts. I held my breath.

The silver locks of Renowden's hair glinted in the moonlight. A part of me was relieved that Blydh had taken someone of his age and wisdom, another part of me wished that Ren had talked him out of the raid altogether. He was surprisingly nimble on land, considering he'd spent much of his time with the Sea Warriors. His stealth put him right at the back of the first watchman.

I could hardly bear to watch, as Ren reached up and grasped his hand over the guard's mouth, silencing the screams as he swiped his blade through the man's throat. Two more of Blydh's men did the same, clearing all the lookouts from the southern corner of the camp. Blydh slipped under the wooden spiked structure and beckoned his men to keep low and follow him. I counted the silhouettes before they slashed into the skins at the back of the Chieftain's tent. He'd taken just eight of his men, including Renowden. For a long moment, nothing happened. All was silent and still and I swear my heart stopped along with the fearsome inactivity.

I stood up, shaking the blood back into my limbs, just as the tent rent open. Three large figures spilled out through the gap, clawing, punching and slashing at each other in the darkness. In the tangle of bodies, I couldn't see who remained lifeless on the ground when the other two stood up and charged back into the tent. The commotion awoke all those in the Chief's shelter. I had a feeling that Brea would have her own tent. There was no sign of her at all, but I did recognise two of the other men drawing their weapons and facing up to Blydh and his men.

One of the young warriors was my banished nephew, Paega. He brandished the long sword he'd stolen from a hiding place in the mining community. Its shining surface was unmistakable. The man to his left, was Paega's uncle from the Priest Sect. He was a renowned warrior of some standing. This was exactly what Blydh had been hoping for, a chance to fight his half-brother on an equal footing. He encircled Paega, drawing him further from the restrictive space and the shreds of skins from the tent. Renowden faced Paega's uncle, while the rest of the men swung their axes about keeping all others at bay.

By now, word spread about camp that they were under attack. More warriors rushed into the Chief's tent to help, but found themselves funnelled into a narrow gap between the shelters. It was too tight a space for more than a few men to enter the fray. At least that was one factor on Blydh's side. Renowden and his foe were evenly matched. Barring exhaustion, neither man seemed able to gain an advantage over the other.

Blydh shifted his axe from hand to hand, lunging and then pulling back from Paega's reach. When he tired of taunting the lad, he lifted the great bronze blade over his head and brought it down with all his might towards Paega's head. His brother had time to position himself, raising the long sword to meet the axe. The noise it made on contact was chilling. The bronze axe cracked, and then splintered into a dozen or more pieces.

Kewri gasped at my side. "How in the name of Cernonnus…?"

My heart pounded out of my chest. Paega looked at his blade as though he had no idea of its power. It gave Blydh a moment to absorb what had happened. How was this possible? Our forged bronze was the best in the land. His axe was stronger than any other in our tribe. Armed with nothing more than the wooden handle and a knife, Blydh dodged his half-brother's ineffectual swipes to his torso and retreated to find another sword.

Renowden held his own, while three of his comrades fought bravely alongside, slaying more than five men each. Despite their superb efforts, those that were killed were replaced by the never-ending stream of warriors piling through the tent. Blydh took one of their spears, jabbing it into any man who dared to approach. Paega melted into the crowds and disappeared. He'd had his taste of battle and found luck, or the gods, on his side. He clearly was not about to tempt fate.

Blydh lunged with the spear, sticking one man through the face, another through the gut and slashing the throat of a third. He did not notice a fourth man sneaking up behind.

Ren was still battling the Priest Warrior. He reached into his pocket and pulled out a fistful of dry chalk, throwing it into his opponent's face. The temporary blindness was enough for Ren to drive his blade right into the man's chest. Paega's uncle fell to his knees, gasped through the foam of blood oozing from his mouth, before crashing to the floor.

Shoving his foot on the man's shoulder, Renowden wrenched his blade from the bloodied torso and turned to help his Metern. Blydh was defending himself from three men at once. Ren decapitated one with a single back-handed swing of his blade, another Blydh stabbed in the eye. Neither he nor Blydh saw the warrior approaching from the shadows holding a massive hammer.

"No, no, no!" I cried, seeing the horror unfurling before my eyes.

Renowden turned to see the hammer connect with Blydh's skull. The crunch was sickening. The blood spurted in all directions, spattering Renowden's face and chest as Blydh toppled to the floor. I swallowed back bile. Tears fell in torrents down my face. It was all over, it had to be.

Kewri peeled off his cloak and jumped down into the river. "He ain't dead, Fur Benyn. I saw him move."

Leaping to my feet, I was all set to follow, but Kewri barked at me to stay where I was. I watched the sweet giant wading through the strong currents, just as Renowden skewered Blydh's attacker with a spear. There were too many to fight. While the two injured protected Blydh's body, another two warriors fought the barrage of Duros at the mouth of the tent. Renowden grasped Blydh by the wrist and dragged him towards the ramparts and back to where they came.

Kewri stomped as fast as he could across the grass, punching out anyone within the vicinity. He was a one-man killing machine. When he reached our warriors, he crouched down, grabbed Blydh by the arm and yanked him over his shoulder. Ren and the three remaining warriors ran. Kewri neither slowed nor tired. He grappled Blydh's body until he was cradled in his arms, keeping his head above the water as they crossed the River Sid. I untethered the horses and waited close by.

How could my nephew survive such a devastating blow to the skull? At the very least, his head would be fractured, blood loss severe, but we had to try. Paega reappeared with fresh torches, hurling rocks and shouting insults over the field, but he did not follow them. Neither did he seem especially bothered by the death of his uncle, lying mangled at his feet.

We had to get as far away from their warriors and the camp as quickly as possible. It would not take them long to summon a hunting party of vicious fighters on swift steeds to track us. With Renowden's help, Kewri pushed Blydh onto his massive cart horse and climbed up behind him. Holding Blydh upright between his arms, he took hold of the reins and kicked the pony's flanks. I shared my horse with Renowden, sending the others south to collect their own and follow as quickly as they could manage.

Between mine and Ren's knowledge of the area, we were able to lose anyone who might have followed, until we were deep within our own territory. Kewri was covered in congealing blood. Blydh's head lolled on his chest. Every few moments, I asked the giant if my nephew lived.

His reply was brief and the same each time. "He has a strong heart. I can feel it."

Beyond all our expectations, Blydh's heart was still beating when we made it back to camp. The horses almost collapsed from the strain, and we were all twitchy with panic, but we got behind those eastern gates as dawn broke on the horizon. I slid down off my pony and fussed about the giant, trying to help him lift my nephew down from the cart horse. Renowden followed me into my hut, bringing my healing kit and knives. None of us had much hope of him surviving.

I touched Ren's arm. "You'd better fetch his mother and brother." I whispered. "They'll want to say their farewells before he heads off to the Summerlands." I could hardly see from the pooling water in my eyes.

"What about Kerensa?" He asked. He was right. The girl had more than ambition on her mind. I truly believed that she loved him. I nodded and then returned to Blydh as Kewri laid him gently down on my bunk. Turning to my massive new friend, I tried to mouth the words, thank you, but my trembling mouth would not perform.

He gave me a half-smile. "Tell me what you need to fix him. I'll find a way to get it."

How could I repair that kind of damage? Kneeling on the rushes, I reached over him and peeled off the blood-stained cloak, leather tunic, and undershirt. Barring a number of small cuts and bruises, his body was clear of major trauma. His head was a whole different matter. I poured some of Tallack's salt into warm water and stirred until it was fully dissolved. Tipping a little at a time over the top of his head, blood, dirt and fragments of skull rinsed from his hair onto my bedding.

I could see his brain clear as day. Three shards of bone were embedded within its surface.

CHAPTER TEN

The more I rinsed poor Blydh's scalp, the more of his brain I could see. Putting my ear to his chest, I could hear his heart thumping strongly. Other than a massive dent in his head and being unconscious, he seemed to have kept enough blood inside to keep him alive. His face was not pinched into a frown or wincing from pain. He must have been hovering between life and death. We needed to act fast.

Cryda stumbled into my hut, falling to her knees and wailing in her grief. Tallack was behind her, struck dumb from the tragic sight.

"He lives still." I muttered. "His heart is beating."

Tallack slipped around to the opposite side of the bunk, grabbing his brother's hand and shooting me with an intense glare. "Then you must heal him, Aunt. Do whatever it takes. He cannot die."

"I've never had to deal with this sort of injury before. Usually, a blow this severe is fatal." I trembled from the pressure. What they were asking of me would surely spell Blydh's doom, only I would be the cause and not his hubris with the Duros. Cryda and Tallack both fixed their stares on me. They were not giving me a choice.

I turned to my friends. "Ren, would you sharpen my blades, please? Kewri, I need more salted boiled water and as many lit torches as you can find. This hut is too dark for me to work and I fear moving him again into the daylight." I poured the rest of the water over his scalp and picked out the bits of rock and twigs until I had clear sight of the damage. When Renowden returned with my blades, I soaked them in more salted water and then heated them in the fire.

Tallack stood up and hurried to the door. "Wait." He commanded. "We must make a sacrifice to the Morrighan, may she allow him to live, and to Airmed, may she speed his recovery."

I didn't argue. How could I be sure that I hadn't brought this tragedy about by angering the gods with my bitterness and hatred? Cryda went with him, wittering about how she should make a separate offering to secure the gods' favour. As soon as they were both gone, I decided to make a start on what could only be a fool's errand. It was easier to work without their beady eyes questioning every move I made.

With Kewri's help, I positioned Blydh so that the top of his head was at the end of my bunk. I sat on a short stool and smoothed his wet hair down. Starting a little further away from the worst of the crush injury, I sliced into his scalp carefully, until I could feel solid bone meet the tip of my knife. Scraping a bit at a time, I was able to remove a flap of skin with his hair attached from a portion the size of my palm. I laid that over his face. Somehow it calmed me when I couldn't see his ashen features.

Renowden passed me the jug of boiled water. It was warm enough to melt the salt, but not so hot as to shock Blydh. The amount of fractured bone was frightening.

Ren sucked in his lips and shook his head. It didn't fill me with confidence. I took my time lifting each shard from the soft matter, doing all I could to prevent further damage. As the pieces shifted, I asked Ren to trickle a little more liquid across Blydh's brain until every chunk was removed.

By the time I had finished, Tallack and his mother had returned, to see poor Blydh's skull wide open and his skin and hair over his face. Cryda almost swooned. Tallack went wild, grappling the air to get at me, but Kewri held him back. Thank goodness he was there, or I might have become the next sacrifice.

"Please, Nephew. This has to be done. He can't go on with ragged bone stabbing his brain." I implored, hoping to allay his fears, but then, I had no guarantees that my treatment would work.

Ren placed his hand on Blydh's chest. "He's still alive, Chief. That has to be a good sign." His words had great impact on Tallack, the oldest of his crewmen and clearly someone who earned Tallack's trust. The Chief stopped fighting against Kewri's grip, signalling his agreement.

Cryda rushed to her son's bedside and asked for the intervention of Airmed, Goddess of Healing, over and over again in a form of chant. The blood splashes on her clothes were evidence of the slaughtered animals given in offering. I hoped that it would be enough.

The next part of my procedure was more dangerous than the last. I announced what I needed to do in case they thought me mad and tried to stop me. Blydh's skull was splintered in such a way as to leave several pointed sections of skull. I intended to smooth off the edges using a small chisel as a file, leaving a gap of a little smaller than the size of a hen's egg.

It was not as easy as I thought it would be. Even with Renowden holding Blydh's head still, and using my sharpest chisel, I struggled to chip away at the shards without digging into his brain further. It was after my second slip, that Ren suggested a different tool. Of all the items I had in my knife wrap, the one tool that was missing was a flint edge. Grinning, Renowden ran back to his shelter, and retrieved a stone with a remarkably sharp side.

"It's sometimes better than a bronze blade for stubborn parts of animal skins. I wouldn't be without one." He shrugged.

Unconvinced by his praise for the tool, I dunked it in salted water first, in case it still had flesh on its surface, and then gently scratched at the bone. The rounded end of the flint felt good in my hand, easy to wield and control. As the sun reached its highest limit in the spring sky, I had smoothed as much of the gap as I could. All that remained, was to find something that I could use to replace the missing part of the skull.

Tallack and Cryda had not moved. Their repetitive chanting was distracting at first, until its mellow rhythm fell in time with my taps and scratches. Now I needed their attention.

"Cryda, I know that Blydh assured the sun for Delen at her naming ceremony, and that his gift to her should be part of her chain of protection for her entire life, but I ask you now for her sun disc. It is all I can use to cover his soft brain."

To see the former Ruvane of our tribe crumple, was almost heart-breaking. I was asking her to save the life of her first born, by breaking the most potent part of her Delen's protection. Without the sun disc, the little one would always be vulnerable to wicked spirits that might have escaped the Underworld during the ceremony.

I could see from her expression that she needed time to think about it, but the longer we waited with Blydh's head open, the less likely he was to survive. Moving to her side, I rested my hand on her shoulder. "Delen is a strong child. She would be more than capable of fending off unwanted spirits. Just remember who her father was. No one dare confront the child of Aebba the Wild."

Cryda gaze shifted to the floor. She was not convinced by my assertion. What was she hiding? Was my suspicion over Delen's true parentage correct? Was she really the daughter of a visitor from the mountain people? This was not the time for explosive information to come out. I had to push her to make the right choice. "Cryda, I need the sun disc. You must fetch it for me now."

I guided her by the arm to the doorway, and sent Kewri to hurry her along, for Blydh's brain was starting to dry out. Resting my ear to his chest, I listened to his heart beat. It was much faster than it should be. Was he aware of what I'd been doing to his skull? Was this the last stages of his death?

At that point, despite my former disbelief, I too began chanting, asking for Airmed to keep him alive and for the Morrighan to release her grip on his life. Cryda returned with the gold disc within moments. It was mucky already, the golden sheen dulled with baby dribble. I buffed it up and checked that it was large enough to cover the hole. It was, with a little bit to spare all around.

Ren stopped me from sliding it under the edges of Blydh's open scalp. "Fur Benyn. It's a good idea, but one jolt and the metal plate will shift under the skin. His brain would then have no protection at all."

I hadn't considered that. His suggestion was to clip the edges of the golden disc and bend them down to form a lip. For this, he volunteered himself, since my hands don't have the strength that his do. While he shaped the disc and polished its surface, Kewri held Blydh's head still for me to score a groove in the healthy bone around the hole. The disc slotted into place, with only a couple of adjustments, allowing me to return his scalp back where it belonged. After a lengthy session of stitching, I had done all I could.

Cryda stood up and watched the eldest of the twins for a few moments, expecting him to spring back into action. "Why isn't he waking up?" She cried. Tallack took his sobbing mother into his arms and shushed her gently.

"He might wake up, he might not. Cryda, this was always going to be a risky procedure. He is in the hands of the gods now." I chose my words carefully, but she still howled without control.

I heard Tallack whisper into her hair. "I never thought that he'd go through with the raid. I seriously thought he'd see the numbers of warriors and tents and turn back."

This was a time for them to be alone. I dumped my bloodied knives into a bowl and dowsed them with the last of the salt water. Kewri carried it outside for me. Ren followed us. It was only after I had washed and cleared everything away that I realised the level of my exhaustion. My back ached, my arms and hands were sore and my stomach moaned like the dead. Thankfully, it was a warm and sunny day. I lay on the grass next to my goat pen and stared up at the clouds.

Would the Morrighan take my nephew from me after all he had endured? Only time would tell. The whole compound was in a sombre mood, the news of Blydh's situation spreading across camp within moments of our return. I closed my eyes for a few moments, wondering what Brea and that treacherous nephew of mine, Paega would be plotting. How long would they wait until they mounted their attack on us? Sitting up, I watched the easy pace of life my tribe had adopted in recent cycles. They'd grown soft. None of the women had trained or fought alongside men in generations.

Heaving myself up off the ground, I called out to the nearest guard in a watchtower to the west. "Ho there! Are the recruits in training out there?"

The guard shook his head. "No Fur Benyn, nor on the northern side."

"Why's that?"

"Chief Blydh's warriors are all giving their offerings and speaking with the gods." It was a decent enough answer, but not one I wanted to hear. There were no sounds of wood choppers, nor saws, nor anvils. Work across camp had ceased, despite the urgency for us to be fully prepared. I could scarcely keep my eyes open, but I threw one foot in front of the other and returned to my hut to warn Tallack. He sent me away with a barrage of harsh words. Tears tumbled down his cheeks.

What could I do? I needed to watch over my patient, but no one was left to direct the battle preparations. There was only one option available; pretend that I was delivering Tallack's orders. I went to Ren and explained the difficulty. As ever, he was more than prepared to help, despite his need for rest and stitches to close his nicks and scrapes. I gathered the men together, both the Head Hunter Clan and the Sea Warriors, and issued orders. Some were to ride out to scout for Duro attack, others were to gather defence materials and food, while the rest rushed to complete the final ramparts and fletch as many arrows as possible.

I then did the same for the women. Splitting them into groups, I had a rota of women in the watch towers, with the sharpest shooters training the youngsters at the targets. The older folk butchered and cured meats and fish, while the children gathered rocks to hurl in baskets. It was all I could do to keep everyone busy. Ren, I tasked with the most important job of all; to secure the fresh water spring and fence it off from animals. If it came to a siege, it would be the only water that could not be fouled.

Before he set to ordering a group of men to create a stone wall around the spring head, he pulled out a handful of bronze fragments from his pocket. I knew where they had come from. The pieces were forged and shaped on one side and jagged on others.

"Give these to Chief Tallack and let him know that Blydh fought valiantly. If the worst comes to the worst, he will have his place next to his father in the Summerlands." Renowden tipped the bits into my cupped palms. I didn't have the heart to tell him that Aebba was not yet in such a lofty place with the gods.

When I entered my hut, I saw that there was no change in Blydh's condition. Neither Tallack nor Cryda had attempted to move him into a more comfortable position. My nephew sat on a stool near to his brother's head. His eyes were raw and dry, his gaze trained on Blydh's face. Cryda was further away. Her tears were continuous and fresh. I was at a loss as to who I should comfort first.

Stalling for time, I banked the fire up with logs and poured ale for them both. Cryda didn't want any. Tallack took the cup from my hands without registering the offering.

Eventually, he seemed to shake himself from his daze. "The last words we spoke together were not kind. We have done nothing but bicker and argue since you and I returned from Skotek."

He was right, but it helped nothing to point out their stupidity. Twins were supposed to be close. Some say that they have the ability to read each other's thoughts. It was obviously not the case for Tallack. He misjudged his brother's tenacity and fondness for raids. As I moved to pat his shoulder, the metal in my pocket clinked together. Tallack frowned, looking down at my tunic. There was no way to avoid the conversation now.

Taking out the bronze pieces, I laid them out across my hands for him to see. "It's what was left of Blydh's axe." I said meekly.

Tallack picked them up and examined the sharp remains. "What did it hit to cause this much damage?"

"A long sword. The one we saw Paega with on the moors at the Duros' first camp."

"You said it had been yours…" His look turned severe, as though he regretted forgiving me for keeping secrets over Brea. Here was yet another half-truth I'd not revealed. I was rapidly losing his trust. That I could see in his eyes.

I confessed all to him; how I'd found the silvery coloured sword in the lakes near to Stonehenge, and how I had planned on presenting it to the new Chieftain after the trials. He understood that I couldn't favour one twin over the other, but he was cross that I'd asked my slave to hide it in the mining camp rather than show it to him.

He seethed quietly for a time, while I bathed the oozing humours from Blydh's head and checked that his heart still pounded in his chest. Tallack turned the axe pieces over in his hands. "Aunt Mel, do you think that Paega has somehow enchanted the blade? He is the leader of the Priest Sect now; he surely has the ear of Cernonnus like his grandfather before him."

"Are you suggesting that the two-faced little toad has cursed us? You think he wields the mighty force of Cernonnus himself?" It was a horrifying notion, especially in light of my recent hateful mutterings about the gods. I had to dispel that fear from our Metern or we would never prevail against the Duros.

"How could any god favour Paega over Blydh?" I forced myself to smile, making it into a joke. Tallack did not laugh with me. Resting the back of my hand against Blydh's forehead, I checked to see that he was not too hot with fever. So far so good.

Before I could sit down and rest, the door skins were drawn back and Faolan stepped inside. He strode over to Tallack and offered his arm in greeting. Tallack stood up and grasped the big man's forearm. I could see his expression had altered. It was not like the Novantae Chief to poke his nose into family matters.

"I've come to see how the lad is doing, what with him supposed to become my kin when Sorcha arrives." He leaned over the bunk and peered down at my sleeping nephew. "I've seen a lad survive a blow to the head like this before. He was plain off his napper though, could hardly walk and kept shitting his bed."

I glowered at his tactless comments, standing between him and Tallack should things take a nasty turn.

"Still, Blydh might be alright." The Skotek oaf beamed. "But if he wakes up barking like a dog, I shall expect Tallack to wed my girl in his place, or my men and my ships are out of here."

CHAPTER ELEVEN

A vein in Tallack's temple began to throb. It was tempting to let my nephew beat the Novantae Chief with raining fists, but I feared that Tallack would not come out of the fight unscathed. Cryda stopped sobbing long enough to hear the selfish ranting of the old man. She picked up my ale cup and threw it at his head, screaming at the top of her voice to get out. Faolan retreated, snorting his disgust at their treatment of him.

Tallack's teeth clenched together. I could see his anger strengthening. He was preparing to go after him. It took all my strength to push Tallack back, leaning my full weight against his chest.

"Just stop and think for a moment. He is a blowhard and a thoughtless kyjyan, but we can't afford to lose his support, or his ships. Let him cool off for a bit, and then call a meeting of the elders in the Long Hut. They will back whatever decision you make." It took several more attempts to beg him not to antagonise the old rogue any further.

Cryda didn't help matters either. She encouraged Tallack to stick his knife through Faolan's gizzard, and take all his ships as soon as they arrive at the estuary. I hardly needed her to put ideas like that in his head, especially ones that spoke to that sailor's heart of his. Any chance to extend his fleet made him flush with excitement.

Blocking the doorway with my body, I struggled to hold him inside. That was when I heard the first groan coming from the bunk. Tallack had not noticed, he still grappled with my fingers trying to prise me from his path.

There it was again, another groan. Blydh was starting to wake. I shoved Tallack away and hurried to the bed, shortly followed by Cryda.

"Can you hear us, Blydh?" I spoke as softly as I could manage. Blydh simply moaned again, pulled an agonised face and returned to his former inert self.

"That's good, isn't it, Meliora?" Cryda whimpered. I shrugged. This was the first of this kind of injury where the patient lived long enough for me to attempt treatment. I inwardly thanked all the gods that he'd made it this far. Airmed the Blessed Goddess of Healing must have guided my hands. This was hopeful indeed. As much as I desperately needed to sleep, I sat by his side and waited for another moan, a word, anything that would indicate that he was still with us. If Faolan's rude proclamations were anything to go by, Blydh may survive, but be little more than an animal.

Tallack was torn. I could see that he wanted to stay with his brother, but he also wanted to find Faolan and clear the air. At least my short delay tactics had given him time to think things through. "I'm going to find Kerensa. She ought to be here, Mother. Don't you agree?"

Cryda did not answer. She did not care for Kerensa, considering her too lowly a match for her first born and Metern of the Dumnonii. She was just the daughter of

Alchemy Clan leader, Kenver. Cryda expected him to wed the kin of a large tribe, one that could extend our number of allies, trade partners and raise our status within the midsummer gatherings.

Poor Kerensa had attempted to visit him as soon as we got back from the River Sid. Tallack had shooed her away, claiming that she had no right to be there. He'd had most of the day to ponder over the sacrifices his brother had made for the tribe. Perhaps it was enough to realise that Blydh deserved love and happiness as much as the next man. Perhaps they are growing into their roles as Meterns after all.

I watched him slink out of my hut. His temper had all but disappeared with Blydh's moaning. It did not take long for Kerensa to push through the door skins and sink to the floor in floods of tears. She had not seen the extent of his injury. Now his head was bound with bloodied wraps, she could see how grave the situation was. While Blydh had his mother and lover to care for him, I left the hut to check that Tallack had not stirred further trouble with the Chief of the Novantae.

Every bone in my body felt twice its weight as I trudged back across the mud and filth to the Long Hut. Tallack was sitting in his bear carved seat, settling the clamour of voices all about him. I noticed that someone had moved the Ruvane chair back between that of the Chieftain's.

The tribal elders had already gathered, awaiting news of Blydh's recovery. When they finally simmered down enough to hear the Chief, Treeve attempted to sneak into the seat at his side. Tallack snapped his head around and gave him the most vicious glare. There had been enough argument over the Ruvane chair without stoking the fires further. Treeve backed away. I thought he would have the decency to leave the hut entirely, since he is not even a high warrior, let alone an elder, but he stayed and sulked near to the door.

It took a little while for Tallack to explain all that had happened, from Delen's ceremony, to the failed raid and how I had picked out the skull bits from their Chieftain's brain. He went on to announce Faolan's intentions to go back on his word. The elders were outraged, yelling their disapproval and sucking their teeth with disdain. I knew how they would respond. These are not men of action, but of simpering words. They have the ability to sound important without actually having to put themselves in harm's way.

The majority of brute force was undertaken by our young warriors, many of whom never lived long enough to become respected elders. These men also know how to tame an angry Metern, bent on revenge. They handled Aebba the Wild and his mood swings for many cycles. I hid at the back of the hut, and narrowed my eyes at Treeve. If I could not participate in their discussions, I could at the very least hear what was being decided.

"Chief Tallack, I understand your reluctance to trust the Skotek Chief. He has, as you said, reneged on the formal arrangement that Blydh and he agreed upon, but we do need his ships and the support of his warriors." It was one of the elders who rarely spoke at these gatherings. As a result, his opinions were worthy of consideration. He had hit upon a crucial point that Cryda had missed. She suggested in my hut, that Tallack should over throw the Novantae the moment they arrived and take their ships. As attractive as that sounded, we did not have enough to fight the Novantae Sea Warriors, let alone man their ships as well as our own. We needed more people to fight the Durotriges and the Ivernii. In short, keeping them as allies was essential if we were to hold our ground.

Two other elders said virtually the same thing, couched in different words. These were the elders who liked to sound clever, but hadn't spoken an original thought for most of their lives. They were also the first to take credit when another's suggestion worked out for the best. Tallack listened to all the elders in turn. I could see that he found the whole process exceedingly tedious.

I glanced about the room, looking out for Treeve the trouble maker. He was not at the back of the hut. I scanned the rest of the crowded room, but could not see him anywhere. Just as I was about to step outside into the late sunshine, he reappeared with Kerensa in the doorway.

"See, they are backing the Novantae. Faolan will be forced to marry Blydh. You will never be the next Ruvane. You may as well give it up now." The spiteful little sailor smirked. Kerensa shook her head, craning to hear what Tallack was saying to the old men.

The Chief stood up from his tall chair and raised his hands to silence the elders. "Please, let's keep this civilised and sensible." He pointed towards the first man to speak up. "What you say is true. We need allies more than we need enemies right now, regardless of how attractive their ships would be next to my Phoenician vessel."

He waited for the mild titters to subside. "And as much as I hate to admit it, Faolan has us at a disadvantage. We can't afford to offend him. In bargaining with Blydh, he was assuring his daughter the place of Ruvane in our tribe, with successive generations maintaining an alliance with the Novantae and all the trade routes for our tin in Skotek." He took a deep breath, as though he was wrestling with his own mind. "Therefore, whether my brother recovers or not, Faolan's daughter will bind with one of us. If Blydh recovers fully and is back to his old self, then Sorcha will wed him. If…" Tallack swallowed back his emotions. "If Blydh is only half-well, then I will bind with her. Either way, she will become Ruvane."

I kept my sights on Treeve. At this announcement, he paled, then screwed up his nose into a scowl. He muttered just loud enough for Kerensa to hear, but I caught it too. "Not if she's dead, she won't." He left the Long Hut before I could catch hold of him. I had to warn Tallack of his lover's duplicity, but it was news he was not likely to believe. Perhaps it was all bravado. These young lads and their bold notions rarely get beyond bluster. Although that's what Tallack thought when Blydh announced his plan to raid the Duro camp.

Pushing between the elders, I launched myself through the doorway, but Treeve was gone. Kerensa shrugged when I asked her if he'd mentioned where he was heading, folded her arms across her chest, and skipped back towards my hut.

My mind was foggy, my body so tired I could barely stand and I was half-starved with hunger. I spun around, looking across the island for inspiration. All I knew was that Blydh had to recover, and Tallack needed to rein Treeve in before he could ruin our carefully crafted alliance with Faolan.

Just as I resigned myself to rest before making any further decisions, a scout rode into camp. He was one sent a few days before to mind the northern routes to and from the River Sid. He skidded to a halt and dismounted.

"Fur Benyn. I've just heard from another scout sent to relieve me. Is Chief Blydh…?"

"No, he lives, just, but he's a long way from recovery. What have you to report?"

"The Lady Brea and the Chief of the Duros have been away from their camp at the Gittesham Stones. They were on their way back to the River Sid when I started back."

"It was definitely the Lady Brea you saw?"

"Clear as day, Fur Benyn. There's no mistaking that one, if you know what I mean."

I did know what the warrior meant. After Aebba's death, her mild manners and tolerance vanished, replaced by a brash young woman with lofty ambitions. Her attitude and clothing altered overnight. If this warrior said he saw Brea at the stones, I had no reason to disbelieve him.

"That must be why they haven't retaliated yet. Those stones are not far from their camp though. They will be preparing their approach any day now." Where were Faolan's ships? Had they been intercepted by the Ivernii before they could make it around Land's End to help us? Our defence strategies were even more important than ever.

I thanked the warrior and sent him to the Long Hut to inform Tallack and the elders of all he'd seen. Staggering into my hut, I made sure that Cryda was watching over her son, and then collapsed onto the bunk meant for patients. My hunger would have to wait until I'd slept.

Within moments, the world about me disappeared. I know not how long I dozed, but it was dark when the squeals woke me. Cryda and Kerensa were flapping about Blydh as though he was on fire. Rubbing my eyes and straining to see, the grogginess subsided.

"What is it? What's all the noise?" I pulled myself up and crossed the rushes to see for myself. Blydh was awake, but his left eye looked strange. Cryda and Kerensa were skipping about hugging each other. Shoving them aside, I leaned in and took a closer look. The black circle inside his eye was massive, far larger than the one on his right. That spelled trouble. "Can you hear me, Nephew? Do you remember what happened?"

He blinked a few times, moaned and closed his eyes again. Panicked, I rested my hand on his chest. His heart was still as strong as before, even if his skin felt clammy.

"He'll be back to himself in no time at all, won't he Meliora?" Cryda remarked. Her former dislike for Kerensa had suddenly vanished. Now she seemed thrilled to have her at his bedside, the two women bouncing around with joy. Such a fickle woman. It was too soon to celebrate. Although he was able to open his eyes, we still had no idea if he had any awareness, let alone whether he could speak or move.

It was late. I could tell from the frost gathering on the tips of the grass as I walked back to the Long Hut. Tallack presided over the elders and all his Sea Warriors, treating them to fine roasted meats and more ale than could be spared. What was he thinking? We needed to maintain our stocks of food in the event of a siege. There was no getting through to these youngsters the necessity of preparation. Despite my annoyance, the smell of slow cooked pork basted in butter was too much to bear. I sneaked a bowlful of rabbit stew and ripped a hunk of pork from one of the platters at the top table. My stomach rebelled from the long abstinence, but I was determined to get it down me.

Tallack watched me tucking into the food. "How fares my brother, Aunt?"

I swallowed my mouthful and sat alone at the table laid out for Kerensa, myself and the Chief's man friend, Treeve. He sat next to Tallack in the Ruvane's chair as though he had every right to be there. I squinted at the upstart, but he just smirked defiantly.

"Blydh opened his eyes just a while ago, but then went back to sleep without saying anything. I'll redress his stitches as soon as I'm fed."

Tallack stood and lifted his cup of ale, encouraging his warriors to stand with him. "To my brave brother, Chief Blydh. He'll live to fight and defeat the Duros yet." His warriors cheered, they all drank and sat back down. Tallack was in one of his irritating loud moods.

"See my incredible aunt there," He gestured to me, although there was no need. Everyone in the compound knew who I was, especially the accident prone and sickly ones. "She galloped off to be at my brother's side in his time of need. Without her, Blydh would surely have succumbed to his wounds."

My mouth was too full to correct him. In truth, Renowden and Kewri were the saviours. Without their strength and quick actions, Blydh would be on a spike in the centre of the Duro camp. By the time I had cleared my mouth enough to speak, he'd moved on.

"My traitorous half-brother has stolen an unbeatable weapon of the gods. A truly magnificent sword, forged by Cernonnus himself, and gifted to my aunt during the midsummer gathering at Stonehenge. Is that not so, Aunt Mel?"

"Well, not really it was…"

"As she performed the ritual cleanse in the lakes near to the sacred grounds, Cernonnus sent the shining blade through the water to find her. Being the dutiful kin of Meterns, she kept it safe for Blydh and me, so that we could take possession of it when our trials were over."

"But that's not what..."

"Paega, spiteful and shameful brute that he is, stole it from her to side with our enemies." He banged his cup down on the table. The ale splashed all about him. "Now Paega believes he has the gods' favour. The sword of Cernonnus shattered my brother's axe, but did not kill him. Cernonnus did not want Blydh to die."

I sighed. He knew his story to be false, yet would not let me correct him. Now the ill-advised raid would become part of our spoken history as some message from the gods. He hadn't finished his point, and I'd given up trying to put things straight.

"We will not let this pretender, Paega keep this sacred blade. We'll forge a new weapon with which to take it back, and offer a sacrifice worthy of all the warriors waiting for us in the Summerlands. What say you all?"

The roar of cheers and stamping was unbearable. It made my head thump. I had no idea how he would find out what made the sword so strong. He'd only seen it from a great distance. The rest of his knowledge was made up of what I'd told him. It was certainly made of no metal that I'd ever seen before. Maybe it *was* from the gods.

"We should give a large sacrifice to honour Cernonnus, Chief Tallack." Young Treeve piped up. I didn't like the devious smile he wore as he spoke out. "Perhaps a high status maid warrior, someone who would please the gods, and who would be grateful that Blydh was spared."

We all knew whom he had in mind. Kerensa may not be of Chieftain blood, but she was a clan leader's daughter, and someone Treeve would rather have killed.

It irked me more than I imagined. "Maybe a young Sea Warrior would suit the gods better. Would you like to volunteer, to show your loyalty to your Chief?"

Tallack roared with laughter.

Treeve was spitting with fury. "Are you going to let her talk to me like that?"

Tallack patted Treeve on the knee. "Don't be so sensitive. She's teasing you."

I wasn't, but hey, if it kept Tallack on my side I was prepared to let it go.

Tallack thought for a moment, tapping his finger to his chin. "He does raise a good question though. Something so precious and important as a weapon of the gods would need a sacrifice of some magnitude. Who should we choose?"

CHAPTER TWELVE

The entire hut fell silent. Both Tallack and Blydh had the authority to choose anyone within the tribe as an offering to the gods. The more senior position the chosen victim held, the greater the sacrifice. Despite my recent doubts over their existence, I was beginning to think that the whole terrible incident with Blydh's wounds could have been avoided if I hadn't goaded our deities beforehand. I dare not speak up, nor look directly at my nephew for fear of him choosing me.

"Aunt Mel?"

My stomach lurched. Was he picking me for death, or asking my opinions? Keeping my eyes cast down, I said, "Yes, my Chief?"

"Can you not think of a suitable gift to honour our god of the Underworld in payment for his favour in the battle to come?"

I could feel his and the elders' stares warming my skin in anticipation. Was he really asking me to pick a person from our tribe to die in a grotesque way to sate a god's vengeful thirst for blood?

"Well?"

Such an impatient lad, he wouldn't give me time to think of an alternative. The faces of all the people I had seen about the compound that day flashed before my eyes. None deserved to die. That was when the vision of the white hart flitted through my mind, the secret sighting of the lonesome deer. Would it be sufficient? Did we have enough time to hunt before Brea and the Duros marched west for our lives? It was all I had to offer. "With respect, Chief Tallack, would it not be better to offer something pure and unsullied by human hands, something that Cernonnus could identify with himself?"

Tallack edged forward in his tall chair, intrigued. "What have you in mind?"

"When I was in the woods not a quarter moon ago, I saw a lone white stag as tall as a horse. His antlers had not yet dropped for the spring. I believe he revealed himself to me for this very purpose. It was the spirit of Cernonnus himself, telling me to retrieve his sword from Paega."

I amazed myself how quickly I could spin a yarn. From the expressions on the men's faces all around me, I knew that they were taken in by my tall tale.

Tallack grinned at me. "Well, Aunt, you are full of surprises. We will track this white beast at dawn, and I will have a pair of axes made from our finest metal using the hart's antlers for the handles. We have our work cut out for us, men. This stag must be captured alive for the ritual."

I wanted to stay and tell him to send a hunting party, not to go himself. There was so much still to do. It would be far safer to send a few skilled trackers after the rare creature, leaving our Chief to direct the training in camp. I stole a glance up at Tallack. His rosy cheeks and raucous laughter put me in mind of his father. Aebba would not be moved when he'd had a skin full of ale and neither would Tallack. I had worn out my luck. Picking up the last of the bread and meats, I scurried out of the Long Hut.

Renowden and a couple of the Sea Warriors had completed the wall around the spring head and were washing themselves in the crossing of the shallow stream near to the west gate. They looked beaten and in desperate need of rest.

"Here, have this between you and then get some sleep. We will need all the men armed and ready to fight at a moment's notice." I handed the bowl to Ren and slunk back to my hut. Blydh was awake, but as far as I could tell by torchlight, his left eye was still blown.

"Has he said anything at all? Does he recognise us?" I asked Kerensa, but her features gave me all the answer I needed. Blydh stared off into the distance with a vacant expression. I sat on the bunk next to him and peeled back the dressing. My stitches were holding well and not leaking vile smelling humours. I counted that as a blessing, although there did seem to be a lot of swelling around his scalp flesh which put pressure on the catgut.

"Where's Cryda?" I said, fetching a cup of water to try and tempt him to drink.

"She's gone to feed Delen and get a little rest. That new slave of hers brought the babe over here, but I sent her back out. I didn't want the crying to disturb him."

Holding the back of Blydh's neck I tilted his head up and touched the cup to his lips, hoping it would trigger a memory of how to drink. It didn't. The water spilt down his chin and onto his chest. Without another case like this to compare recovery times to, I had no idea what to expect. Every attempt I made to pull him out of his daze, upset Kerensa even more. At length, I decided he would fare better without her tears.

"Get yourself some sleep, child. I'll send for you if he takes a turn for the worse." I didn't need to ask her twice. Alone with my patient, I tried to assess how bad his senses were. I took a lit torch and moved it from left to right in front of his face to see if his eyes would follow. No luck there. I clapped my hands together behind his head, but he didn't react at all. After a while I gave up. He was starting to smell ripe and he'd pissed himself again. It took some time to clean him up, and with the help of Kewri, get him into a sitting position on my bunk.

Kewri was so patient and kind, I am beyond grateful to him. He held Blydh in his arms while I changed the bedding and gently laid him back down beneath clean furs. As he let go of his legs, Kewri accidentally brushed Blydh's foot. My nephew jumped, as though he'd been tickled. I uncovered his feet and stroked the undersides. Blydh did it again. His whole body jiggled from the sensation. He had feeling in his legs. I took out my bone needle and pricked his thumb. Blydh pulled his hand away.

I was overjoyed with these responses. It gave me a little hope that he would recover further. Maybe when the swollen flesh had settled back down, he would fully wake. Kewri had rested during the afternoon and was happy to watch over Blydh while I got more sleep. I know I created a fuss over my nephew's orders for him to follow me about for my protection, but I thank Cerridwen and all the goddesses combined for his help. The soiled bedding could wait until daylight. My poor body was beyond exhausted. Until it got the rest it needed, I was not fit to help anyone.

Kewri let me stay in my bunk until past dawn. When I awoke, Tallack was at Blydh's bedside looking grief stricken. My first thought was that Blydh had died during the night and no one had told me. My chest fluttered in deep anxiety until Kewri raised his hand to me.

"He lives, Fur Benyn." He smiled that big lazy grin of his and repeated the same phrase as before. "He has a strong heart. I can feel it."

That was all I needed to calm my fears. Breathing deeply to still my racing pulse, I rose from my bed and splashed cold water on my face. "Did he say anything during the night?" I asked Kewri. The giant shook his head.

Tallack said nothing, just stared down at his listless brother in pity. It was hard to judge what he might be thinking. They had been such a close pairing that even when they were pitted directly in competition with each other for the Chieftain Challenge, Tallack and Blydh helped one another through the trials they faced equally. When their cheating half-brother was denounced, they formed a strong pact to become the very first joint Meterns of the Dumnonii. I really thought that it would be a special bond that would last their entire lives.

Now I wasn't so sure. The arguments and differences of opinions over how the tribe should be managed had strained their relationship. Was Tallack mourning the past, or feeling guilt at hoping Blydh would never recover? None but the gods would have the answer to that question, but it hovered in my mind all day.

At length, Tallack left my hut without uttering a word. His men met him near to my door holding the reins of his horse. I had to bite my tongue to stop myself calling after him. He was the Metern. If he chose to hunt a rare white deer instead of training his warriors, what could I do to alter his mind?

Kewri spooned some porridge into a bowl and offered me some warm ale to wash it down. It suddenly dawned on me that neither Tallack nor I had given him what he'd asked for after he'd saved my life. All he wanted was a warm bed and a roof over his head.

"Kewri, when you have slept, can you bring some wood to build another bunk for yourself. I think we can squeeze you in over there by the fire." That huge grin reappeared again.

"I'll sleep later when it's built." He put down his bowl and lumbered out of the hut in search of the materials he needed. Perhaps I would feel safer knowing that he is around, especially if Brea and her savages break through our defences.

After a quick rinse of our bowls and cups, I checked on Blydh again. He needed to drink water or his innards would dry out. I tried again to pour a little from a cup into his mouth but he almost choked. Coughing up bubbling spit and water, it seemed to jolt him awake. His hand thrashed in front of his face, pushing the cup away.

"Blydh! Can you hear me? Nephew?" I almost shouted it.

Blydh groaned a long mournful growl. His mouth opened and he croaked. "Not water. Ale." He spluttered. I was so happy; I almost fell off the bunk. Clapping my palms together in glee I held his face in my hands and kissed each cheek.

"Get off me woman. I need resin. Get me poppy resin." The words were slurred, but I understood enough to make me wildly ecstatic.

I dashed to the doorway, shouting to anyone I could find. "Fetch the Lady Cryda, send a scout after Chief Tallack, Blydh has woken." Hurrying back to my patient, I took a small pinch of resin and mixed it in water, making sure not to give him too much that his senses would be addled. When I got back to the bunk, Blydh was waving his hand in front of his face.

"What is it?" I asked, almost predicting his response.

"I can't see out of my left eye."

Given all that his body had endured, he was lucky it was only one eye. I didn't think he would live long enough to get back to camp, let alone recover as well as he had. What could I say to the lad? I handed the cup of resin water to him and let him sip. Cryda and Kerensa arrived within a few moments, fussing about his bed and kissing him like a child. I thought it best to allow them some time alone with him. He could tell them about the blindness in his left eye. I had no way to fix it for him.

Tallack came skidding to a halt a short time later. He'd left his hunting party to snare the white stag without him, in order to speak with his brother. I went down to the stream and soaked the bedding, allowing the current to do my work for me. All around, tribal members toiled away at the orders I had laid down days ago.

The watchtowers were stocked with baskets of rocks and new arrows, the grain store was above ground on stilts and filled with traded wheat and oats, the dried fish and meats were guarded from temptation and the fresh water supply assured. We were in good shape, but for the clueless recruits and the absence of our allies, the Novantae and their ships.

The longer we waited for those Skotek tribesmen to arrive, the more I started to think old Faolan was not true to his word. All he had to do was wait until we were at our weakest, when the Duro's attack had taken its toll, and he could sail up the estuary and claim our lands and mines for himself. That is supposing he could do so before Brea and her horse lords could take them from us instead. So much was riding on his tribe's help, yet they were nowhere to be seen.

I washed what filth I could from the bedding and laid them out to dry in the weak sunshine. There would be few chances to gather new bedstraw in the near future. I returned to my hut for a large blade with which to gather more, but Tallack blocked my path.

"Come with me to the forge, Aunt. I want you to explain that mysterious sword to the smith." He said, grabbing my arm and turning me about. I had no chance to counter his demands. The forge was a kind description for the shack where they heated the ingots of copper and tin to make bronze. There were a number of apprentices lurking about hoping to learn the skill of the old smith. If they could gain his ability, they too would be more valuable to a tribe by staying in camp, rather than learning to fight.

I peered at the short weaklings and grinned. Who could blame them for avoiding conflict? If the old smith chose them to train, they would build a strength far greater than the average warrior in time. It was a cunning way to appeal to the womenfolk in camp. They were onto a good thing.

Tallack called out to the smith, who had his back to us sharpening a blade on a whetstone. "Ho there! I have a commission for you." The smith saw us and stopped his labours immediately. Looking pleased with himself, Tallack tried to explain his need for a metal that had a silvery appearance and could crack a bronze axe into fragments.

The smith shook his head. "Begging your pardon, Chief Tallack, but it ain't silver. Even if we could get hold of enough to make a blade the size you describe, the metal is too soft for weapons. The cost of such an item would be enormous."

"But my aunt here saw just such a blade with her own eyes." Tallack pouted. "Tell him." He nudged me in the arm.

"I did, but like the smith says, Nephew, it could not be silver. Perhaps it is a metal known only to the gods." I could see that Tallack was building up for a tantrum, just like his father used to when he couldn't have his own way. The smith looked petrified. I needed to diffuse his anger and direct it elsewhere. "When we beat the Duros, you can have the Sword of Cernonnus for yourself. Paega doesn't deserve to have such a weapon after his treachery."

"Hmm." Tallack pondered my words, narrowing his eyes. "Until that time, I want Blydh and I to have matching blades, curved like the Phoenicians and really huge. How long will that take you?"

The smith glanced down at the ground. It was another foolish request. "Chief, bronze weapons of that size are too heavy and easily crack. I could make you both new axes. We have enough metal for those."

I sensed that his suggestion would not satisfy the splendour Tallack had in mind.

"Fine, but not like the usual axes. There's no strength in relying on an angled stick with a tiny capped blade stuck on the end. I want a big curved blade, with antler handles running through the metal at the sides. Make me a mould so that Blydh's is the same as mine. Together, we will be unstoppable."

The smith raised his brows. There was no point arguing with Tallack. His mind was set on a curved weapon of such a size that all who looked upon it would tremble. It did not occur to him that it might be too heavy or brittle to use. I gave the smith a piteous smile. There were far better uses for our limited metal supply than to create two unwieldy axes. Still, at least they would be valuable enough to use as payments to Cernonnus, should the worst happen and our Chiefs needed entry into the Summerlands. Not that dwelling on such terrible thoughts was a healthy occupation.

Content with his order, Tallack headed back towards the Long Hut, and no doubt, too much ale and more tall tales. When was he going to train the recruits? While I laboured away at my chores, taking in the washing, grinding more powders and mixing tinctures, seeing to the goats and such, young Treeve came barrelling into the compound panting as though he'd been running all day long. In fact, he had only run along the river bank from the estuary to our southern gate.

Bent double and panting, he yelled up to the watchman. "Call the Chief. There are ships heading towards the river."

My relief washed over me in a soothing wave, until I saw the look of panic on the boy's face. Why would he be so frightened of our allies finally making port? That was when it hit me. "What colours are they flying, Treeve? Is their banner blue for the Novantae?"

Gasping, he spat on the ground. His face was red and pinched. "No Fur Benyn. Their banners are green."

CHAPTER THIRTEEN

My heart froze. Our Skotek allies had abandoned us to the Ivernii and Duros dual attacks. How could we possibly man Tallack's ships and the compound defences at the same time? The watchman blew a long blast on the cattle horn, calling everyone able bodied to the grass outside the Long Hut.

Tallack did not look amused. He strolled from the Chief's hut holding a whole roasted pigeon in one hand and his ale cup in the other. When Treeve pushed through the crowds to Tallack's side, his bravado fell away.

"Ivernii ships nearing the bay. We are too few to fend them off. We need all the Sea Warriors and as many bowmen and women as can be spared." I gasped, hurrying towards him.

I knew that preparing the compound would not be enough. Now that battle was imminent, neither of our Chiefs had a plan of attack nor defence. The older warriors could fight, but not in any coordinated way. Having the Ivernii thin our numbers by surprising us must have been Brea's plan all along. With the Iwerdon tribe bearing the majority of early casualties, the Duros could simply walk in and take over the few of us left who survived. It must be why they had waited before retaliating.

Tallack didn't seem to be in control. He was more used to trade negotiations and ordering men about ships than organising a battle. Blydh was the Head Hunter, experienced in deadly skirmishes and successful raids, barring his latest venture. Men and woman about camp didn't know which way to turn. Some collected their weapons and scaled the ladders to the walkway near to the top of the compound walls. Others hovered next to Tallack awaiting their orders. Looking about for guidance, Tallack breathed heavily. The future of our tribe lay in his hands.

Faolan appeared from the undergrowth of the wooded area to the east of the island. He was still pulling up his leggings as he walked. "What's all the fuss about?"

Treeve repeated his message to the Skotek wolf, which prompted a crazed grin on the Chief's face.

"So, what are you all waiting for? Get to the ships and fight the kyjyans!" He let out a howl worthy of his name and slapped Tallack's back. "Shall I go with you, or stay and defend?"

It was a critical moment. Did Tallack trust Faolan enough to leave him in charge of our compound, with our young and sick, with the food and metal stores and enough hostages to last a lifetime?

I could see Tallack's indecision. He stared hard at the Novantae Chief, weighing up his intent. After a lengthy pause, he said. "Come with me, Faolan and watch my ship cut right through their fleet." I was relieved to hear it, but then who would protect the island? Tallack called out again. "Where's Renowden?"

"Here, Chief."

"You will stay behind and assure the safety of our people."

I was going dizzy with holding my breath. Tallack was beginning to make sensible decisions. There was hope for us yet. He divided the able bodied into two groups. Those who could swim, shoot and fight went to the row boats in the river, and from there to the ships in the bay. Those who could not swim stayed behind to man the defences in camp.

That left me between the two. Where could I best be of use? Tallack rushed off to the boats, leaving me to decide for myself. Kewri stood behind me, holding my medicine kit and the reins to our two horses. I guess he thought I should be close to the action.

Normally, I would have baulked at the idea of putting myself in the line of fire, but seeing how Kewri made short work of the Duros during Blydh's raid, I was in no doubt that he would put himself in harm's way to protect me.

Mounting my horse, we set off at a canter. It didn't take long before we had over taken the row boats, their winding route slower than our direct path on land. As soon as we were clear of the marshes, Kewri led the way across the flatlands of homesteaders' properties to the coast. As we passed the wider parts of the bay, we called out to the sailors making ready on Tallack's ship.

The enormous Phoenician craft was a prize in any tribal hoard. Tallack made sure that there was always someone aboard to raise an alarm if a raiding party attempted to take her. With the threat of the Ivernii ever present, my nephew had increased the number on watch to more than a dozen. They now hurried about the deck in preparation.

One of the smaller vessels rowed closer to us on the shoreline. It was a seasoned canoe crafted from rough-hewn planking and sealed with a leather hull treated with birch tar. Since Tallack got hold of the Phoenician vessel, he had less need of the smaller boats. They were mostly used for short trips relaying goods and passengers to the Phoenician craft. I wondered what the Iverni ships would be like by comparison. Were Tallack and his men in for serious trouble, or could we fight them off unaided?

Kewri and I waited until his men came close to the riverbank and told them that Tallack and his warriors were not far behind us, before we galloped off to the coastal path. A couple of things in our favour were the enormity of the estuary and the strong currents that were hidden within. Strangers to these waters would easily be thrown off course, or swept out to sea with the force of the tide. The bay itself was deep and riven with shifting sandbanks to beach those who did not pay attention to its ways. Again, there we had the home advantage.

It was roughly a quarter day's walk to the beach from the island, but it took much less on horseback. With our ponies well fed and rested, plus the salt flats drier than usual from the kind weather, we cantered to the headland in no time at all. Kewri dismounted as soon as we reached the beach. I was too stunned at the sight before us. The Iverni ships were not huge and ornate, like Tallack's, but they were plenty in number. As far as I could tell, each smaller craft held at least a dozen men or more.

Their sails were tied and oars extended as they approached the narrow gap at the river mouth. I hoped to Cernonnus that Tallack and Faolan had formed some sort of plan against such a number of men. I counted as many as thirty crafts before the bobbing waves made me lose track. How were we to out manoeuvre half such a number?

Kewri tethered our horses and walked across the dunes looking for driftwood. We would need a fire to stay warm in the biting winds, depending on how long we would need to stay around to tend to any wounded men. I sat at the dry high-water mark in the sand and pulled my cloak about me. Feeling utterly helpless as they rowed ever closer, I suddenly wondered what I'd do if one of the Ivernii swam to shore with an injury. Would I feel compelled to heal their wounds too, or would I be overcome with extreme hatred for my enemy and command Kewri to kill them? I felt the pressure of that question pressing down on my chest, but I said nothing. I would have to make that decision if and when it happened.

Until the time when I could offer my skills, all I could do was watch and wait. If the sea battle looked to be favouring the Ivernii, Kewri and I would have to ride like the wind back to camp.

"You don't think that the Duros are attacking the island at this very moment, do you?" I asked Kewri when he returned with the sticks and driftwood. He dropped his armful of supplies and shrugged. For a few moments he considered my words, frowned and said; "Do you want to return now, Fur Benyn?"

I looked at the sky, the ocean and the sand for inspiration, but no guidance came to me from the gods. "I don't know. What if right this very moment, Lady Brea and her Duro Chief are slashing and burning their way through our family and friends?"

Kewri scratched the back of his neck and pulled a face. How would he know? I was not helping matters with my anxiety. We'd made a decision to be on call should Tallack or his men need us. That was all we could do for now.

The land at the end of the River Exe is relatively flat, little more than salt marshes and sand dunes. There were no high points where we could view both the estuary and the bay at the same time. As the sun moved into our line of sight, we watched the Ivernii boats approach the river mouth. It was a tense time. Would Tallack wait for them to paddle into the estuary, or sail out to meet them in the bay?

When it looked like they would enter the river, Kewri strapped the wood to the backs of our ponies and we walked along the beach to see where our men were stationed. The last time I had travelled in a boat with my nephew along the river, he'd let the current take us on a winding journey along the deeper channels. Now that the Ivernii boats were close, I could see old Dathi, their Chief leading his men in a more direct path. Did he know how shallow the waters were at this time? Was this the basis for Tallack's plan, hoping that they would become stranded on a sandbank at low tide? It was a risky gamble, since the ocean was nowhere near fully out.

Kewri led us back along the coastal path, by-passing the salt marshes and sending the waders and gulls shrieking into the air. If the Ivernii hadn't spotted us before, we had certainly announced our presence with all the noise from the bird calls. Now that we were alongside the widest stretch of the river, it was easier to see the whole estuary. Where were our men? The Phoenician ship sat at anchor in the central and deepest part. The smaller crafts of our fleet surrounded it, but all were still. From such a distance it was difficult to see who, if any, men were aboard.

Was Tallack going to let the Ivernii sail right up and take possession of our most prized vessel? In a flat panic, I kicked the pony's flanks and hurried further inland. Had something befallen our tribe?

That was when I saw the flicker of light on the Phoenician ship. Where the sleek curve of the stern arched up and over the deck, a chain hung down on which a metal basket for small fires was suspended. This glowed brightly. Someone had lit the stove.

I pulled back on my horse's reins and stopped. Kewri did the same. As Dathi of the Ivernii gazed in wonder at the proud lines of our foreign beauty, I saw the bowmen sneak along the deck to set their arrowheads aflame. Tallack planned to surprise them all.

My stomach flipped and sent a burning surge of bile into my gullet. It was a risky strategy to employ, since it allowed the enemy to completely surround our boats in order that they should be close enough to fire upon. Was this Faolan's idea, knowing what was at stake if they failed? The funnelling wind stung my eyes. Was it strong enough to extinguish their arrows before the flames could catch hold of the Ivernii warriors and the wood of their boats?

They were almost at the point of no return when a single arrow let loose from the Phoenician ship. As soon as it was air born, the game was up, it was all or nothing. It soared high over the boats and rippling water and thudded into the hull of an Ivernii vessel. This was Tallack's order to fire. His men laying in the smaller crafts sat up, nocked their arrows and loosed them at will. It rained bolts from all directions, some aflame, others simply seeking the hearts of men. The plan seemed to be working for a few moments. The Ivernii flapped about in shock trying to scoop water onto the burning darts while others ripped them from the hulls and threw them overboard as more fell from the skies.

The first few volleys took out more than ten of the Ivernii warriors, but their crewmen took action. They stowed their oars and lifted shields above their heads. Overlapping the wooden protection, the blazing arrows embedded but the flame soon burned out. It needed something else to get the wood to catch.

It was as though Tallack was channelling my thoughts. Some of his men hung over the sides of the ship and threw bladders of watery grease over the shields and men. That got it going. Those with oars reversed their trajectory, steering them away from danger. The men holding the flaming shields slung them into the river. They were exposed once more.

I jumped for joy on the bank side, thumping Kewri's arms to join me in celebration. He did not move. Turning my gaze back to the fleet, I saw what Kewri had noticed. While our men attacked from the starboard side of the Phoenician ship, they had not paid attention to the Ivernii crafts approaching their port bow.

With hooks and lines, they grappled the planking of the ship and dragged their own craft close enough for their warriors to board. Carrying blades and axes, the sneaky Ivernii were cutting their way through our men before they knew what had happened. Necks were opened, bellies slashed, and entrails spilled out onto the decks in a slippery mass attracting the gulls in massive numbers.

More of Tallack's crewmen scrambled to join in the fight, paddling their smaller crafts closer to protect their Chief and the best ship in the fleet. Those aboard tripped on the long oars, others fell overboard, some swam to the small boats, only to be bludgeoned over the heads by the wicked Ivernii men.

Our numbers were decreasing every moment, warriors, youngsters, and women falling at their hands in equal measure. The muddy river took on a dark colour where their blood churned in the currents. I held my hands over my mouth in despair. There were so many of them. Their nimble boats swarmed between our larger unwieldy ones, delivering their most able fighters to the most vulnerable of our crewmen.

It was every man, woman and child for themselves. Tallack's plan and coordinating orders were abandoned. Staying alive was all that counted now. The Phoenician ship was overrun with feral Iwerdon head hunters, Dathi's most elite force. They each bore tattoos on their foreheads like a mark from the gods. The distance was too great for me to see what the markings showed, but each one of them fought with the might of twenty or more of our recruits.

One of their largest warriors stepped up to young Treeve, lifting his axe above his head in readiness to strike. Tallack dived into the path of the falling weapon, shielding the young crewmen from harm with his short bronze sword. He was much taller than my nephew, with the hardened muscles of a mature warrior. He would not be so easily dispatched.

One of our smaller boats began to sink. A thrown axe cut a chunk from its hull, letting in the River Exe and tipping out all its occupants. Weapons sank beneath the bloody waves while the dead floated out to sea.

Tallack and the huge warrior rounded each other in the stern of his ship. Treeve cowered between the storage boxes snivelling. Bow women discarded their bows and picked up the spears and pikes from their dead menfolk. They were fierce, with as much, if not more, to lose than the warriors before them. They jabbed and stabbed anything in their paths.

Tallack made the first move, lunging towards the vast warrior with his blade. The wily man stepped aside, letting the youthful Chieftain scurry right past him. Each man turned quickly. Tallack stooped to grab a fallen pikestaff, wedging it under his arm for stability.

My breathing quickened. He was no match for this seasoned foe. He had neither Blydh nor Renowden to guide him and little experience on which to draw. I knew that Tallack would not back down. There was no way he would allow the Ivernii to take his ship while there was still one warrior left to fight.

Another of our boats tipped and sank beneath the surface. Our enemy cared nothing for capturing our fleet for their own use. Their only interest was killing as many of our people as they could find.

The warrior on the Phoenician ship swiped his axe about Tallack's head. It missed by a hair's breadth. The next blow would be more carefully gauged. Tallack darted to the warrior's side, keeping the pikestaff blade between them. For every giant stride the man took closer to my nephew, Tallack hopped backwards and jabbed the pike towards his enemy. I could see the man losing his patience. This was closer to a dance than a fight.

Baring his teeth, he snatched the pike into his hand by the sharp end until it sliced into his flesh. Without so much as a whimper, he yanked it from Tallack's grip and slung it overboard. Now all that stood between this maniac and death, was a small bronze blade and Tallack's wits.

Even at my distance I could see the warrior grinning. He backed Tallack into the tightest point of the stern. Treeve crouched beneath Tallack's legs, tucking his head to his knees. I could hardly bear to watch, as the warrior moved in to strike the fatal blow.

CHAPTER FOURTEEN

Two of our most loved warriors were at this man's mercy. I could tell from his casual stance that he relished every moment of his impending victory, the Ivernii head hunter who killed the Chieftain of the wealthiest tribe in the land. An accolade that would stand him in good stead for the rest of his life; he would take home my nephew's head as his prize, along with the Phoenician ship to add to their fleet of small boats.

I knew that he could afford to take his time. There was nowhere for Tallack to run nor hide. His tiny blade was no match for the heft of the warrior's axe. With all the swagger of victory, he knocked the short sword from Tallack's clutches, took his axe in both hands and lifted it above his head. Before it reached its highest point, young Treeve scooted forwards on his knees and buried a knife up into the warrior's groin.

The cry could have curdled blood. Treeve twisted the blade before wrenching it free of the man's parts and plunged the knife in again. On Treeve's fourth shove of the blade, he cut through the vessel in the man's thigh. Blood gushed all over him as Tallack slipped past the warrior's thrashing axe and retrieved his sword. It took moments for our Chief to slash his throat and put him out of his misery.

At last I could breathe again, but the skirmish was far from over. Those who were still able to fight, swam towards the Phoenician ship. Other's too badly injured made their way to shore. The rest were carried with the tide, face down and losing their organs and tissues to the fish below.

Our men were gathering to their leader aboard our greatest vessel. Where was Faolan? He was conspicuous by his absence. How had he come to be away from the fight after Tallack's express orders to follow him?

There were still at least ten Ivernii boats surrounding our men. Dathi was in their largest craft, directing his men from the rear of the fleet and out of the direct line of fire. Few bowmen were left to pick off those enemies swimming from capsized boats.

Those of our warriors who remained, were outnumbered and completely surrounded. Some of the Ivernii still shot arrows up towards Tallack's crew, others threw grappling hooks with an intention to board. Treeve took hold of the dead warrior's axe and ran around the deck cutting any lines that managed to take hold. They were closing in fast and then there would be no opportunity for escape.

Kewri laid his hand on my shoulder and then gestured to the injured on the shoreline, gasping, rolling about in the mud and silt, and all bleeding from devastating wounds. I had to help them, but my mind wouldn't concentrate. It'd been a long time since I had tasted the bitter air of a battle field, and my strength was not what it was when I was young.

The wounded cried out for my assistance. I had to respond. Kewri led the horses down behind me and began building the fire for hot water. I unpacked my bone needle and catgut; plantain paste and bindings and sat on a rock to begin my work. Those who could walk without complaint waited until I had assessed the condition of the seriously injured. How some of them made it back to shore with half their guts hanging out I'll never know.

One woman lay with her face split in two. I could smell the foul stench of death leaking out of the slash in her belly. There was nothing that could save her from the Morrighan now. All I could do was to take a pinch of poppy resin and slide it under her tongue without adding any water.

I gave her enough to numb her of every sensation and held her hand until the gods came to take her into the Summerlands. She was no older than my niece Derwa. When her groans of agony subsided, I closed her eyelids and moved onto my next patient.

This was grim work indeed, but it kept my attention so fully, I had to look up to see why our tribesmen were cheering. It took a moment for me to focus, but there at the river mouth were the sails of more ships. These bore the blue banners of the Skotek tribe, the Novantae. At last, our allies had arrived just in time, although a quarter moon ago would have been preferable.

As soon as the Ivernii saw the arrival of so many ships coming to our aid, they abandoned their attack, took to their oars and rowed like the spirits of the Underworld were on their tails. Having the smaller vessels, they were able to cut right across the shallow waters near to the sandbanks, thus avoiding steering into the path of the much larger Skotek ships in the deeper parts of the estuary.

We were saved. I wasn't sure how I felt about my injured patients standing guard over the riverbank with their blades in hand ready to cut the throats of any Ivernii who might make the mistake of swimming to shore, but at least I could treat people without fear for my life.

It took me the rest of the day to tend to all those who were nearing or close to death. The walking wounded I stitched and patched and sent them back along the river path towards the island. I asked Kewri to return to the compound to fetch the Chieftain wagon for the dead. He refused to budge.

"Send one of the warriors on your horse, Fur Benyn. I won't leave you here with the Ivernii in these parts. They may come back and stick a blade between your ribs while you're not looking." He folded his arms and wouldn't be swayed on the matter. I must admit, I did feel exposed there on the shore with no cover from trees nor cliffs. As soon as I agreed, one of the less hurt men volunteered to ride back.

It was a long time before he returned with a cart, and it did not belong to the chief. I laughed when I saw the rickety old thing he'd borrowed from the smith. It still had bits of wood and a dusting of sand and clay in the back.

"Why in the name of Cernonnus didn't you take the Chief's wagon?" I asked the warrior. Had Tallack returned to the island? Who was in charge there now?

"The hunters had taken it out to move the white stag from the forest into the compound. It was all I could find." He said, jumping down to help Kewri lift the sick and dying aboard.

"And the Chief?"

"Didn't see him. Chief Blydh is still in your hut, Fur Benyn, recovering. There was only Ren about the place."

Where were they all? I squinted in the darkness to see across to the Phoenician ship. The tiny fire at the stern still burned brightly, but I would have expected a guard to have stayed aboard as a minimum. Black shadows against the muddy waters were visible, bobbing up and down with the choppy movements of the tide. Those I took to be the smaller ships of the Novantae.

Our fleet had taken a serious beating. Only two of our smaller boats were still afloat, plus the foreign vessel, but that required significant repairs before it would be safe to take out to sea. The Novantae had timed their arrival to perfection. They lost not a single man nor boat in the skirmish.

The thoughtful warrior had the common sense to tether three horses to the rear of the cart. At least I could ride alongside my patients while two crewmen rode behind us for protection. Kewri rode up front while another steered the cart. There was no room for the dead in such a small wagon. Tallack would need to send another party of his men out come dawn for the bodies.

The journey back to camp was bumpy and exceedingly painful for those in the wagon. Their injuries were dire. I'd given them as much resin as I had dared to give them, but I doubted they would make it through the night.

As we reached the southern gate and crossed the shallow tributary over the gravel banks, I noticed that the row boats were missing from their jetty further downstream. When the watchman called down for the gates to be opened, I saw that the row boats had been lifted from the stream and carried into the compound. It was a shrewd move, but one that informed me that Tallack and his surviving men, must have returned with the Novantae tribe.

The whole island was surprisingly dark and quiet. Few torches lit our way and no noise came from the Long Hut as I had expected. Our losses did not deserve celebration, but I wondered why the usual hospitality had not been extended to the new guests. Faolan's family had provided me with much comfort after my slave's sudden sacrifice at their settlement. Faolan had even given me his hut as my own, treating us to unrivalled generosity. Tallack should have done the same in return.

The moment the gates were secured behind us, I sent Kewri to feed and water my goats and to make sure that the horses were turned out in their enclosure. Exhausted and confused, I made my way to the Long Hut to find out what had happened in my absence while the warriors carried the dying back to their families.

The wood panel was wedged in the doorway over the draped skins. It was hardly cold enough to warrant those kinds of precautions. I walked around to the rear entrance, where the cook slaves attend the roasting pits, but that too was shuttered. Annoyed and frustrated, I kicked out at the wooden panel until Renowden came to dislodge it from my path.

"What's happened? Where's the chief?" I rasped.

Ren didn't answer. He pulled a face and flicked his head towards the top table and Chieftain seats. I hurried inside and noted that Ren returned the panel to plug the doorway behind me. The torches were lit inside, but they burned low, as did the central fire. Tallack sat in his bear carved seat with Treeve at his side. Both were coated in thick dried blood. Faolan and his daughter

Sorcha took the guest seats next to the wolf's head chair belonging to Blydh.

Ren stood behind me and muttered into my ear. "The Chief didn't want the elders or warriors to attend this private meeting."

I snapped my head around to look at Ren. What could be so delicate that it could not be discussed in the presence of the elders? Surely anything that critical should include Blydh's opinions too.

Tallack looked grim. He massaged his temples and peered up to see me. "How many did we lose, Aunt?"

I looked directly at Faolan as I answered. "Difficult to tell exact numbers, Nephew. Many were washed out to sea, but certainly many more than we would have if the Novantae had hastened their journey here."

Faolan opened his mouth to object but Tallack silenced him by butting in. "Nevertheless, Aunt, they are here now and prepared to keep to their promises." He too glared at the old Skotek wolf, before lowering his gaze once more. I took that to mean that Tallack had said all that he was going to on the matter, but I could not hold my tongue.

"I did not see you in the ships, Chief Faolan. Where were you today?"

He scratched at his ginger whiskers and looked towards his daughter as though she could rescue him from my interrogation. She just stared into the distance as though he was the last person in the world whom she would assist. "I was concerned that my old legs would not make it in time to the boats so I borrowed a horse but got turned about in the forest. By the time I found my way back, the battle was over and my boy Ealar had arrived with our ships and men."

I narrowed my eyes at him. "The forest is north of here, the estuary south. How did you manage to ride in the opposite direction to our row boats?"

He stammered his words and coughed. Feigning a dry throat, he took a swig of ale from his cup and took his time swallowing. A loud banging on the main door panel saved him from answering me. Renowden rushed over and lifted the shutter out of the way. One of the watchmen muttered something to him. He leaned the panel against the thatch of the hut and returned to where the guests were sitting.

"The hunting party are back with the white hart, Chief Tallack. Should I send them out with the cart to the estuary to collect the fallen with the others?" Renowden waited for Tallack's nod of permission, before issuing his orders to the men.

It was a solemn evening all round. The slaves delivered the food to Tallack and his guests and left to see to their own meagre offerings. I left soon afterwards. It was clear that there was still much to be said, particularly with regards to the Novantae's part in the bloodshed, but this was not the time to press my luck. I piled two bowls high with meats and bread and returned to my hut.

Kewri took his food from me with deep gratitude, although I deserved none. Blydh was less thankful, chewing a little of the goat meat before spitting it across the floor in complaint. Nothing I did for him seemed to make him happy. At first, I thought it was frustration.

I'd seen something similar before with warriors who were too injured to fight, only to have their friends and family slain in their stead, but this was different. His anger seemed to be directed towards me, though I could not fathom why. Everything in my power to do for him, had been done. Short of direct intervention from the gods, nothing would return his sight to his left eye.

Kerensa stayed for a while, fussing around him and encouraging him to eat the food I'd brought. Her smile was borne of knowing that Blydh was less attractive to the Novantae as a husband to Faolan's daughter. She was a fine-looking woman herself, dark haired with toned muscles and a keen mind. She wore a necklace of connected feather quills. They were stacked neatly in a row forming a plate against her breast. A tiny tin bead separated each of the white tubes. It was something she always wore, night and day. Whenever I remarked upon its unusual appearance, she would smile and say;

"It's my treasured possession."

Certainly, the tin beads were worth a fair price, but the feather stems were common enough and the design easily copied. Perhaps it was valued for a memory or sentiment. Whatever its origin, she would not be pressed on the matter.

She stayed until late into the night, but returned to Blydh's shelter when the moon was high. I busied myself with redressing Blydh's head, although he fought me every step of the way, and then turned into my bunk to sleep. I'd had more than enough of the day and wished it to be over with.

Come morning, the camp was alive with activity. It was not a happy place to be. The men dragged wood into the compound through the northern gates, while the widows and children cried over their dead loved ones at the stream. There they prepared the bodies for the pyre that would send them into the Summerlands. Few elders could remember a time when women were among the fallen in battle.

I recalled those days well. Women warriors were often fiercer than the men, but they were born into a tradition of training all the children to hunt, shoot and fight from the moment they could walk. The age of Aebba had left our tribe weak. Our children lacked the killer instinct of our forefathers. My brother taught me to fight. He was a fair few summers older than I, and already a warrior when I was born. It did not stop him from putting a blade in my hand and insisting that I learned how to slice throats. It was many cycles before I was able to convince him that I could best serve by stitching wounds instead of causing them.

Kewri was heaving enormous lengths of wood from the river for the pyre. When he saw me, he tipped his head to one side, signalling that he had something to tell me. I wandered closer to him and the group of men building the pyre.

"Fur Benyn, I think you should speak to that young lad over there. He said he saw Chief Faolan before the battle yesterday."

The lad overheard Kewri and approached us both. He was keen to share all that he'd seen.

"That big Skotek man with the fuzzy red beard took one of the Chief's horses and galloped off towards the woods. He didn't look lost to me." The lad shook his head gently.

"What makes you say that?" I asked, curious as to this boy's intentions. We have our fair share of lads who think they're men before their time.

"I say he knew exactly where he was heading. He carried a pole with the white banner of peace flying at its top."

CHAPTER FIFTEEN

I could hardly believe what I was hearing. "Are you absolutely sure, lad? It was definitely Faolan riding the forest trail to the north of our camp bearing the white banners?"

He nodded so emphatically, there was no room for error. There was only one explanation for this peculiar sighting; Faolan went to treat with the Durotriges while our men were being slaughtered in the estuary. I was so incensed I couldn't speak. I asked the boy's name and told him not to leave the compound until either Chief Tallack or I had spoken to him again. He was my only proof that Faolan was a duplicitous traitor.

That would account for the delay with the Novantae reaching our shores. Were they further down the coast all along, just waiting for a signal to sail into the river mouth? It wouldn't take much to figure out the extent of our scouts' reach. Fuming, I returned to my hut to think of a way to tell Tallack that would not anger him into acting unwisely.

Blydh was still being an awkward patient. Each time my back was turned, he tried to get out of the bunk to walk. Every attempt he made resulted in him crashing to the floor. With Kewri helping to build the funeral pyre, I was left alone trying to heave him back into bed. It was very tempting to give him enough poppy resin to keep him quiet for a few hours, but I couldn't afford to get the dosage wrong. The last thing I needed was to send him into an eternal sleep.

Running around after my nephew made my head spin. I couldn't think clearly. As soon as Kerensa appeared to check up on his progress, I charged her with the unhappy task of cleaning him up and remaking his bed. When Kewri had finished his labours, I intended for him to carry Blydh back to his own shelter. I was more than content to dress his wounds twice a day but to have a constant stream of visitors plus his growing anger towards me was not in either of our best interests. Kerensa could watch over him until he was back on his feet.

After I'd refilled my healing kit, I went to see how the injured from the estuary were fairing. Two had made it through the night and looked set to make full recoveries. The third had just enough time to say his farewells. His family were making offerings to the gods when I arrived. I slipped the warrior's mother a few grains of tin to pay Cernonnus for his crossing into the Summerlands and some dried valerian to soothe her frayed temper.

Kewri and a dozen other men worked all day to build a pyre large enough for all our dead. In the end, they had to stack the bodies on struts like shelves or the fire would have been large enough to engulf all the shelters and woodland on the island. At the southern end of the compound, I saw the strong posts hammered into the ground enclosing the majestic stag. The men succeeded in trapping the white hart, and brought it onto the island for sacrifice.

I'd hoped that my nephew's thirst for blood had been sated after losing so many the previous night, but he was determined to complete the ritual. I watched him yelling at the smith near to the southern gates. He expected his axes to be ready so that he and Blydh could anoint the blades with the deer's blood. I should never have told him about the mystical sword that Paega stole. Now he was obsessing over matching the weapon with two of his own; a pair of axes blessed by the God of Death himself.

Sorcha moped around the camp, watching the horses gambolling about their enclosure as though she was debating whether to take one and ride off into the wilderness. I can't say that I'd blame her. Her father was about to give her to a stranger in return for a trade agreement. That's if he hadn't also promised her to the Duros for another reason, such as betraying us and taking over our lands on behalf of our enemies.

The whole situation made me sick. There had to be a way out of our deal with the tricky Skotek Chief. What I find so hard to stomach, is that he was so kind to both me and Tallack while we rested at his home settlement. You couldn't have found a more loyal and generous man. What had made him turn on us so quickly?

Standing next to the skittish white hart, I tried to calm myself, tipping out a handful of grain from my pocket; a final meal for my vision of the gods. He didn't deserve to die, but then neither did anyone else from camp. If only we knew for sure whether the gods existed or not, we could ask them what gifts and offerings they would prefer.

Sorcha leaned on the fence and lowered her head to her hands. Was she in tears? Making my way over to her, I touched her shoulder and the skinny maid jumped with fright.

"Shush now. It's only me."

She lifted her face towards mine, letting the tears fall freely down her cheeks. She had no need to tell me what was on her mind. It's an age-old problem for the daughters of Chieftains in this land. They could be as strong and courageous a warrior as their brothers and twice as intelligent, but they would still be considered as chattel for their fathers to sell to the highest bidder. As tall as she was, the girl threw her arms about me and held on as tightly as a limpet, sobbing into my neck. If I thought we'd get away with it, I would have gladly given her a pouch of tin and a horse with which to flee.

My own memories of a similar situation crowded out my reason for a time, before I came to my senses. Faolan would blame me for Sorcha's disappearance, and by association my nephews. It would most likely begin a feud that would last for generations to come. Knowing that did not make it any easier to hear her despair. At least she would not be forced to bind with a rough man twice her age with gout and stinking sores. Both Tallack and Blydh were young and attractive, even though one had lost the sight in an eye.

When at last her upset petered out, I took her by the hand and led her into Blydh's storage hut. The guard on the door didn't even blink as I pushed my way past him. I suppose I do abuse my privilege in the tribe at times, but on this occasion, I deemed it necessary. There were no cups next to the jugs of ale, for fear that the guard on duty might be tempted to drink his way through the entire stock. It didn't mean that we couldn't take a few swigs straight from the jar.

"How did the discussions go with Chief Tallack last night?" I asked her, hoping to gain an insight into the mind of her father.

"Not well. My father wanted Blydh for my husband until his injury. I still haven't seen him, so I don't know how bad the scars are or the effect on his temper, but now my father is demanding that Tallack binds with me, or he'll take us and our ships home to Novantae lands in Skotek."

"Do you not like Tallack, Sorcha? You seem to get along nicely when you gave us both shelter during the winter."

"He's not a monster, I know that. He's nowhere near as bad as the son of the Carvetii Chief, who father first wanted to give me to. He looks like his mother was a wild hog with rotten tusks." She grinned for the first time since her arrival. I couldn't stop myself giggling at her comparison.

"It's not that, Fur Benyn." She continued, handing the jug back to me. "It's, well…Tallack doesn't much like girls, does he?"

And we all thought my nephew had been discreet. Once my chuckling started, I found I couldn't stop. "Oh, believe me, child. Tallack does like girls, and boys and most likely anything else that takes his fancy."

Sorcha's eyes widened along with her rosy pink smile. She burst into cackles of her own and snatched the jug of ale to pour down her throat.

"At least he won't make unpleasant advances towards you. It could be a blessing in disguise."

I have no idea how long Sorcha and I were in there for, but it was dark when we staggered out laughing and tripping over our feet. A different guard watched us zig-zag across the compound towards the northern end of the island. That was when I remembered the funeral pyre. I tried to shush Sorcha, tugging on her sleeve and whispering as loud as a wolf howl to be quiet. Our revelry was disrespectful to the dead.

The glowers and scowls we received put paid to our amusement. Every member of the camp encircled the pyre, waiting for Tallack to light the kindling. Doing my best to focus my blurry eyes, I scanned the area in search of the white hart. It was not near to the pyre, nor tethered nearby. My best guess was that it had been spared for the evening, whether because Tallack's special axes were not ready, or he thought it inappropriate to mix the funeral rites with a request for favour from the God of Death, I knew not.

Suitably chastised, Sorcha and I held one another upright as Tallack said a few words about all those who had fought with honour and courage, before lighting the dry rushes under the wooden structure. While we all tried to ignore the smells of roasting warriors, and show our respect, Kewri shuffled closer to me.

"Where have you been?" He muttered quietly. "I looked everywhere for you."

Sorcha almost lost her composure. Her snort turned into a chuckle, thinking about us rolling around Blydh's ale and meat store for most of the day laughing until our bellies and faces ached. I jabbed my elbow into her ribs and she regained control over herself. This was a tragic occasion for so many people of our tribe, not least since for the first time in generations, women were among the dead.

A vision of the woman whose guts spilled out over my shoes, whom I held until the poppy resin carried her on swift winds into the Summerlands, flitted through my thoughts. That memory served to sober me up in moments. The realisation that it was only the beginning of our troubles, took me past sobriety and into extreme anxiety.

I had spent the day getting drunk with a friend to ease her woes, when I could have been preparing tonics and tinctures and seeing to the ails in camp. Guilt piled up inside like the stacked bodies on the pyre. Opposite where we stood, Faolan and Ealar glared at us. I suppose they too had searched for Sorcha. Tallack was too wrapped up in his own thoughts to notice, but young Treeve was not. He stood next to my nephew like a dog scent marking his territory.

I recalled his words to Kerensa when the idea of Sorcha binding with Tallack was first raised. Threatening to murder one of our guests does tend to linger in the brain somewhat. Was he just mouthing off, or was he serious? After seeing him repeatedly thrust his knife into an enemy's balls, I have no doubt that he is able to kill but would he really end the life of a noble daughter through jealousy?

Most of the affected families remained around the pyre until it burned low. I staggered off to see if Tallack had closed the Long Hut for more discussions or whether it was open to all his warriors and elder families. If there was to be another important discussion regarding the Duros and the part Faolan's men would play in the war to come, I wanted to be there.

By the time I had made my way back towards the huts, the ale had worn off to leave me with an aching head. I nipped back to my own shelter for a little willow to chew and found Blydh sitting on the edge of the bunk, trying to pull on his leggings.

"Kerensa told me all about our defeat. We lost too many of our people. I should have been with my men. Help me up woman."

My initial shock was not that Blydh was doing all he could to return to his warriors, but that his former fondness for me had vanished along with his calm temper. I was no longer his Aunt Mel, just a woman to be ordered about like any other. It gave me a cramping pain in my chest, that I should lose the love of my nephew after so many summers of warmth. Faolan warned me that he might be altered if he recovered, which was surprising since his heart was unharmed. It puzzled me how feelings should be seated in the head and not the chest, but there was no time for pondering the human body.

What confused me more, was why Brea and her tribe of Duros had not attacked us while we were dealing with our fallen warriors. Our defences were down and our numbers weakened in grief. It would have been the perfect moment to surround us with their superior numbers and killed us all. What was the delay?

I tried to help Blydh back into the bunk, but he gave me such a volley of abuse, I stood back and watched him struggle on his own. Rather than return to bed, he wrestled with his tunic and leggings and attempted to stand.

As much as I wanted to see the little ingrate fail in his attempts, my familial bonds are too strong to allow him to falter for long. I fetched my stick and called to Kewri outside to come and help our injured Metern.

In truth, I was glad to have Blydh out of my hut. His hateful words were taking a toll on my love for him. He could recuperate in his own shelter.

I watched Kewri and my nephew hobbling over to the Long Hut and followed on some distance behind them. The door panels were stacked to one side, allowing the elders and warriors entry to hear what Tallack had to say.

Kewri lowered Blydh into his carved tall chair and retreated to a respectful distance. The great lummox nodded at me as I entered, letting me know that he was keeping his beady eye on me. I slipped into the crowd of elders' wives standing at the back. The top table was full to bursting. Tallack and Blydh sat either side of the empty Ruvane chair, with the Novantae visitors sitting to Blydh's left. Treeve and Renowden sat to Tallack's right hand side, squashed onto a bench fit for one.

Cryda wandered about in the small space next to the back door, nursing and jogging the babe to quieten her down. Derwa and her mountain man sat at my normal bench below. The heat inside the hut was almost too much to bear. I took my cloak off and hung it over my arm. Other ladies of the elder families did the same. The stink of old sweat almost over powered us all.

Tallack leaned across to his brother and whispered something into his ear. Blydh nodded and then tried to stand. The moment his backside left the chair he lost his balance and crashed back down into the seat. Kewri lunged forwards to help, but Tallack gestured for him to stay put.

"Rest brother. Speak from where you are." Tallack was filled with concern. His eyes glossed over as though the sight of Blydh in reduced circumstances was his own fault. It could have also been the result of guilt, but I couldn't be sure of either. All that I knew was that over the space of a full moon's passing, they had bickered and argued until Blydh's course of action almost took his life. Perhaps this terrible turn of events would see their sibling bond restored.

Blydh took a mouthful of ale and swallowed. Clearing his throat, he addressed the visitors, elders and his men. He began by thanking them for all the well-wishing and his gratitude for the offerings made to the gods in his name. This was met with a good deal of foot stamping and cheers that he was on the mend.

"I also have to speak with regard to our recent losses. There is nothing more tragic than losing fine warriors in battle, unless it is to lose warrior women too." Blydh said, casting his only working eye over the crowd. They knew not of his impediment. To them, he was as fearless and dangerous as ever. I silently wondered how his altered state might affect his abilities in battle.

When the murmurs died down, he continued. "Of course, this tribe has not lost women warriors since my grandfather's day, when every boy and girl in the tribe were trained in warfare tactics, use of spear and bows and defence strategies. The blame for the loss of women in the estuary this quarter moon falls squarely on one person alone, my Aunt Meliora, who had no right to send untrained women into battle."

CHAPTER SIXTEEN

I couldn't believe what I was hearing. Every set of eyes trained on me, as the women of our tribe moved from my side, showing me cowering at the back of the hut. My own nephew blamed me for taking control at a time when his own brother was too struck with anxiety over Blydh's injuries to make a decision. Now he was encouraging others to cast me as the villain for my initiative. The women were untrained because he and Tallack could not agree on a division of labour, not because I stated the obvious fact that we simply did not have the numbers to fight against our enemies.

He had conveniently forgotten that the reason our neighbouring tribe were after our blood was a direct result of Blydh's order to kill his own half-sister. Add that to the fact that the treacherous Lady Brea was spurned by Tallack and war was inevitable.

They were all still looking at me, expecting me to apologise or atone for the sins laid at my feet. What could I say to confirm my innocence? Every phrase swirling about in my head was likely to anger Blydh all the more. Swallowing my fear, I stepped forward.

"It was my suggestion to arm the women, yes. They need to train as hard as the men if we are to survive what's to come. I make no apologies for my part in the tragedy, just as Blydh shouldn't have to apologise for losing men during his failed raid that almost killed him." Looking up to the broken man in the wolf's head seat, I summoned my courage and continued. "I know not how I've offended you, nephew. I did all I could to patch up your skull, for better or worse. Hear me now, Chief, if you waste time casting blame about instead of making sensible preparations, then we are all done for."

His snarl was instant and violent. He spluttered with a rage that would not be quelled, struggling to get to his feet. Tallack raced from his tall chair to intercept his brother, muttering soothing words into his ear and persuading him back into his seat.

What was clear to me most of all, was that I had lost the ear of my nephew. I ambled from the Long Hut, hiding my tears from the world in the fabric of my cloak. By the time I was half way across the compound to my hut, Kewri had caught up with me.

"Fur Benyn…?"

"I'm fine, Kewri. Go back to the gathering. I will need you to be my eyes and ears at this time." I didn't look back at him, but I knew that he was standing with his arms limp at his side, unable to choose between comforting me or following my orders. When I said nothing more, he turned and retraced his steps.

For all my previous moaning about being cramped, my shelter suddenly felt cold, empty and unwelcoming. I tried to bank up the fire and sort out the bedding to occupy my mind, but Blydh's angry face came back into my thoughts to crush my spirit. My time of usefulness in the tribe was coming to an end.

How long would it be before I was branded a burden on our people? I could better serve the tribe by waiting on the moors for Cernonnus to call me to the Underworld. There would be no sacred space in the Summerlands for me. I was never a true warrior like the shield maidens and fierce champions of my forefathers and without the grace of my family's tin supplies, I would not have any wealth to pay my fare.

I am ashamed to admit that I indulged in self-pity. I ate a little ground oatmeal steeped in warmed goat's milk and crawled under my furs for the night. Kerensa or Cryda would have to see to Blydh's wounds while his rage was still so hot.

The sound of hammering woke me at dawn. My tongue was stuck to the roof of my mouth and my head was sore from the ale. When I went outside, I saw Kewri skewering the soft ground with hazel poles. From the shape they made in the soil, it looked to be the foundations for a new hut next to mine. He was building himself a home. Was this his subtle way of informing me that he'd abandoned me too?

The crushing ache in my chest pained me all the more, knowing that I'd lost his respect. All around camp, people were busy at their chores, laying boardwalks over the muddiest stretches of ground, fletching more arrows and smelting more bronze, sharpening blades and practising their aim at targets in the training ground beyond the western gate. Each of them had purpose and knew their place within the tribe. It seemed that the dual Meterns had settled their differences after all.

I wrapped some cheese and a little dried pork in a waxen cloth and loaded my pony up with all the possessions and medicines he could carry. Kewri didn't even notice I was gone. I took the northern gate towards the forest, stopping to pick the new shoots and leaves of useful plants as I walked. As soon as I was clear of the woods and marshes, I veered west along the beaten trail heading for the northern fringes of Dartmoor.

It being a well-trodden route, some of the travellers noticed me passing by. I was fairly well known in these parts, especially those with sickly children or ailing old folk under their roofs. One or two homesteaders stopped me, asking for aid and trading what little food they could spare for my ointments and tonics. I cannot afford to be as generous as I once was. Hunting is for the young. I would have to ration what little grain I had and make it last me.

When the spring sunshine was high overhead, I stopped to eat my cheese and give the pony a rest and a drink before the long climb to the top of the hill. This was always the worst part of the track. Despite wanting to stop several times before reaching the peak, I knew that it would be unwise to do so.

Plenty of travellers have been robbed as they tired from the lengthy hike. For the rest of the day, I kept good pace through the homesteads of those whose young folk now trained in our compound on the Exe. If only they knew that I was kin to the Chieftains, I'd not be welcome through their lands.

Crossing the River Taw through the dense forest was a little tricky, what with the fading daylight and my eyes playing tricks on me. At one point, I felt sure that I was being followed by woodland sprites. No doubt they hoped to lead me into a forgotten dell for some unknown mischief of their own.

I passed through unscathed and began the steep walk up to the moorland peak between boulders and rocks. As the sun set below the ridge, I could hear the priests beginning their nightly rituals. Their fires were a welcome sight, as were their shelters that looked large enough to accommodate visitors to the Nine Maiden's and their stone brothers. Before I came into view, I slipped a couple of copper beads into my pocket from the pouch hidden under my medicines. I was keeping what little tin I had left for emergencies.

At the entrance to the sacred site, I tethered my horse and stepped up the avenue towards the priestess awaiting near the end. She greeted me with early meadow flowers and a little bread in exchange for my copper beads, and ushered me into the circle.

I was glad that I hadn't stopped for a ritual cleanse in the freezing waters of the River Taw, since the priestess looked me up and down, and judged me to be a lowly old medicine woman without kin. Her pity for me induced her to return my copper beads into my hand. Beckoning me towards her fire, she ladled hare stew into a bowl and sat with me while I ate.

"May Cerridwen bless you, priestess." I said, patting her hand. After such a long walk, I was ravenous. It was salty and strong in flavour, but the meat was surprisingly tender. She even offered to smear a little of the skimmed lard onto my bread. It didn't do to be so suspicious, but I couldn't fathom why she had singled me out for her kindness. There were others who looked to have travelled far longer than I and all they received was a chunk of bread in exchange for their offering.

The priestess waited until my bowl was empty and shooed away the noisy drummers and pipers dancing all about. "How may we help you this night?"

It was a long story and one that I didn't really want to divulge, but I knew that I had to make my peace with the gods or be damned for all eternity.

She sensed my reluctance to share. "Have some ale and have a think about it. We can come back to your requests when we've dealt with the simple ones."

I looked across to the other fires around the circle. There was a couple with a babe in arms that coughed as though it were its last breath, an older man with an injured cart horse, and several warriors. When one of their number turned around, I saw the mark of the Durotriges Tribe tattooed on his neck. They had come to ask the Morrighan's blessing for their planned assault on our lands. I bowed my head in case they recognised me from my trip into their camp before the last midsummer gathering. Not that they would remember an old crone like me.

It made me wonder if my niece Wenna had the same markings when she was bound to their Chieftain. I didn't recall seeing it on her neck, but then who knew whether it was a choice for them or not?

I took the priestess's advice and sipped her ale at her fire while her maidens and priests led the warriors into the circle. Why had they ridden into our lands to seek the god's blessings? Surely there were plenty of sacred spaces for the Durotriges to speak to the Morrighan in their own territory?

Whatever their reasoning, they were deeply focused on the ritual. Each man paid for a sacrificial offering, and carried their creatures to the maidens standing in front of the short stones. They were exceedingly pretty young girls and quite a distraction for the men.

The priestess had to bark at them to hand their ducks, rabbits and geese over to the young women sitting on the stones. After a fair bit of screeching and flapping, the girls held the birds and animals tightly in their arms, while the priests intoned the blessings.

"We ask the Morrighan to watch over these men in battle, to favour them with her good grace, and to seek out their enemies to drag into the Underworld in their place." The priests looked up towards the stars and babbled and wailed in a garbled tongue, speaking the language of the gods. It was hard to believe that such animal noises could be understood by our sacred deities but who was I to judge? Whether they could hear the priests or not, I had to make amends for my past insults.

The warriors waited for the signal from the priestess, before they unsheathed their blades and slit the bellies of the animals for which they had paid. The squawks and screams of the creatures lasted mere moments. Their blood and entrails spilled down the maiden's legs and the drummers and pipers started their noisy playing once more.

The priestess danced around the circle waving her arms in an elegant manner. At each maiden stone, she dipped her thumb into the animal blood and made a mark on the tiny brother stones either side of the girls. Her second time around the circle, allowed her to anoint the warrior's foreheads with the sacrificial blood. This took some time, since there were nine warriors, nine maidens and a whole host of brother stones to mark too.

I'd begun to think the priestess would run out of blood. When all was done, the men ate and drank and celebrated their coming victory.

The priestess returned to face me. "Are you ready to speak your woes, Fur Benyn?" I looked at her in shock. How did she know my nickname? Was it sheer coincidence that she'd chosen to call me a name bestowing respect or did she really have the ear of the gods? I must have betrayed my surprise for she giggled and returned to the bench at my side.

"I grew up at the compound on the Exe. Don't you remember me, Fur Benyn?"

She had long straight hair clipped to the side of her heart-shaped face, bright eyes and a clear skin. Concentrating hard, I tried to place her from my memories. It wasn't until she gave me the benefit of her beaming smile that I recognised her. That unmistakable gap between her front teeth. "Little Endelyn?" I gasped. She chuckled all the more. "But you were a tiny tot when I last saw you. How in the name of Cerridwen do you remember me?"

"Everyone in camp knew you, and those beyond the walls too. You used to give me honeycomb in the late summer and berries in the autumn. I could never forget you." She poured me more of her ale and squeezed me about my shoulders with her draped arm. "I knew who you were the moment you walked up the path to the stone circle."

This was why she had returned my beads and treated me with extra kindness. I was humbled indeed. There was she eking out a living as a moorland priestess and I came from the wealthiest family in the whole area. My shame must have registered on my face. She took both my hands in hers.

"Tell me, Fur Benyn, why are you all alone on a chilly spring night in the middle of the moors? Where are your kin? Something is troubling you; I can tell."

She was right, but how could I relate all that had happened? She knew my family almost as well as me. What if they were the cause of her isolation in this bleak and inclement place? "Perhaps it was stupid of me to come all this way. I thought I might be able to appease the gods. I made the mistake of insulting them, and now my family are suffering hardship as a result." I hung my head expecting her to be furious with me. Her entire life revolved around speaking with the gods. "You know, Fur Benyn, I don't believe that they are as vengeful as people make them out to be. Think about Cerridwen. She understands every stage a woman must pass through, all that they must suffer in bringing new life into the world, the trials and tribulations of changes to our bodies and the despair when our loved ones are lost to us. She is not just maiden, mother, crone, but contains all the knowledge of the world within her. With that level of understanding, how could she condemn any of us? Cerridwen embodies forgiveness, as only a mother can."

Although I had no living child to my name, she made sense to me. I see it in Cryda daily. Tallack and Blydh could go out on a rampaging killing spree and she would forgive their sins in a moment. Her love for them was absolute, as my own had been all those summers ago. "It comforts me to know that one goddess still favours me. How can I make amends to the rest?"

"Am I to assume that your insult was in declaring that you no longer believed in our gods?"

She was more astute than I realised. I nodded.

"And was this declaration while you were under some sort of extreme fatigue or ague of your own?"

"Someone close to me was killed." I muttered, feeling the rush of heat scaling my chest and neck at the thought.

"Then your outburst was understandable at the time, and you have come all this way to seek forgiveness. I don't think you are to blame for the misfortunes falling on your kin. If I remember them correctly, they are all fairly headstrong and therefore responsible for their own actions." She stood up, still holding my hands. "A small offering and an incantation should clear the air. Come along."

I recalled her little face clearly now. She was always a clever little thing. I took the copper beads from my pocket and offered them to her again.

"No, this is on me. No one else gave me honeycomb, Fur Benyn." She winked at me in the flickering light from the fires surrounding the circle. The maidens were still sitting on their stones, completing the ritual for the parents of the sickly babe. It was my turn next. Endelyn waited for the couple to make their sacrifice and let them wander towards the stew pot and the revelling warriors.

She chose a duck from the wooden boxes near to the stones. Carrying it around its fat middle, she held it firmly with one hand clutching the top of its neck. The bird fought against her, kicking out and making an awful racket. "Do you have a blade, Fur Benyn, or do you need to borrow one?"

I produced a small bronze knife from my kit and followed her into the stone ring. The pipers and drummers began. The priests stood by confused, as Endelyn strode to the very centre and stood on top of the sacred burial stone. She was going to perform the ceremony herself, in my honour.

When she was ready, she nodded to the musicians to halt their playing so that she might ask Cernonnus and the Morrighan for forgiveness. The lit torches surrounding her in the centre of the circle cast shadows across her pretty face. She looked less like the charming little girl with honey dripping from her chin now and more like a powerful priestess with the ear of the gods.

She flicked her head at me, summoning me closer with the knife. All the maidens looked on in awe, as though this was an exceedingly rare occurrence for the top lady to get herself dirty on behalf of a penitent.

"May we all bear witness to this offering. It is given in the spirit of forgiveness. We ask that all the gods bless this noble woman and all that she does for others, in the name of Airmed, Goddess of Healing." She looked down at me. "Is there anything that you would like to say to the gods while they are listening?"

I felt ridiculous, standing there in my dirty travelling clothes in front of priests and maidens and nine warriors, all listening to the silly old women say sorry to invisible deities. Still, I'd walked a long way to make peace, I wasn't about to spoil the moment. "I shall never take the gods for granted ever again, nor call them to account. My life is theirs to do with as they see fit, in return for their lenience on my kin."

"Bless you." Endelyn whispered, her smile fixed and comforting. With a raise of her eyebrows, the drummers bashed out a rhythm for me to pace forward and end the unfortunate duck's life. This I did as swiftly as possible, with as little bloodshed as could be managed.

"There." She said. "All is right in this world once again, Fur Benyn."

The relief I felt was indescribable. She passed the dead duck to another priest and together, we began walking towards the fires. That was when I noticed one of the warriors staring at me. I turned away quickly, but it was too late.

"They called Wenna's aunt, Fur Benyn." He said to the other warriors. "She was the medicine woman from the Dumnonii. Healed the rotted arm of a friend of mine. She looked exactly like her." He pointed directly at me as they approached.

CHAPTER SEVENTEEN

They were so huge compared to my feeble little body. Nine large warriors surrounded me and the priestess, three had already unsheathed their blades ready to do serious harm. Endelyn shoved me behind her, shouting at them to abide by the terms of peace in the sacred space, but I knew that would not hold them off after all the sacrifices made that night. The maidens fled, shortly followed by the cowardly priests.

I could hear a distant rumbling of heavy hooves on dry chalky ground approaching. Was this the rest of his warrior friends? What possible gain would they achieve by slaughtering an old woman and the unarmed priestess? My puny blade would be useless against their mighty force, unless they meant to capture me and deliver me to the Lady Brea and her hulking great Duro Chieftain? Either way, my life would be forfeit.

As I stared into the chilling eyes of my foe, a peculiar calm came over me. I had made my peace with the gods. They would accept me into the Underworld for the price of my bronze blades and a few beads. The rumbling grew louder, but I closed my eyes to it all. I would not die screaming in fear, but as a daughter of Chieftains. Holding my head high, I waited for the blade to be thrust into my gut, or for my head to be sliced from my shoulders so that it would end as quickly and painlessly as I had taken the life of the duck.

The thundering hooves were at a gallop now, and it was one heavy horse. Peeking from beneath one half-opened eyelid, I tried to see what was the cause of the delay in dispatching me. When I saw who was cresting the top of the ridge, I almost broke down sobbing. Kewri kicked the carthorse into top speed, covering the distance between us in a flash. He held no blade, nor axe, nor bow. His fists and strength were all that stood between me and certain death.

Without a single thought for his own safety, he hurled his enormous mass from the fleet-footed horse onto three of the waiting warriors at once. His fists whirling, his elbows jabbing, his head butting, he laid them out cold before they could strike him with their short swords.

Rolling from their crushed bodies, Kewri was up in a flash. I'd never seen him in action before. It was thrilling beyond words. For such a huge man, he was nimble on his feet.

The first lunge with a blade he side-stepped, smashing his fist into the man's face with such force, I heard the lower jaw dislocate as teeth and blood shot from his opponent's mouth.

Before the next warrior could raise an axe in fury, Kewri reached behind and took hold of the chin of another, yanking the Duro fighter right over his head until his neck snapped. Kewri released the dead man as he reached shoulder level with his body, knocking down the rest of the Duros like a child's game.

There were three left standing. None of them dared to move. Kewri stomped closer to them and all three ran for their horses, mounting and galloping away before they could pack up their belongings.

As far as I could tell, Kewri had a small cut on his hand and another graze on his forehead from the initial head butt and crush, but in a fight against nine armed warriors, he was unharmed.

When the riders had vanished into the darkness of the moors, he came to check me over. Resting one hand on my shoulder he leaned back and looked me up and down, assessing any damage. I had to grin.

"Don't ever do that again, you hear me?" He bellowed at me, before surrounding me with those huge arms and hugging me until I could no longer fill my lungs. My arms were pinned against my sides.

"Can't breathe."

He lessened his grip but still didn't let me go. "Sorry."

"Kewri, as grateful as I am to you, I'm not your responsibility." My voice was muffled by the folds of his tunic. I wriggled free from his grasp to gather my things together. The priestess was astonished by the entire spectacle. "Are you alright, my dear?" I asked her. She nodded with her mouth still wide open in shock.

Kewri rested his bloodied fists on his hips and pouted. "You are my responsibility, which means you cannot just wander off whenever the mood takes you. From now on you are not to leave camp without me, is that clear?"

It was hard to keep a straight face. He was just a young recruit as far as tribal hierarchy was concerned. To order me about was comical, but his concern was genuine. My heart melted. "Thank you for rescuing me, even though I didn't know that I'd need it. You are kinder to me than I deserve."

He fidgeted and smiled. “You do deserve it, Fur Benyn. You look after everyone in camp and yet, no one looks after you.”

“You’ve protected me admirably since that day on the training ground. It’s the second time you’ve saved my life, Kewri. I owe you. No wonder you wanted to build you own hut to be away from me.”

His smile wrinkled up into a frown. “You mean the shelter I started next to yours… that’s for your patients. I’ve already got my bed in your hut.”

That tipped me over the edge. I sniffed back the tears. I started to introduce him to Endelyn, so that we could come to some sort of an arrangement over the dead bodies and injured warriors that were left.

Kewri interrupted me. “Begging your pardon, but we don’t have time to figure all this out. The Duro’s are marching towards our compound as we speak. I was sent to fetch you back…I mean I would’ve come anyway, but Chief Tallack was right mardy when he found you’d gone. We all thought you were in the forest picking your herbs and that, but you didn’t come back.”

It was the most I’d ever heard him say in one go since we’d met. He was all fired up from his fight. “But the horses haven’t rested.”

“They can rest when we get back. You have to come now, they need you.”

“Why, what’s happened?”

“It’s Chief Blydh. I think that gold plate you put in his head has slipped. He keeps passing out cold.”

I didn’t need to hear anymore. I thanked the priestess, gave her all the copper I had hidden in my medicine kit, and apologised for the additional burdens. She didn’t seem at all bothered by the dead Duros, but then she was born a Dumnoni and she’ll die a Dumnoni. I dare say the Duros will always be our enemy and there were six fewer to attack our compound on the Exe.

Kewri took some of the load from my horse and helped me up onto its back. Despite my long walk and aching bones, we had no other option but to ride hard through the night to get home. The route was still fresh in my mind, making navigation easier. The tricky bits were through the dark wooded regions, where the moon could not light our way.

We stopped once to water the horses and ourselves, before pushing them on until we reached the soggy marshes near to our homeland forest. Here, Kewri whispered to me that we should make as little noise as possible. It was likely that the Duro scouts would be in the area and would hear us cantering along. My horse was frothing with sweat and panting hard, but we could not stop. Picking our way through the lesser known tracks of the forest, we followed the tributaries that I knew well, and that led directly to the island.

As we neared the northern gates, I noticed that both crossings that Renowden had designed and made, were out of action. The first was lifted into an upright position, the second was dragged away into the compound before the gates were shut. They were battle ready and awaiting the Duro attack. My pulse raced. I found myself trembling from my gut all the way to my fingers, but on we trotted.

Kewri led the way around the island towards the western gate. This too was barricaded with spiked ramparts across the shingle ridge of the stream. We hurried to the southern gate, wondering all the time if the Duros were watching us and waiting for an opportunity to pounce. We were lucky. We made it to the watchtower and called up to the man on duty. Within moments, the gates opened just enough to let us through, before slamming closed again. A large post was hoisted across the gates securing us inside.

My relief was immense. I never thought that I would be welcome within these walls again. It just shows what an irrational old woman I can be at times. There were many bridges to build with the twins to regain their favour. It started with repairing Blydh's skull. I'd been thinking about how best to help him all the way home. That's if he would let me try.

The camp was deathly quiet. Even the warrior shelters were silent, with a few pacing up and down the stream nearby. The pyre at the northern end still smouldered after all that time. It made me think of how fire might be used against us. I wondered if Tallack had also considered that in the preparations. Grabbing my medicine bag, I sent Kewri off with the horses and ducked into the Long Hut.

It was filled with the most senior warriors, tribal elders and our two Chiefs sitting in their tall chairs at the top table.

Tallack saw me enter. "Where the kyjya have you been? I sent scouts out combing the forests and hillsides looking for you."

"I went to see the priestess at the Nine Maidens." It made perfect sense when I decided to go, now it sounded as though I was a child seeking her father's attention by running away from home.

"You chose now to restore your faith in the gods? Cernonnus keep me from clouting you…" Tallack's voice trailed off. Maybe he realised that he'd sounded just like his own father. "You're here now and that's all that matters. Blydh's head's not right. Show her brother."

I was frightened to approach Blydh. The change in attitude had shaken me to the core. His actions were erratic and confusing, but as I drew nearer, I could see that his left eye was facing a different direction to his right eye. That was the one in which he had no vision. Were there more fragments of bone shifting inside his brain?

Blydh leaned forwards for me to look at the top of his scalp. The swelling had reduced, easing the pressure on the stitches, but there was an odd shape to the top of his head. Kewri was right, the plate had shifted under the skin. I'd been lucky the first time, poking about in our Chieftain's head. What if he did not survive a second time? Would I be held responsible for his death? I stood out of arm's reach and held my hand over my mouth. It hid the fact that my hands were shaking.

"Well?" Tallack asked with more impatience than normal. "Can you put it right?"

I stared into Blydh's eyes trying to figure out his state of mind. "I can't make any promises, but I will try. That's if you're willing to trust me, Nephew?" He raised his head up. It was hard to tell if he could see me. His face twitched with a distinct lack of control but he nodded a fraction in consent.

"I will need some help and a few things." I began to say but Tallack cut through my request.

"Fine, take whoever or whatever you need to get it done." He flicked his hand towards the door dismissing me to my duties. Blydh was not the only one to have altered in his personality. The strain of ruling our tribe was starting to affect Tallack too.

Grabbing Renowden on my way out, I asked him to collect some items and bring them to my hut. Kewri was hovering at the unfinished shelter wringing his hands together regretfully. He couldn't have worked any harder to get it finished, there was no need for apologies.

"Can you go and help Chief Blydh back to my bunk? We will have to open him back up again."

Before I could carry wood from the stacks beneath my eaves inside to make a fire, a distant rumble travelled through the skies. Were the gods angry at us or at the Duros for marching on our compound? Either way, I knew that they were not far off. I had to work quickly before the fighting began. Perhaps my visit to the Nine Maidens was not wasted after all. Cernonnus and the Morrighan were warning me of their approach. There was even the chance that they would send a torrent of rain to render the soils around the island too boggy for the warriors to trudge through.

Kewri practically carried Blydh and for once, our Chief was silent and compliant. He sat on the edge of my bunk and winced, stifling a whimper.

"Is the pain very bad?" I asked him.

"I can take it, Aunt Mel." It stopped me in my tracks. I was back to being his Aunt Mel. Was it fear that mellowed his temper, or the shift in the golden sun disc? He looked up at me with huge sorrowful tears welling in his eyes.

"Blydh, you understand what I need to do?"

Another pained nod followed.

"Then you must drink this." I handed him a heavy dose of poppy resin mixed with water. "I can't have you moving about while I put the plate back."

He accepted the resin and sank it in one long gulp. Laying back on the rolled-up furs, he let his head fall back over the end of the bunk so that I could reach him easily. I rinsed off my blades in salted water and then heated them in the flames. Kewri and I waited for him to drift off into a resin induced sleep all the while listening to the storm rolling closer and closer. For every crack of thunder, my heart beat twice as fast, for I knew that the Lady Brea and her men were fast on its heels.

Twice I sent Kewri out to the northern watchtowers to ask for any signs of their arrival, both times his return filled me with dread. Renowden returned just as Blydh dozed off. He held in his cupped palms the items I had asked for; tiny pins made from silver.

"And the tools?" I asked.

Ren tipped the pins into one hand and reached to his belt for a delicate hammer from the forge. "It's the one used for Cryda's jewels." The second item was a sharp pin made from bronze stuck into a wooden handle. I knew that the smith had this tool, for I had seen him use it to make holes in the leather belts. Ren emptied all that he'd brought into a bowl of salt water until I was ready for them.

Kewri knew what I needed him to do. He took the leather strapping I had laid out and tied Blydh's arms and legs to the bunk. I couldn't have him thrashing about while his skull was open. I softened the catgut stitches with a cloth soaked in warm water and then cut through them. The scalp flesh had already begun to knit to his bone. It tore away as I pulled it, making a sickening noise. With the flap of hair and skin rested on Blydh's face, I could see how the sun disc had shifted. The shallow groove at the back of his head was not sufficient to hold it in place.

My reluctance to complete the job saw me rinsing him down with salt water and peeking into the folds of his brain looking for any bits of skull I might have missed. I couldn't see any, but that didn't mean that there were none, only that I couldn't find them. With a growing sense of foreboding, and the thunder cracking over our heads, I took the pin tool from the bowl and with as much care as I was able, made small holes in the bones at the outer limits of the sun disc. Ren passed me the silver pins as I tapped them into place with the jewellery hammer. When I had surrounded the entire disc with tiny nails, I began tapping them flat over the golden plate.

Kewri held two torches above my head to give me enough light to work, for the skies were dark with storm and the rain washed down in rivulets past my door. I was just fastening the last pin when Blydh stirred and his eyes flickered open. I froze with the hammer no more than a thumbnail's distance from his skull.

CHAPTER EIGHTEEN

Blydh's head flopped to one side and then backwards. He groaned a long and mournful cry, drowned out by the god's wrath overhead.

Renowden's quick thinking saved the moment. He held Blydh's chin and pulled down on his jaw while trickling in more resin water. The top up was all it took to send him into a peaceful slumber.

Before I could begin to stitch him back up, Tallack scurried into the hut soaked from head to toe. "Are you not done yet, Aunt? I wanted him to see the axes. They are finished. What do you think? Aren't they magnificent?"

Was it only the young who could be this oblivious to the perilous nature of this treatment? One small slip and I could have killed him at any stage in the procedure. There was no way that Blydh was going to jump up miraculously cured. He'd be lucky if he regained his wits at all. I took a deep breath and let it out slowly. This was my Metern and I had to humour him no matter the situation.

"Blydh is repaired to the best of my ability, Chief Tallack, but he won't be fit to fight for a long time." I glanced up at the axes. They were huge and heavy, with curved edges and a dimpled surface. It was doubtful that Blydh would even have the strength to lift one, let alone fight with the Duros. I noted that the handles were made from antlers. "You sacrificed the white hart last night then?"

Tallack let the axe handles slip through his hands until they rested on the rushes. "No, it still lives and will stay in camp until those kyjyan horns have grown back. Then we'll have a proper ritual." That confused me. I screwed my face up in puzzlement, looking at Renowden to explain.

"The buck's antlers fell off for the spring moult. Cernonnus obviously doesn't want this creature killed." Renowden smirked, hiding his smile from Tallack.

I said nothing. Perhaps it really was the spirit of the God of Death who visited me in the forest and who grazed in our enclosures with the horses. I took it to be a good sign. Having a god wandering about the compound gave me a sense of calm. Cernonnus must have heard my apology at the Nine Maidens. Why else would he send such vicious weather to deter the Duros from attack?

"I will sacrifice him though," Tallack sniffed. "When the time is right."

Ren rolled his eyes at me, making me chuckle. "Is there anything else that needs doing, Chief? Fur Benyn's finished with me now."

Tallack tapped one of the axe head's with his toe. I could tell that he was itching to try out his new toy. "Not sure. Are the rock baskets full on the battlements?"

Renowden nodded.

"And the row boats carried inside the gates along with those movable bridge things you made?"

"They are."

Tallack pulled a face. "Have I forgotten anything, Aunt Mel?"

Now he asks me. It was a bit late to get my take on the largest raiding party our tribe had seen since Aebba the Wild's youth. "I'm just a healer, Nephew. What would I know about war?"

Tallack sat on the edge of the bunk next to his brother as I completed the last of the stitches. "You remember the old ways. When grandfather increased our territories to beyond the River Sid."

I nodded. "I do."

"Then tell me what to do. I need your guidance."

"Blydh almost banished me for making suggestions when I had no right to. I dare not offend him again."

He looked up at me and then at Renowden. Ren took the hint and shuffled around the tight space and ducked beneath the door skins and out into the teeming rain. Kewri didn't know what to do with himself. I needed him to hold the torches for light, but he was uncomfortable staying. Tallack took them from him and flicked his head towards the entrance.

When we were alone, Tallack returned to being the sweet-tempered boy I knew him to be. Maintaining the pretence of being Tallack the Fearless took a toll on him. He looked exhausted and the Duros were not yet at our walls.

"Fire will be their greatest weapon. We are trapped here with nowhere to run. They will surround the camp and shower us in flaming arrows until everything is ablaze and there is no food nor shelter. If they burn down our walls in several places, we are done for. We don't have the numbers that they do."

His forehead puckered into a panicked frown. "What are our options? Should we make a run for it and go further west?"

"And have them believe us cowards? They would run us down and slaughter us all. We have mothers, babes in arms and too many elderly to outrun them. We stand and fight, but that means all of us. Arm everyone who can swing an axe. Give everyone blades that they may protect themselves if the worst comes to pass. And prepare for the prospect of fire."

"How?"

"Put the mothers and babes in the Long Hut. It is the most central part of the island. With luck, it'll be too far for flaming arrows to reach. Thank Cernonnus that the leaves are not fully out on the trees at the wooded fringes. We may lose some but probably not all. The critical thing is to shoot the men down before they can get near to the walls to cut or burn them. The river on the eastern and northern edges will help there."

As I told him all the things that my brother would employ to prevent catastrophe, Tallack's expression grew more and more grave. The torches were burning low and the noise from the storm was deafening. I finished smearing plantain paste and binding Blydh's head while Tallack poured himself a cup of ale.

"You think that we will lose?" He said, with grim resignation.

I shrugged. "Only the Morrighan has those answers, and we have no idea whether she favours us or Brea." It was not a name I should have mentioned at that time. Just when I was starting to win back the affections of my nephews, I mentioned the woman who killed their father and got away with it unpunished due to my reluctance to speak out. "Better make sure that there are plenty of buckets next to the streams so people can start putting out blazes." I said, quickly changing the subject.

Tallack finished his ale. "Anything else?"

I thought for a moment, debating whether to tell him my suspicions over the devious Novantae Chief, Faolan. I'd heard nothing about him or Sorcha since my return from the moors. Having made the wrong decision before, I chose to confide in Tallack. "I think Faolan is plotting with the Duro's behind our backs."

Tallack stared directly into my eyes, but I held his gaze. This was no tall tale. I had the evidence from the young scout who saw the Skotek Chief riding with white banners away from our boats. I laid out the details of my suspicions and the possible reasons for their betrayal. Tallack listened with a solemn expression until I'd finished.

"He is a reliable scout; I know the lad well. If he says he saw Faolan with the colours of peace, then I believe him." He said, slumping down on a stool by the fire. "What are we to do?"

"Are all the Novantae in camp right now?" I asked.

"No, Faolan sent Ealar back with some of his men to watch over the boats in the estuary. Why?"

"All the boats, your ship too?" I watched as the pieces fell into place inside his mind.

"You think Ealar was sent to take my ship?"

"I think he has a greater plan in mind. If he has made a pact with the Duros it can mean only one thing; Faolan will try to kill our family and then take over the whole tribe, our lands and our mines?"

"But we made a fair deal." He whined. Sometimes I wish I was young and naive still.

I tried not to snort, but I couldn't stop myself. "Faolan is only interested in Faolan. You think he cares if he breaks his word with us? We have few warriors and vast lands and wealth. What would you do in his place?"

Tallack stared at the floor, thinking through all the potential ways that Faolan could gain the upper hand. "I agreed to let his men defend my ship. All my warriors are here in camp."

"Then send someone you trust to take a few strong men to secure it, or you'll find that the Novantae are the proud owners of a swift Phoenician vessel and on their way home to Skotek."

Tallack ran from my hut before I could discuss any further tactics with him. I needed to enlist more help, but Blydh was too weak to be left alone. If he was sick from the resin, he could choke. His arms and legs were still bound to stop him from scratching at his scalp. I stuck my head out between the door skins and shouted above the roar of the thunder. "Kewri!"

Bless him, he was under the goat shelter, soaked through. I sent him to fetch Cryda, Derwa and her Ordo husband, Glaw. While he was gone, I took a fair portion of the resin I had left, knowing that it would leave me short, and mixed it with a little water and crushed valerian root. Cryda hurried into my hut cursing me for daring to summon a former Ruvane in such a manner. She was followed by Derwa and Glaw not long after. All were genuinely concerned about Blydh and had no idea that I had to open his head for a second time. Cryda thought it was my reasoning behind fetching her. It was not.

"Cryda, do you have any of that Frynkish wine tucked away anywhere? It's really important. If you have a secret stash, I must know at once." The urgency and tremble in my voice made her sit up straight and pay attention. Panic kept me from succumbing to fatigue.

My body ached but there were more important matters to attend to than sleep.

"I have a little left. Why do you need it?"

There wasn't really time to explain my plan, but I knew that they would not help unless they were aware of all the threats ahead of us. I rattled through my suspicions and gave them the same evidence that I'd presented to Tallack.

They too came to the same conclusions. My relief at having secured their help did little to settle my churning gut. It took another cup of ale each before I'd laid out the full details of my hurried aims, but they were all keen to play their part. I just needed to catch up with Tallack and appraise him of my plan.

Leaving Kewri in charge of Blydh's care for a while, I pulled on my cloak and went in search of my nephew. The new boardwalk was such a blessing now that the storm was creating puddles the size of huts around the place. If only there was time to complete all that were needed.

Scampering down towards the southern gates, I passed the horse pen where the white hart stood regarding me. Where once his antlers stood proud, there were now pink nubs. Their loss seemed to make the stag more docile. Although still wary of people passing by, it did not startle nor flee as I approached. Lifting the soggy cloth of my hood from my eyes, I looked at the beast with great reverence. "If you are the spirit of Cernonnus, guide all my kin to victory and I will find a way to set you free."

He raised his head and treated me to a long soft grunt, his ribs tightened and his breath fogged the air about his nose. This was not a buck in panic, nor warning me to back away. The God of Death had accepted my bargain.

Almost distracted from my mission, I stood in the rain for far too long thinking about his unusual white fur and pink skin around his nostrils. He was the mystical connection to the gods, sent just for me. After a short time, something spooked him and he moved off into the trees at the side of the enclosure.

I turned around to see what had alarmed him. The warrior maiden who almost caved in my head with an axe was watching me. I hadn't seen her about the camp for a while, but then I hadn't been looking out for her. Slopping through the mud, she joined me on the boardwalk.

"I just wanted to say that I wasn't aiming for you that day. I hope you know that and I am sorry if it scared you." Despite her apology, the offending weapons were all about her. A bow and quiver hung from strapping across her back, a blade rested at her belt and she held the very axe that almost took off my head. She was an impressive young woman, older than some of the other recruits and less fleshy. I imagine that she would be a formidable foe and was glad to have her fighting with our tribe instead of against us.

"I know you never meant me harm, but I thank you for saying it nonetheless." My errand was urgent, but something stopped me from moving on. This maiden had hidden talents, of that I was sure. "What do folk call you?"

She smiled, glancing down at her weapon, almost in embarrassment. "Senara, Fur Benyn."

"Born of the Dumnonii?" I squinted at her, concentrating on any trace of falsehood in her response.

"Parents are homesteaders east of Dartmoor."

That was good to hear. She was of our tribe and used to tough conditions. I had no doubt that she knew the land around our compound better than most of our warriors. "Can you ride?"

"As well as any. I can shoot a squirrel out of the tallest trees and from a running start." She puffed out her chest and jutted her chin forwards.

"Can you sneak up on a fellow without them hearing?" I asked with a view to co-opting her into my battle campaign.

"On men and boys, easily. Maybe less so for stags like him." She pointed to my godly spirit and grinned at me. She'd been watching me interact with the beast and formed opinions of her own. I liked this Senara. She could be invaluable to my plans.

"Would you be prepared to take orders from an old lady?"

The grin didn't falter. "Rather that, than be bossed about by those kyjyan men."

That was all the confirmation I needed. I picked out a horse for her to take and handed her a little tin for her troubles. Before she mounted the pony, I gave her my instructions and shouted up to the southern watchmen to let her come and go as she pleased. They obeyed without question.

When the huge gates swung open, I saw Tallack walking across the shallow section of the tributary close to where Renowden, Treeve and a few Sea Warriors were boarding a row boat further downstream. I had a feeling that he would choose them to protect his Phoenician craft. Renowden was completely trustworthy. I was less sure of Treeve.

Tallack hastened through the opening just as Senara cantered out into the tributary and across the wide clearing where the recruits trained on chalkier ground.

We strode along the raised planking towards the Long Hut discussing Tallack's part in the evening to come.

"Do you think that's the reason why the Duros have held back from attacking?" He asked me before we could be overheard by the guards on duty outside the Chief's hut.

"Faolan's offer coupled with this rotten storm. If their only weapon against us is fire, then it makes sense to wait until the thatch and fences are dry."

"Treacherous Kyjyan. After all that time we spent up there with his tribe too. I really thought we'd made an ally for life."

"Can't count on anyone except your own clan. Even then, best not to make assumptions, especially in light of Wenna's betrayal."

Tallack twisted his mouth to one side, nodding. By the time we reached the back door to the Long Hut, Cryda, Derwa and her husband were already inside chatting with our visitors. I let Tallack enter first. The moment he saw Faolan and Sorcha, he gave them the broadest smile and offered his arm in greeting to the old Chief.

"This is a day of joy. My aunt has returned and Blydh has survived a second treatment to his skull." He sat in Blydh's wolf chair so that he could be closer to Faolan. "We should celebrate, ay mother?"

Cryda knew this to be her cue to speak. "Indeed, son. Shall I break open the last jug of Frynkish wine?"

Faolan looked at the ale in his cup. "Not on my account, my lady. I am content with beer."

"Nonsense, we should drink to Blydh's good health. Only the finest wines for our esteemed guests." Tallack bellowed, until all the elders and warriors in the hut could hear. They stomped and cheered, making Faolan look rude for rejecting the offer.

"Aye, well, I could take a little nip if it's as good as you say." Faolan sniffed, sinking down the remnants of his ale and holding out his cup.

My niece rose from her bench. "I'll go and fetch it, Cryda. You stay with the babe." Derwa took the horn cup belonging to the Novantae leader and left through the rear door to speak with the slaves.

Glaw removed the green rock from his pocket and turned it over in his hand. I'd seen him do this so many times, I assumed it had become a habit. It drew his full attention as though it was more prized than pearls, greater than tin or gold.

"I'm very glad to hear that your boy is recovering, Lady Cryda. It's a fearful thing to watch when your offspring are sick or injured, but you must prepare yourself should the worst happen. As I said to Meliora there, I've seen such a wound like this before. The lad was never the same again. Couldn't feed himself, shit the bed all the time, really he'd have been better off dead."

I could see Tallack's eye twitching as he held his emotions in check. Cryda took a long slow breath, closing her eyes to his harsh words. When she finally exhaled, she looked up at Faolan and tried to smile. The whole plan rested on their ability to act naturally. Their awkward postures and stilted conversations were making Faolan uneasy. He was a shrewd man and not one to underestimate.

Glaw sat sullenly at the end of the lower bench examining his rock. Faolan watched him for a few moments, captivated by the Ordo's obsession.

"What have ye got there, lad? Give it here and let me look at it." Faolan commanded.

"It's just a rock. Nothing special." Glaw seemed reluctant to hand it across. Faolan flicked his hand towards him, urging him to release the peculiar object. Its surface glimmered in the flickering light, tricking the eyes that it was shining green. Glaw had no option but to pass it to Cryda who then walked it over to the Novantae leader, or risk making a scene that would ruin my plans. Faolan weighed the rock in his palm, bouncing it up and down. A tiny sneer bloomed on his whiskered face.

"Where did ye find this then?"

Glaw scowled at the old man, his eyes narrowed to slits. Everyone in the hut stopped talking to hear his answer. "While I was down in the far west on the Lizard Peninsula hunting."

"Is that so? And you know what it is, I presume?"

Glaw looked at Tallack and then back to Faolan and nodded.

"And I'm guessing you haven't told your new kin here that they have copper on their land?"

CHAPTER NINETEEN

Faolan's statement hit us all hard. Surely it couldn't be true? Had Derwa's husband found copper deposits near to Land's End and kept it a secret from us for all this time? His own people would know the rocks as well as their own faces. Their tribe boasted the largest copper mines in all the land. If this was indeed true, not only had he deliberately deceived us, but had been flaunting it under our noses this whole time. No wonder he hadn't gone back to the mountains with his new wife in tow. He was considering how best to handle this development.

Tallack burned with rage. I could tell from his sour face that he wanted to grab his new brother by the neck and choke the life from him, but he knew that it would ignite a feud between us and the Ordoviches. We already had enough tribes who counted us among their enemies without adding to the number.

Glaw cast his gaze to the floor. Whatever plan he had hatched up could no longer work in his favour. He was found out. His best option to stay in our favour was to come clean over the whole discovery, and as I predicted, he faced Tallack and said; "If you'd like me to, I can take you or one of your kin to the exact place that I found the rock, and explain how we go about processing the metal up in the mountains?" The gesture was too little, too late, but in light of Faolan's betrayal, it was an issue that could afford to wait.

"That's good of you, brother. As soon as the Duros are dealt with, we'll take you up on that offer." Tallack almost spat the word, brother, through clenched teeth. This meeting was not working out as I had hoped. Far from appearing a united force, all we'd achieved was to show the Novantae how fractured our family had become.

Derwa returned a short time later with a wooden board on which sat several cups, including Faolan's own fashioned from horn. She bent her knees and held out the tray to our guests first. Faolan swiped his own, while Sorcha took the cup closest to her. Derwa smiled as she turned to hand out the rest to her family and a couple of the most senior elders. That was when I knew that she had successfully laced and delivered the resin and valerian mixture.

Everyone waited for Tallack to stand and announce a blessing for his brother, when we would all drink to Blydh's health and ask for the gods to watch over us all. As he did so, I kept an eye on Faolan and Sorcha, to see that they were drinking their doctored wine. I knew it would take a while to have an effect on them, but there was no way of knowing whether Derwa had taken note of my dosage instructions.

Cryda did a brilliant job of distracting everyone's attention, parading little Delen around and encouraging people to hold her and give her a cuddle. With all the familial bonding going on, no one noticed when Faolan nodded off to sleep in his chair. Sorcha's eyelids grew heavier and she began swaying to stay upright. It was my turn to act.

"You look exhausted child. Shall we walk together to your shelter?" I bent over Sorcha and whispered into her ear. "I have some more of that ale stashed away. I'll bring that too, shall I?" Winking at her, she giggled and then let me pull her up to her feet. I slipped my arm about her waist and guided her towards the front door of the Long Hut. As soon as I was clear, I heard Tallack give the order for his men to carry Faolan out and bind his limbs together.

The storm was finally beginning to blow itself out, but the breeze was still chilly and carried with it the last of the rain. She didn't even notice that the ale had miraculously travelled from my hut to hers without me walking anywhere. We bundled inside out of the cold and I dropped her onto her bunk. She burst with laughter, rolling about in her furs.

"Please don't make me marry one of your nephews, Fur Benyn. I want to go home. I miss my ma." She whined. I poured her a drink and made sure she was upright enough to take the cup from my hand. "I mean, they're nice, but not like a Novantae man. They're rugged, with big, strong arms and tangled beards and fierce warriors to be proud of." Her voice was slurred. I had to be careful that she didn't pass out like her father had. She needed just enough ale to loosen her lips. She drank without encouragement. The resin can give people a raging thirst. When she shoved the empty cup under my nose for more, I made sure that I didn't pour out too much.

"It's just not fair. Ealar gets to go home, why can't I?"

"I thought your brother was to stay here and manage the shares and transportation of tin from our mine on the north coast?" I had to be careful what I said to keep her talking.

Sorcha stuck out her tongue and shut her eyes tight. "Pah! Ealar can barely wipe his own arse without our mother's help." She lay back on the bunk and lifted up her knees to her stomach. Tears of laughter rolled down her cheeks. "Greum will take over here, while Ealar and Father go home."

This was it. The old wolf was playing all sides in his game of strategy. Every eventuality would benefit him and his family directly. If the twins survived, Sorcha would wed one of them and become Ruvane. If he got the chance to kill either of them or both, his eldest son would take over our lands and mines and all our people too. What deal had he made with the Duros and Lady Brea, I wondered?

"Ah I see. Your eldest brother is the clever one, is he?"

She nodded. "Och, he's much more than that. He's the best hunter, best fighter and best sailor in our whole tribe. Well, you've met him, Fur Benyn. Wouldn't you agree?"

"Oh yes, child. Of course. Greum is a fine man. And er… where is he now?"

"Down the coast a wee bit with the rest of our men."

"Is that so? And what are they waiting for?"

"My father's signal."

"Oh? What kind of signal?"

She looked at me with screwed up features. Had I pushed too quickly?

She forced her eyes wide and pulled a face at me. "To light the beacons of course. How else could he see from the ships?"

In her addled state she thought me stupid. If it wasn't such a tense situation, I'd think it quite endearing. As it was, we now knew the extent of Faolan's betrayal. He'd sent for all his men and ships, but only revealed the presence of a few to send the Ivernii fleeing home to Iwerdon. I was itching to ask her just how many men had Faolan summoned and precisely where were they docked, but I needed her compliant and truthful. There was every chance she would exaggerate, that's if she knew the answers to my questions. I would have to rely on my new scout Senara and her stealthy instincts to give me the facts. Until then, we had two hostages with which to trade and the element of surprise.

I stayed just long enough to ply her with enough ale to make her sleepy and then bound her legs and feet together around a central post in her shelter. When I got back to the Long Hut, the elders and my kin were all awaiting my news. It did not take much time to relay all that I'd found out.

Faolan may have bought us a delay from the Duro attack, but only so that he could position himself to take over our tribe and send them running back to their own borders in our stead.

Tallack stood up and paced around at the back of the hut. The elders were all quiet, shaken by the enormity of our situation. None had anything useful to offer by way of a solution. The one person who excelled at strategy was unconscious in my shelter with his head leaking bloody humours. He may have misjudged the raid on the Duro camp, but after two summers of planned attacks along the borderlands with his Head Hunter Clan, Blydh was the best we had.

When the scouts changed shifts, they came straight to the Long Hut to report to Tallack. I feared that they bore the terrifying news that the Duro's were outside our gates, setting their fires and sharpening their blades. Thankfully, the news was the same as it had been before the storm; the Duros had made a temporary camp in the next valley. In terms of walking distance, they may as well have been at our gates.

I tried to eat a little bread and stew but my anxiety balled up in my chest and pained me. The more I thought about the Novantae ships and the Duros in the next valley, the more addled I felt. I was so tired that I could scarcely keep my eyes open, let alone think of a way out for my tribe.

Derwa noticed my nodding head. "Get some rest, Aunt. We'll need to be fighting fit for when…"

Cryda and Tallack both shot her a look.

Derwa adjusted her tone. "Come, I'll walk you back to your hut and watch Blydh for a time. Let's give the elders time to think."

I remember walking back through the boggy camp, wishing that the boards extended to my hut and thinking that the elders hadn't a clue how to solve our difficulties. The rest was a blur. It had been more than two days since I had any real sleep to speak of, and even then, all I could do was nap for a short time.

Derwa seemed all the more attentive since her husband's revelation. Perhaps she took some of the blame for his silence on herself. By all rights, he should have dragged her back to his tribe in the mountains and forced her to perform her duties. Instead, Glaw let Derwa make all their decisions. She treated him with utter disdain and almost rejoiced when he rode off to hunt in the west of our lands. Perhaps if she had met him half-way and tried to build a relationship together, he would have told her about the copper sooner. It would have solved many of our problems of metal supplies, had we known that the deposits were right under our noses.

I kept my musings to myself, yanking off my soaked cloak and muddy shoes and climbing under my furs. Kewri had watched Blydh virtually all day and was as tired as me. The look of relief on the gentle giant when Derwa sat on the edge of Blydh's bed was so noticeable, it made her laugh. It took moments for me to fall into slumber, despite the low moans of Blydh across the hut from me. I had worried myself into a state of exhaustion.

When I awoke, it was still dark outside and the fire was low. It took a little while for me to gain my bearings and see who was shaking my arm. The silhouette was of a young woman, but she was taller and leaner than Derwa. I sat up and realised that it was Senara. She was as stealthy as she claimed. No one else had heard her enter. Kewri, Derwa and Blydh were all still fast asleep.

"What is it? What did you find out?"

She held my cloak out for me to put around my shoulders. I took that to mean that her news should be heard by the Chief and elders too. Retracing my steps across camp, I called out to Tallack in his shelter and heard someone inside grumbling about the intrusion.

I should've spoken to my nephew about that young Treeve. He had notions of high status for himself, which gave me pause for thought. The last of Tallack's bed fellows was now sleeping with the Chieftain of the Duros in the next valley.

"Tallack, summon the elders. We have new information." I shouted, before leaving him to dress. We hurried over to the Long Hut. The slaves had at least kept the fires burning inside. When Senara lifted the door panel away for us to enter, the heat hit us in a great wave. I was glad of it, having come from my warm bed straight out into the cold air. It was long before dawn and none bar the watchmen were about camp. It was fortunate that Faolan's deal with our enemy had granted us this reprieve, but it would not last for long.

If there were any spies in camp, word would reach Ealar and his brother Greum that their father and sister were our hostages. With this knowledge, the Duros would be at our gates within hours. When the majority of elders and Tallack's best warriors had assembled, Senara and I stood before the top table to give the Chief her news. The warriors all tittered behind their hands at Senara as she took the bow and quiver from her back and rested her axe on the floor. I gave them such a glare for their poor attitude.

"If you get injured in the battle, you might find me out of resin when you're howling in pain. Such brave fellows like you can make do with a little willow bark." That wiped the sneers from their faces. If they had to put up with all that a woman has to tolerate, they wouldn't be so quick to judge.

"Chief Tallack." Senara began. It surprised me how confident she was in speaking in front of so many men. It made me wonder whether she had been forced to take charge at her family homestead. Where had she acquired such skill with axe and blade prior to coming here?

"Chief Tallack. Fur Benyn charged me with scouting along the coastal path and to tally the number and whereabouts of the Duros. I come back with all I have learned."

In truth, I had not expected her back so soon. She must have ridden like the wind and fair worn out that poor horse, but then she is half the weight of the menfolk and less of a burden to carry at speed.

Tallack looked her up and down. At first, I thought that he was deciding on her attractiveness, but his eyes rested on her weapons, not the curve of her body. "And what did you discover?"

"There was no sign of the Ivernii ships. Fur Benyn said that they flew the green banners of Iwerdon. None of the vessels I saw had those, but I saw plenty bearing the blue of the Novantae. They have made anchor around the headland near to the mouth of the River Sid."

"How many?" Tallack sat forward, trying to keep his composure.

"More than your fleet, even before some were sunk and all were filled with fighting men."

I faced her. "Did you happen to spot a large unlit beacon on your travels?"

"I did, yes. It's on the highest point of the headland above the salt pans. I thought Chief Tallack might have arranged it to be there, to call back his fancy ship." Senara jabbed her thumb out towards my nephew, puzzled.

"Call it back?" I asked.

Tallack rubbed his forehead. "I sent Renowden, Treeve and a few of the men to take it out to sea. It's too vulnerable to leave in the estuary, even if we do need our warriors here in camp."

That struck me as odd. If Treeve was in the middle of the Channel with Renowden on the Phoenician ship, who was in Chief Tallack's shelter a short while ago? "Were there any boats left in the estuary?" I asked.

"Only the damaged ones and two of the Chief's. No others." She said.

Where was Ealar and Faolan's great ship? Had he sailed to meet up with his older brother's fleet so that they could all move in a coordinated fashion upon seeing the lit beacon?

"And the Duros? Did you get a good look at them?" Tallack continued, while I mused over who his latest conquest might be.

"Yes, Chief. They are over the rise to the east of here, but the marshland extends right along this valley for quite some distance, so they'd find it hard going to come at us on horseback without sinking into the bogs."

"How many would you say?" I asked.

"Hard to tell, since while I watched them, a large party rode away from camp to the north-west, but I'd say more than twice our numbers." She peered around to look at the expressions on the warriors' faces. They seemed more anxious of the Duro attack than Senara did, and she saw them with her own eyes. They were not jeering now.

"They've split into two forces. They'll come at us from either side." I said. The elders murmured in agreement.

"Well, if they come at us from the west, they'll have to cross the cleared training grounds before they can reach us. We'll pick them off with our best shooters." He turned to one of his warriors standing close by. "Did you finish the submerged spikes in the river alongside our eastern wall?" The man nodded solemnly in response. Tallack tried not to appear worried for the sake of his reputation, but the sweat bled through his tunic at the neck and chest. The fire was not kicking out that much heat.

"Well at least we know what we're in for. We can rain arrows down on them from the western battlements and hope that our defence structures hold to our east." He looked at me and then back at the warrior maiden. "Was there anything else you think we should know?"

"Well, I did think of one thing that might be useful, if we can act quickly enough to take advantage of the situation."

CHAPTER TWENTY

"Go on." Chief Tallack urged.

My respect for this young warrior maiden was growing every moment. Not only was she skilled with blade and axe, bow and spear but she was intelligent too. That's rarely the case with the average warrior I've found, but then she is far from average.

"It's just the next valley floor is as boggy as this one after all the rain from the storm and it hasn't drained away. The Duros moved their camp up the shallow hillside to get away from the mud. They are sitting half-way down the western slope."

Tallack glanced at me as though he thought her mad. He hadn't realised the girl's plan. From the look of his warriors, they couldn't fathom it either.

"You mean to roll fireballs of willow withies stuffed with kindling down the slope to burn their camp down before dawn?" I had to state it as obviously as possible or Tallack would have shown his lack of mastery over the situation.

"I do, Fur Benyn, but we'd have to act fast. It won't be long until day break." She said, smiling at me for giving her this opportunity to show her worth.

Tallack grimaced. "But it'd take us just as long to ride through the marshes as the Duros. We'd never make it unseen."

"I know a route through, Chief. If a small number of men follow my horse, we can have them aflame and be back before dawn. But we must act now."

He could hardly argue with the girl. She was willing to put her life on the line to improve our chances of defeating such a number of enemies.

"Fine. Do it, but there is nothing I can do if you get caught." This was the first time he seemed pleased not to be included in the raid. "And if you do, you'd better keep your mouths shut over the Novantae." Tallack picked out half a dozen men to go with Senara and explained where they could find withies and kindling from the Chief's personal stores.

Before he could hunker down with the elders and remaining men to talk siege tactics, I spoke up. "And the beacon, Chief?"

"Oh yes, is there anyone willing to go and knock it over the cliff? We don't want anyone lighting that and bringing the Novantae down on us too."

Another of his men stepped forwards, before rushing from the hut to complete his task. I was left wondering what to do with myself.

I was no use in the stealth raid, and no help in battle talks. Too agitated to go back to sleep, I returned to my hut and made porridge for the men, in the hope that Blydh would wake and retain all his senses. I splashed water on my face and changed my stinking tunic, before setting about restocking my medicine kit with wrappings and tonics and ointments.

Kewri appeared as I fed and watered the goats. He emptied the piss pot and nodded his greetings to me.

"You'd better get over to the Long Hut." I said. "They could use a strapping lad like you in a strategic spot when the Duros get here."

Kewri gently shook his head. "My place is by your side." That was all he said before ducking under the thatch to find his bowl of porridge.

A little after dawn, the raiding party returned, whooping and hollering their victory. I didn't see the smoke myself, but Senara regaled me with a detailed description of the Duros fleeing their burning tents in complete disarray. She said that their horses bolted towards the moors and that many of their tribe were scattered or killed by our warriors as they ran into the woodlands surrounding the dell.

I should have been as jubilant as she, but I was sad. The whole event could've been avoided, had Brea been less ambitious and Blydh in better control of his temper. How many children lost their mothers or fathers before dawn, I dare not contemplate, but then if the situation was reversed, the Duros wouldn't think twice about killing us all.

I heaved a sigh, and congratulated Senara. "I bet the men look at you differently now, don't they?"

She gave me a huge smug smile and nodded.

"Good. Has the Chief given you any other orders?"

"No, Fur Benyn. Was there something you needed me to do?"

Bless her. She had been awake and active longer than I had after my walk to the Nine Maidens. "Rest, child. They'll be plenty for you to do come dusk, I'll be bound."

"I'll just go and make an offering to the Morrighan first, then I'll see if I can find a bunk in the recruits' shelters."

I had completely forgotten the wretched conditions in which Blydh kept the young trainees. She was one of our most valuable assets and she was not sure of a bed. "Make your offering, Senara, then come back here. You can sleep in my bunk until it's time." The smile she shot me etched itself inside my mind forever. That made it two recruits I'd poached from Blydh without his knowledge. If he were to discover my latest infraction, he was likely to banish me for the rest of my days.

With a pocket full of grain from the guarded store, I walked the boards to the horse pen in hope of gaining the attention of my god spirit. His white hind quarters were hard to hide among the leafless trees at the western fringes of the island. His ears twitched when he saw me. I waited for some time at the fence, hoping that he would find the courage to come closer, but he didn't. More than anything, I needed the confirmation that he was Cernonnus and that we were in his favour.

At length, I poured the grain into a little heap inside the boundary and began to shuffle slowly away. Before I was back to the goats behind my hut, I saw him walk over to my own offering and gobble up the wheat and oats. Maybe he is just a deer after all, and I let my imagination run away with me.

Blydh was sitting up in bed when I got inside. He said nothing, but his face was ashen grey and the wound was more swollen than ever. My resin pot was perilously low, but I knew he needed a dose. I mixed it for him and left Kewri to stand guard.

With the remaining porridge and a wooden spoon in my pocket, I trudged towards the shelter where I knew Tallack had tied up Faolan and Sorcha. After all the kindness they had shown me in the past, I couldn't let them starve, hostage and traitors or not.

When I walked in, Sorcha began crying. Tallack's warriors had bound and gagged her and Faolan to a central post which supported the skins covering the shelter. There was no fire for warmth nor any water. Faolan's eye was badly bruised and almost closed with pus and humours. The warriors had obviously taken out their anger on the old man before leaving him to fester in his own filth.

I took off Sorcha's gag first and held a cup of water up to her mouth. She gulped it down almost choking.

"Go easy, there's plenty where that came from. I'll make sure that someone comes often to give you more."

She howled as the tears tumbled down her cheeks. "What have we done? We gave you our home to stay in, fed you our best food and protected you from the wild creatures of the mountains. Why are you doing this to us?"

I couldn't bear it any longer. I slipped the gag back into her mouth and began the procedure again with Faolan. "She told me everything." I said to him.

He couldn't look me in the eye. "I guessed as much."

I let him sip at the water and then gave him a few spoons full of porridge to eat, shovelling it into his mouth like a babe.

"Please, give it to her. She needs it more than I do."

I left his mouth free of the gag while I fed his daughter.

"Why would you do this? We had a deal all thrashed out. We would have made perfect allies." I had to know what had brought about the sudden change in our ties of friendship.

"You're a good woman, Meliora, but you overlook the twin's faults. They are selfish and greedy and care little for their tribe. You have one who would rather smash down fences and kill everyone who speaks against him and the other who cannot decide which side of the bed to sleep on, or who to share it with. You think I want my Sorcha bound to either of them now?"

"You could have just told me that and sailed home with a reasonable tin trade. Why go to such lengths? Call off your sons, Faolan. If you don't my nephews will make sure that your death is long and agonising to deter other tribes from ever betraying us again."

"You think death scares me? I've had my time. My sons will make sure that this compound is razed to the ground."

"You want Sorcha to burn alive alongside you, after the warriors have all had their turn at defiling her? You know that is what will happen, long before your ships and men can get anywhere near the estuary. Your head will greet them on a spike at the southern gates, Sorcha's entrails wrapped around the pole for the dogs to chew." I described a small fraction of the horrors that awaited them both.

Blydh had more than his fair share of Cador the Cruel's traits in him. There was every chance that he would think of something far more devastating and spectacular as a warning to others. That's if he had retained his mind. I spooned in the last of the porridge and let my threats sink in. Sorcha's tears renewed as did her wailing.

The old man sucked in his lips. I could see that he was set in his ways and wouldn't back down. Pulling their gags back into their mouths, I pushed myself up from my knees and grabbed the cup and bowl to carry away. Before I left the shelter, I took one last look at them both. "It's a shame." I said shaking my head. "She would have made a fine Ruvane for this tribe. She'll be lucky if anything remains of her to bury."

As I walked to the stream to rinse the bowl, I thought about how Treeve had reacted to the notion of Sorcha binding to Tallack. He too had threatened to kill her rather than have her take his lover from him. Now I was doing the same thing. This was what I was reduced to in the protection of my kin. The truth is that none of my warnings were bluffs.

Both Blydh and Tallack would expect the Novantae to die in a horrible manner, unless there was a way to call a truce. I suspected that neither of Faolan's sons cared much for their sister, especially when they had the chance to replace their father as Chieftain of their tribe.

There was still time for the stubborn old brute to change his mind and force the Skotek fleet to stand down. Perhaps he just needed time to think about the fate of his daughter in the twin's hands.

Blydh was sitting up in the spare bunk when I walked in to my hut. He still looked grey and gaunt, but then he'd hardly eaten a thing since his injury. He must have been weaker than a day-old chick. Kewri was scraping out the wood ash and piling more logs onto the fire. I sat beside my nephew, wary of his anger.

"How is the pain? Do you need some willow?" I watched the movement of his eyes. The left one was still as it was before. The dark spot in the centre was big enough to cover over the ring of colour.

He cleared his throat. "It's bearable. I'll have some willow later." That was a good start. He hadn't yelled at me, but then he hadn't called me Aunt Mel either. I nodded to Kewri to untie the bindings from one side of the bunk while I loosened those closest to me.

Blydh flexed his hands and rubbed at his wrists.

"I'm sorry, but we had to stop you from scratching the wounds and shifting the gold plate in your head." I leaned back in case he felt like lashing out at me.

He reached up to his hair and gently touched the line of catgut stitches, wincing where they strained against the swollen flesh. Kewri and I sat by as he tested the capabilities of his body, clicking his stiff neck muscles and moving his legs. When he cupped his right hand over his eye, I knew that he was trying to see through the blown left one. Within moments, his hand slumped down into his lap and his face slackened. It was obvious he had not regained its use.

I jumped up and grabbed the axe with the massive curved blade from the end of his bunk. "See what Tallack had made for you." I said, hoping that it would please him. "The handle is fashioned from a rare white hart antler, the spirit of Cernonnus himself. It matches another that Tallack wields. When you are recovered, the pair of you will be formidable." I tried to make my voice sound jolly and hopeful, but it fell on deaf ears. Blydh was not interested. He wouldn't even take the blade from my hands.

"Kewri, pop and fetch Kerensa will you, please? I'm sure that she will want to see Blydh now that he's awake." He did as I asked, but Blydh did not seem keen to see her.

"How far are the Duros from our camp?" He trained his good eye on me, making me more uncomfortable under his gaze than ever. His wits had returned but brought melancholy along for the ride.

"It's all in hand, there is nothing for you to worry about. Tallack has things under control." I slid the axe to the floor and tore a chunk of fresh bread from the loaf baking on a flat stone by the fire.

He pushed my hand away when I offered him the bread. “How far?”

“In the next valley, just over the rise, but a raiding party has already thinned their numbers with fireballs before dawn.”

“Then they will come tonight, be assured of that.” He swung his legs to the side of the bunk and struggled to get to his feet. I didn’t know whether to help him or not, considering his fluctuating temper towards me. Instead I hovered close by, ready to slip my arm under his if he was in danger of collapse. Kewri returned before Blydh could slip on the rest of his clothes. He was alone.

Frowning at him, he shrugged at me behind Blydh’s back. Maybe she was with Cryda or somewhere Kewri would not think to look. Lifting the axe to pass to Kewri, I said; “Can you carry this for the Chief…”

Blydh snarled at me, snatching it from my hand. “I can manage. I’m not a child.”

I guess that answered my question about his state of mind. I needed to keep my distance or fear him using his new axe on me. Tallack may have forgiven me my sins, but Blydh sure hadn’t. Cernonnus only knew how he would react when he discovered Faolan’s treachery. Blydh dragged the axe along the ground, churning up my rushes and the mud in a great wake of mess behind him. Kewri and I watched him stagger about without coordination nor balance in a sweeping arc towards the Long Hut.

In two minds whether to go or stay, I figured that I could never live with myself if he fell and killed himself before my handiwork could heal. This was one of those times when I wished I’d stayed on the moors with the priestess of the Nine Maidens. It’s a simple but bloody way of life.

Hurrying after my nephew, I reached the Long Hut only moments after he'd arrived. The warriors, elders and his mother were all overjoyed to see him up on his feet so quickly. He even managed a faint smile for her, as Cryda smothered him in kisses instead of touching foreheads together as we usually do. It was a sensible move considering the swollen skin on that part of his head.

"Where is Tallack?" Blydh turned in a full circle about the Long Hut in search of his brother, but he was nowhere to be seen. Whether Blydh noticed it or not, Kerensa was also missing. He sat in his wolf's head chair and dropped the axe, while Cryda wove between the crowds to take the Ruvane chair at his side.

It took her less than a few moments to inform him of the latest developments with the Novantae. Why she couldn't have waited until Tallack was present before giving him such explosive information, I will never know.

Blydh was wild. His nostrils flared; his speech slurred so that it was difficult to understand. Red in the face, he rocked his body until he had enough momentum to stand. As soon as he was upright, he tried to stoop for the axe. That tipped his balance, sending him crashing into the table below.

In a tangle of legs and bronze blades, his fall was cushioned by poor Glaw who almost lost an ear for his troubles. The mountain man shoved Blydh until he could find his feet. Blydh reeled from the pain, clasping the sides of his head as he stomped through the group of warriors and elders towards the front door.

Everyone pushed and clamoured to follow him, me included, but I was swamped by the force of the crowd. I knew where he was headed. Turning on my heels, I scurried as fast as my old bones could carry me through the rear entrance and out past the fire pits.

Ahead of me, Blydh dragged his feet, scraping the axe behind him. The noise from everyone shrieking and talking brought others out of their huts. Almost everybody from our camp watched Blydh stumbling towards the shelter where we had Faolan and his daughter held captive.

CHAPTER TWENTY-ONE

Wasn't anyone brave enough to stop him? Where was Tallack? I fought my way through to Cryda and grabbed her arm. "You can't let him kill them. They are hostages, we need them as leverage."

"How am I supposed to do that? He doesn't listen to me." She let her eyes roll as though I was stupid for interfering. If she wasn't going to try and prevent the bloodshed, I had to, there was no other choice. I knew that I was taking my life into my own hands. Sneaking beneath the elbows of the warriors pushing around the shelter, I got inside. Blydh already had the axe high above his head.

"Please, Nephew, I beg you to wait." I slipped around his narrow body and stood between him and our captives. It was a risky move, considering his altered feelings towards me. He was just as likely to dispatch me to the Underworld as them. "Faolan has a massive fleet of ships with all his warriors aboard in the next bay. They could attack us at any moment or side with the Duros until we are dust beneath their feet." I clasped my hands together in front of my chest, imploring him with closed eyes. "Please, Chief Blydh. They have value alive. They are useless to us dead. There is still time enough to forge a treaty with his sons."

"A treaty? You still expect me to bind with this traitorous scum?"

"No, not that. Please, let me fetch Tallack and together you'll be able to convince Faolan to call off the attack."

Faolan sneered up at Blydh, goading him to end his misery quickly. "I'll nae beg for ma life, if that's what ye think."

Blydh rammed the end of the handle into Faolan's face. Blood splattered from his nose, but the old man stayed quiet.

"Think about it, Nephew, if you kill him quickly now, his suffering will all be over. Let him live until a new agreement is made, if you don't get what you want from him, then you can make it a slow passing into the Underworld, without ever claiming his seat among the gods."

Blydh warmed to this idea. He lowered his axe and heaved a sigh. "I don't need my brother to forge a deal with a back-stabbing kyjyan like this. I am just as much Metern of the Dumnonii as he is."

Before we could sit down and begin the talks, a loud and haunting sound echoed through camp. My blood ran cold, sending gooseflesh throughout my arms and legs. It was the watchman's horn blowing from the southern gates. The Duros were in sight of the walls.

A second call sent everyone scrambling for their weapons and running for the posts assigned to them. Only Blydh, Cryda and I were left standing around the shelter, wondering what we should do. A third blow on the watchman's goat horn and the sharpest long bow shooters mounted the battlements. Others stood by with filled water buckets and spears.

Women wept with fright, corralling their children into the safety of the Long Hut, just as I had suggested. All about me, our tribe were following the recommendations I had mentioned to Tallack. I hoped to Cerridwen that I'd thought of all possibilities.

"Cryda," I said, pushing her in the backbone to force her into action. "Get your slave to take the babe into the Long Hut, and for kyjyan sake, find Tallack!"

This was it, the day we'd been waiting for since I first caught sight of the Durotriges camped along our borders on the moors. Would it be just those who were not burnt or scattered from the night raid, or had Faolan's warriors joined them on land to overwhelm us? I admit to feeling more fear than I should at my time of life, but no one wants to die a violent death in a muddy field. There is no honour in that.

I was only half way across the compound when Kewri came running towards me. Before I could give him any instructions, he picked me up with one arm and flung me over his shoulder. I smacked his back and kicked out for him to let me go, but it made no impact whatsoever.

He ran into my hut and dumped me down onto my bed without ceremony. "Stay here and no harm will come to you, I promise." He said, standing guard over me in the doorway.

I rolled off the bunk onto my feet. "You great, giddy lump. How do you expect me to heal the injured?"

"They can come in here." He said, folding his arms across his chest and glaring out between the door skins.

"Move yourself, Kewri. I mean it. As much as I appreciate your protection, you have to let me help the tribe." He narrowed his eyes and wouldn't budge.

"Look," I softened my tone of voice. "If it will make you happy, you can stay by my side as I go out there and do my bit."

He thought about it for a moment and then nodded. Together, we rushed down towards the southern gate to see Tallack climbing the battlement ladder. He was preparing to give the order to fire. A mixture of men and women crouched low on the raised walkway against the high walls. Lower sections were cut out for the bowmen to aim through. As frightened as I was, I was desperate to see how many warriors we were up against. Spinning about, I muttered this to Kewri.

"I know a spot where you can peek out. Follow me." We rushed down the boardwalk, past the horse pen until the fencing changed directions and joined up with the compound walls. Kewri opened the gate to the enclosure and pointed to where a tributary snaked through, allowing the horses and the white hart fresh drinking water. Where the brook disappeared under the wall, Tallack's warriors had forced huge posts into the stream bed to prevent anyone from entering through the gap. There was just enough space between the wooden poles for us to peep through.

The horses bolted, snickering and fussing from the tense atmosphere building in camp. I could see Tallack in the distance at the top of the wall. His arm was raised, waiting until our enemies were close enough to receive a barrage of raining arrows. I peered through the gap, angling myself to see towards the southern expanse of the chalky training grounds.

There was a long line of warriors, all with blue woad painted on their faces and necks. Each one carried a shield above their heads. They had anticipated our moves. What struck me the most, was that there was only one row of men, far fewer than I'd expected. Surely the night raid of fire balls did not kill that many Duros?

"This doesn't feel right, Kewri. There are too few. They must be distracting us from another entry point." I back-tracked and called to my usual pony. He came close the moment I clicked my tongue at him. With a little help, I mounted the horse and gestured for Kewri to open the gate. Cantering through, I kicked my heels into his flanks and made short work of the distance across the island. Passing through the weaving shelters, leather stretchers and butchers huts, I pulled up the reins when I got to the eastern fringes and called up to the watchmen. "Keep your eyes peeled. They are playing us for fools on the southern side." I was right. The moment I'd said it, one of the watchmen blew the goat horn and shouted down.

"Boats heading north." He yelled. Those bowmen and women on the eastern battlements ran down towards the tower to get into position. I felt so helpless. Kewri was puffing and blowing on foot, trying to catch up with me. Before he could sling me over his shoulder again, I dismounted and began climbing the battlement ladder. I had to see for myself.

Their canoes were sturdy, with two warriors paddling at either end while the rest held their shields overhead for protection. The storm had swollen the river levels. I wondered whether the shallow hulls of the boats would clear our defences, rendering them useless.

"Fire at will. Send them all into the arms of the Morrighan!" I bellowed, as loud as I could make my voice carry. Those on top of the battlements, wasted their arrows. Some darts dug into the shields while others bounced off and into the water. One or two of the lower level shooters found their mark, but it made little impact on their progression upstream. While their attention was on our bowmen and women, none noticed the submerged spikes at random intervals. Just as they steered towards the section of the wall closest to the water with their axes, the leading edge of the first canoe hit a spike. Rather than splitting the timber and sinking the vessel as I had hoped, it tipped them all out into the river.

"Now! Let loose your arrows. Do it now!" I screamed. A bolt whipped past my ear in a flash. There were more warriors hiding in the marshland shooting back. I ducked under the battlements before they could better locate their target.

A man at my side caught a direct hit. It sliced through his neck with a squelching thud and protruded from the other side. He had just enough time to raise his hands to staunch the blood flow before toppling from the ledge. Pink foam spilled from his mouth. I shuddered as he hit the muddy ground beneath me. He was the first of our tribe to fall.

There was no time for contemplation or grief. The Duros had spotted the other spikes hidden in the water course. Those that remained afloat steered away from the walls to the opposite bank. They were trapped. If they tried to get out of the water, our bowmen would massacre the lot.

"Keep them pinned down. Don't let them get their axes at our walls." I screamed, hurrying down the ladder to my horse.

Kewri was out of breath. He bent double with his hands resting on his hips having caught up with me on the eastern side. Between the forge and skin stretching racks, I could see the southern gates bowing inward at regular intervals accompanied with a loud thudding noise. What was happening? Why wasn't Tallack protecting the entrance?"

Shielding my eyes from the low sunlight, I could see Tallack's unmistakable silhouette on the battlements, screaming out his orders for the bowmen to shower our enemy with arrows. Climbing back on my horse I cantered towards the gates as the first axe cut its way through the wood. "Kewri!" I called over my shoulder. He was already in pursuit. Two lonely warriors stood on our side of the gate jabbing their spears through the holes the Duros had created. How were the arrows missing these axe men? As the second hole punched through, I saw the shields suspended over their heads by their fellow tribesmen.

The hand of a Duro poked through the gap and threaded a thick bronze chain around the posts. One of our men unsheathed his blade and slashed him at the wrist. The first cut sliced down to the bone. The second followed on quickly and took it clean off.

Our man picked up the hand as a trophy, waving it at its owner through the hole in the gate, laughing. Blood gushed from the stump, pooling on thc ground. Within moments, our warrior's laugh stopped as another sharp shooter struck him between the eyes with a well-aimed bolt.

That was all the time the Duros needed to get the chain in place. I shouted at the remaining man to shatter it with an axe, but my voice was lost amid the clamour and bellowing of the crowd. I peered up at Tallack's shadow, waving my arms about to gain his attention. He did not turn around. He too was firing a bow taken from one of the fallen.

Desperate, and fearing that we were about to be inundated with perhaps as many as a hundred of our enemies, I pulled on the reins and galloped towards Tallack.

Blydh had staggered to the foot of the ladder and was trying to climb. Kewri was at the south gate yanking on the chain, trying to free it from the massive ropes attached on the opposite side. Digging his heels into the soft earth, he pulled with all his might but the chain stood firm. Just as he took his hands away to get a better grip, the slack in the chain pulled taut against the posts.

"Tallack!" I cried at the top of my voice. He turned to see Blydh half way up the ladder. His body swayed from one side to the other like he was addled on ale. The gates were a key part of our defence. "You must stop them from smashing the gates."

Tallack threw his hands in the air. "They have a team of oxen. They are out of firing range."

"Then find a way to cut the ropes." As soon as I yelled it, I knew my suggestion to be madness. The only way that could be achieved would be to lower someone down the outside of the wall with an axe. They would get picked off by Duro bowmen before they could get close.

Another horn sounded from behind us. The northern gate was under attack. Where our men had cleared away the forest for the timber and for better lines of sight, the Duros had found another angle for attack. As I predicted, every arrow arching overhead from the north carried with it the potential to burn our thatched roofs to the ground. Women holding shields over their heads, scurried about, stamping out the fires and dowsing huts with buckets of water from the stream. They could hardly keep up with the constant bombardment.

Blydh saw the northern watchtowers ablaze, and climbed back down. "I'll take command at that end. You find a way to keep them from the gate." He said, though

I knew that he'd never make it in time. The watchman had already succumbed to the flames. His falling body and screams of agony filled all our hearts with dread.

I slid down from my horse and gave him the reins. If he was insistent on fighting, at least he could ride to his enemies and not waste what little energy he had on running while half done in on resin. He stepped up on a wooden post and lay along my horse's back. The loyal old beast began walking immediately, even before Blydh was able to right himself.

Kewri was standing at the south gate with one warrior and the dead body of another. He thrust a spear through the holes every now and then, but I knew that the Duros had retreated under their shields to a safer distance.

I knew their plan. They would wait until all their forces could join them. When they were all assembled, they would force their oxen to pull down our gates, allowing them to swarm into the compound.

I cupped my hands around my mouth to direct my yell. "Tallack, pull your men down here. They must form a line of combat. The gates will fall."

He shook his head. "It'll stand. We can thin the numbers better from up here." Obstinate fool. What good are men half way up a wall when a massive horde were set to stampede through our camp?

Without my horse, I hurried as quickly as I could between the flaming arrows and churned mud to the gap in the wall. From my westerly position, I could see men running from the northern side to join up with those at the south. It was exactly as I'd feared. One tug from those oxen and there'd be no one to stand in their way.

How could Tallack not see their game? The arrows were little more than distractions to keep us busy firefighting. At least there appeared to be only Duro warriors. From what I could make out, every one of the men had the distinctive neck tattoos visible under the blue woad.

Perhaps Faolan's sons were holding back in the knowledge that their kin were inside. Several of the warrior's tents were burning next to the eastern wooded area. That was where all our pigs and chickens foraged.

Torn between hurrying across once more to set them free and heading south to reason with Tallack, I chose my nephew. We had to stop them from entering in one huge mass. I stuck two fingers in my mouth and blew a shrill whistle. Tallack turned and scowled at me.

"The gates… send everyone to hold the gates." The chain links clanked against each other and bit into the wood. A loud creak sounded as the poles bowed from the strain. Tallack screamed to his warriors to slide down the ladders in all haste and prepare to fight. At last the headstrong young Metern was listening to me.

The creaks and groans were followed by an enormous crack, as the posts gave way, wrenching a gaping hole in the panels. This was it; we would stand or fall defending our homes. Our men and women grabbed their spears, axes and shields and staggered their positions across the smashed gateway. I could see them hurtling towards us in a great wave of fury. At the head of the line was the leader of the Duros and my nephew, Paega the Wily.

CHAPTER TWENTY-TWO

It was a shock to see my banished nephew at the front of the warrior line, running at top speed towards us bearing the mystical sword that he'd stolen. He was not one to put himself in danger at the best of times. Perhaps he too thought that the sword was blessed by the gods and would protect him from all harm. It had, after all, shattered Blydh's bronze axe as though it was made from clay. From Tallack's expression, he believed it too. He held his newly commissioned axe up high, swapping his grip over and over, revealing his nervous state.

Kewri back stepped nearer to me. "You shouldn't be this close to the action. Move away before I carry you out of here."

"Dear boy, do stop treating me like an addled child. I have to see what's happening. Tallack is too mixed up in the action to figure out their plan." From my slightly elevated position on the island, I had a perfect view of the team of oxen across the training ground and a woman mounted on a dappled grey horse. Even at that distance, I knew it was Brea. She had planned the entire attack.

Our best warriors rushed forwards and engaged the leader of the Duros and his men in bloody battle. Spears ripped through guts, knives slit gizzards and entrails were spilled. The whole camp stank of innards, attracting rats and dogs in equal measure. Mangled bodies fell on top of others as our men ploughed through theirs. It was just as Senara had said, our lands were too marshy for them to have approached on horseback. That helped to even the score. The Duros may be skilled horsemen, but they were less formidable on two feet.

Paega spotted Tallack on the left side and strode towards him holding the god sword with both hands. Steadying his stance, Tallack gritted his teeth and waited for the first move.

Over confident, Paega swaggered to his younger half-brother and they began their dance. "You are no match for me, Tallack. Surrender as Chieftain and I will spare your mother."

That only angered our Metern more. He lunged at Paega swinging his axe upwards towards his chin. The blade scuffed the tip of his jaw, sending him reeling backwards to regain his balance. Before he could retaliate, Tallack spun around in a giant arc, his new axe flying at head height.

When he was facing his brother once more, the axe connected with the shiny blade of Paega's sword flicking it from his grip. It soared through the air and dug into the mud with a twang some distance from them both. Disarmed and witless, Paega fell to his knees.

"Please, brother. Forgive me. This was all Brea's idea. I was content on the moors until she met up with us and forced us to align ourselves with the Duros. Please Tallack, have mercy." He wrung his hands together in front of him. What a pathetic sight he was. He had learned nothing and changed little over the years. I knew from the moment I watched him claim the auroch bull from the twins in his warrior quest that he would come to no good.

Tallack curled his lip in revulsion and walked over to the sword. "This blade was never meant for you, brother." He spat on the ground, missing Paega by a fraction. "If it was truly yours it would have protected you from the swift death I now offer by its keen edge." He lifted it from the soil and rested the tip of the blade to Paega's neck.

"Nephew." I interrupted from behind him. "Do you not think that justice would be better served if your brother had the honour of the death blow?"

He looked over his shoulder at me. "You're right, Aunt. That seems fair considering I now bear the sword. We'll let Blydh take his life." He altered his stance lowering his weapon from his brother's throat. "Kewri, find something to bind him with and stick him with the Novantae. All the traitors together in one tent. We should burn it down with them inside. That would serve them right." Tallack admired the sword for just a moment, before giving me the broadest grin. "It has finally found its true keeper. I wield the blade of Cernonnus. Let no one stand in my way."

Our women shooters knelt behind the line of fighting warriors and fired a volley of arrows at the Duro horde. I encouraged them to keep going, while Kewri dragged Paega by his bound wrists to the other hostages.

Blydh returned on my horse. His scalp oozed pus and blood, his skin was clammy and pale. How was he able to continue? He must have been in extraordinary pain. Together we watched as Tallack cut through his foes as though they were made from butter. The blade was the most incredible thing I'd ever seen. It sliced through bone and sinew better than any butcher's knife, better than an axe, better than the curved Phoenician blades of the foreign travellers I'd known.

Warriors fell like stuck pigs. Tallack channelled the gods themselves, killing all who stood in his path to protect our kin. As the numbers of our enemy declined, most turned tail and ran. The hairy Chieftain of the Duros was left standing all alone next to a heap of his dead men. He opened his mouth wide and roared, clenching his fists around his short sword and axe. He would not flee, nor would he allow us to take him alive.

Surrounded by those of my tribe who'd survived the onslaught, the Duro Chief walked in a circle, evenly spaced from Tallack's strides. Either of my nephews could have ordered their warriors to stick him with a dozen spears, or grab him from behind and slash his neck, but this was a matter of honour. A Chieftain should die at the hands of another.

I knew that reasoning with Tallack would do no good. He had a reputation to uphold, especially since his brother was in a critical state. While one was weak, the other must show their strength. Tallack also knew that his long sword would lead him to victory and a fresh head to suspend from the gates.

"Don't make it too quick, Brother. I want to see that kyjyan suffer." Blydh said standing at the front of the circle of warriors surrounding the pair.

"I'll do my best, but if Cernonnus wants to dispatch him with haste, who am I to argue?" Tallack was getting cocky. That was not a good sign. Even with a decent blade, he still faced an experienced warrior who stood head and shoulders above my nephew. This would not be an easy fight. I sent my hopes and fears up to the Morrighan to spare him from defeat. All things considered; we had come through the ordeal relatively well, thus far.

They were still posturing, edging around each other. Were they both having second thoughts, sizing up their weaknesses or just taking the time to catch their breaths after the frenzy of fighting earlier? The Duro made the first move. With his left hand he jabbed at Tallack with the short blade, while swinging the axe in the other hand.

Tallack stepped backwards out of the reach of both while blocking the axe with the mystical long sword. The two metals clanged together with a deafening ring. The Duro looked surprised, as though he expected Tallack to crumple from the force. Before he could regain a solid footing, Tallack forced the shaft of the axe down to the ground and stamped hard against the wood. The handle splintered under his foot.

The Duro let go, staggering backwards. It was now sword against sword, except that the Blade of Cernonnus was twice the length of its opponent's.

"Finish him off, Tallack. I tire of this dance." Blydh shouted from the side-lines. It whipped the rest of the warriors into wild shouting and howling. They jeered and bellowed and jostled the Duro whenever he got near to the edge of the circle. One got close enough to grab his braided hair. He cut it off close to the nape of his neck and held it aloft for the crowd to see.

Unsettled and distracted, the Duro swished his short blade from side to side in front of him to deter Tallack's lunge, but the reach was simply too short. They parried for no more than three swipes, before Tallack's patience left him. He waited until the big man thrust his blade out again.

In one deft move, Tallack side stepped the brute and drove the great mystical sword through the Duros chest. The sound of crunching bone and gasping breath lasted but a moment. He hung there, suspended from the silvery blade, until his dead weight forced Tallack's grip towards the ground.

We all watched him choke on his own blood, just as our bowman had done on the eastern battlements. With one final gasp and a wide-eyed stare of panic, the gods dragged him away to the Summerlands. His bravery, however misguided, would be rewarded with a seat next to the warriors of old.

I knew just how ill-advised he was, for Brea watched from her safe distance beyond the training grounds. With all competition dispatched, she would now be free to take over as sole ruler of the Durotriges. Perhaps that was her aim all along. After Wenna had attained their devotion, the Duros were used to a woman ruling over them.

Tallack lifted his foot onto the dead man's chest and levered the sword of Cernonnus from the body. Blydh did his best to hug his brother, but his fever had taken hold. His knees buckled beneath him. Tallack rushed to lend his support and save face in front of his men. They broke the tight circle to face the broken south gates. We all watched Brea turn her horse around and trot away with her remaining warriors.

Blydh was furious. Dribbling and rolling his head about, he tried to lift his axe from the mud. "I'm coming for you, Brea. This is not the end! You hear me! I'm coming for you!"

Tallack struggled to keep him upright without losing hold of his sword. Kewri and I offered to take over, leaving our victor his spoils. The moment I turned my back to follow Kewri and Blydh back to my hut, I heard the thud of the long sword as it severed the Chieftain's head.

Blydh was burning up. I pulled his arm over my shoulder while Kewri held him about the waist. Leaving the axe in the dirt, we dragged him standing upright to my hut for treatment. There was no way I would let Kewri pick him up again. Not only would the men in camp have seen, but I feared that he might lose the top of his head.

All about the compound, women wailed over the loss of their sons, husbands and in some cases, daughters. Others formed human chains to carry water to the burning stores and huts, while others stripped the items of use from the dead Duros before stacking the bodies for burning.

The puddles and flooded areas were awash with blood. Our victory had come at a heavy price, but it could have been far worse without our defences. Renowden's moving crossings had put paid to their northern incursion, while the submerged spikes proved adequate in deterring their approach from the east. They would not be so keen to take us on again.

As relieved as I was to know that they were running back to their own lands, it did not solve the problem of the Novantae in the next bay. In many respects, they posed a far greater threat than the Duros had. They were hardened to the cold and wet conditions and were fierce and relentless fighters. They would not be easy to defeat. With Renowden out at sea protecting the Phoenician ship, I feared that Tallack would not have wise counsel to steer his course.

When we drew level with the Long Hut, Cryda saw us and raced to Blydh's side. She hadn't even noticed that the battle had been won, or that a third of the compound was ablaze. All that mattered to her was her first born. The light was failing by the time we got him settled and warm. I managed to get him to drink a little willow tea before he began thrashing about in his fevered state. Cryda clung to his hands for a time, trying to stop him from clawing it his scalp, but he was too strong for her. As upsetting as it must have been to watch, I instructed Kewri to bind him again to the posts of the bunk.

I went through all my stores of medicines and the bag looking for wild hops to bring down the fever, but I was completely out. The stitches were straining against the puffy tissues and it smelled foul. It really needed some crushed rose hips mashed into a few globs of honey to draw out the vile humours, but it was the wrong season for such things. I had to make do with willow, and hope that I'd made it strong enough to break his sweat.

"Is Kerensa not here?" Cryda said, moving out of Kewri's way as he tied the leather bindings at Blydh's wrists. "I expected her to be at his side. They got pretty close while they were at the mining settlement in Bentewyn. I thought it had run its course when he rode back here to rebuild the compound." She looked both sad and perplexed. I couldn't decide whether she was happy that he'd found someone to love or whether she disapproved of the union.

"I've not seen her for quite some time. I wonder where she went." It hadn't crossed my mind with all the turmoil of the battle. I had more than my hands full with Blydh, plus a growing line of injured people waiting under the new shelter for me to treat them.

"I suppose that we must give more offerings to the gods for favouring us in this way. To own the truth,

Meliora, I didn't think we'd prevail. The stories in the Long Hut would have made your hair curl. I was nearly frightened out of my wits."

I looked at Cryda in her pristine tunic and combed hair, bejewelled with gold and tin beads. She had hidden for the entire skirmish with the young children and old folk. What could she possibly know of fear? Where was she when our warriors and shield maidens were putting their lives on the line for us? I said nothing. There is no reasoning with her when she gets into these moods.

"I suppose we can sacrifice the white stag now. Won't that be a blessing to the gods?" She piped up with a macabre grin spreading across her face.

"No. That mustn't happen." I reacted too quickly, giving away my fondness for the creature. "Tallack says he's to remain in camp until his antlers have regrown." I hadn't forgotten my bargain. Somehow, I had to find a way to give him his freedom.

"But that won't be until late summer, early autumn. Surely, he won't make us wait that long? I bet he'll taste divine with some purple carrots and roasted tubers."

It pained me to hear her speak of my spirit animal as an offering or worse still as her supper. If she had seen his splendid stance in the forest that day, maybe she would think differently.

"Can you watch over Blydh while I treat the others out there?" I just needed to be away from her prattle, to clear my head and think about how to deal with the remaining danger. Kewri followed me outside. I was quick to set him to work with the rest of the tribe, stacking up the Duro bodies on the forge cart and wheeling them out to the southern training grounds for burning.

At least while I was under the shelter of the new hut, I could see all that was happening around camp. Having no walls yet came in handy after all. The injuries were varied. Some lay on the ground, their wounds seeping faster than I could stop the flow of blood. Try as I might, two more were lost to me before the sun was fully down. One had a splintered ankle that was so bad, only an axe could put it right.

The poor soul bit down on a piece of leather while his friends held him down. It was a job I loathed most in the world, but it was either lose a foot, or die weeks later from the stinking rot. What made it worse was that I had to walk from my fire in the hut with a glowing blade to close the wound. By the time I reached the man, it was half cooled and didn't fully seal the vessels. Despite the agony he'd endured, he had to wait until the knife was heated a second time to finish the job.

All about me, people talked of their relief that the whole raid was over. Were they unaware that the Novantae still lay in the next bay awaiting an order to attack? We'd defeated the Duros, but what we did next could make or break us. We were still in terrible danger.

What preyed on my mind most of all was the fact that the Duro's seemed to know that Faolan's plan to kill Tallack and take control had failed. How could they have known he was our captive? Did we have a spy in camp?

CHAPTER TWENTY-THREE

Our tribe worked late into the night. They sorted through the pockets of the dead and stripped them of anything useful. Our strongest men gathered the Duro bodies into a massive heap on the southern training ground outside the walls.

Tallack threw the first torch on the mound, grinned at the array of heads swinging from the watchtowers and walked back inside the gates. They would have to wait until daylight to be fixed. The families of our fallen collected their kin and mourned over them in private. There would be another pyre built to honour them and a feast to send them into the Summerlands as the heroes and mighty warriors they were.

When I was finished doing all I could for the injured, I sneaked to the unguarded grain store and took a few handfuls to the horse pen. After so much rain the ground was soggy underfoot, but the sky was clear and all the tiny shards of light peeped through the holes from the Summerlands. I liked to think that the gods were celebrating up there too.

The white hart peered out from between the trees to see me. He looked even more spirit-like in the moonlight. Checking all around that I could not be overheard, I held out the grain on my palm.

"It's me, god of gods, Meliora. I came to thank you for sparing my kin and leading us to victory this day. Although our troubles are far from over, I will honour my pledge to set you free." It was the perfect time. The southern gates hung in tatters and everyone was either in mourning or watching our enemies burn. He could slip past them all and out into the wilderness once again. I scattered a little of the wheat on the ground in case he wasn't sure of my intentions. The entrance to the pen was wide open. "Come on." I said backing away and sprinkling more grain on the ground.

Thinking that my presence alone had frightened him, I returned through the enclosure gate and hid behind a hut, hoping that he would seize his chance. I waited for as long as I dared before the horses noticed the opening, but barring the odd snuffle and ear twitches, he didn't move.

The crackling noises of burning men quietened and at length, our warriors began to file back into the compound. The opportunity had passed. Sighing, I returned to the gate and closed it, depositing the rest of the wheat inside the fencing. Before I was a few paces away, the stag wandered across the grass and dipped his head to the food. Perhaps he'd chosen to stay. Maybe Cernonnus had not finished with me yet.

My mind turned back to more pressing concerns. What had Tallack decided to do about Faolan and his heavily armed sons? My feet were soaked in muddy water and blood when I got to the Long Hut. There were still many children, nursing mothers and elderly in the benches closest to the front door, too scared to return to their own huts.

Tallack had ordered his slaves to cook a large pot of stew and make flat bread for all those still in and around the central hub of the compound. A few would have to sleep there too, until their homes could be rebuilt after the fires. The cooking smells made my stomach turn, for it was fairly similar to that of the burning bodies outside.

When all was said and done, the outcome could have been significantly worse. Snaking through the crowds, I made my way towards the top table. Derwa and Glaw were sitting in their usual seats on the bench just below.

"Ho there, you two. I didn't see Glaw among the warriors. I was afraid he'd be counted as one of the fallen." I said, knowing full well that the devious little mountain man was nowhere near the fighting. He'd stayed in the Long Hut with the women and children. What shook me more was that Derwa defended his decision.

"He's the heir to the Ordoviches Tribe. Neither the Ivernii nor the Durotriges are their enemies. Why should he have to fight against them?" Her petulance was astounding considering she couldn't care two hoots about him before. If anything, I'd have thought her desperate for him to fight, so that she may be freed from her unhappy marriage after he was killed. That girl never ceases to vex me.

Tallack was in his tall chair looking decidedly lonely. The visitors' seats were empty, as was that of the Ruvane and of course his brother's wolf chair. He watched over us all, holding the handle of his sword as though it was alive.

Most of his warriors were still with their families or outside with the fallen. He hadn't cleaned himself since killing the Duro Chief. Blood was smeared across his forehead and leather tunic. His hands were black with mud and dried humours. It was hard to see a section of his clothing unstained by those he'd slaughtered.

A slave poured more ale for him, but he didn't drink from his cup. As I moved closer, he spotted me. "Aunt Mel. Come up here and give me the news."

How could I refuse? When I climbed up the platform to his level, I was unsure where to sit. Every space seemed to be cursed. Tallack appeared to read my mind, for he patted the Ruvane seat between the two tall chairs of the Chieftains. I perched lightly, feeling exposed and vulnerable to criticism. I was aware that our whole tribe could see me.

"How's my brother?" He asked. I was glad that this was uppermost in his mind, since he had not checked up on his state for some time.

"The fever has set in. We can only hope that this doesn't addle his brain or steal him away from us. Your mother sits with him now. I shall take over later."

He nodded slowly, taking it all in with alarming dispassion. Had he grown used to ruling from the top table alone, or had the number of violent deaths of late numbed his sense?

"Our defences held up well." He muttered.

"Thank the gods."

He shifted in his seat to face me. "Now you believe in them? Kyjya, Aunt, make up your mind."

"I believe that they favoured us this day. I don't know if that state will last. We still have the Novantae to deal with."

He glowered into his horn cup. "Do you think I don't know that? According to your scout, who is a brilliant find of yours by the way, Greum and Ealar have more ships than us and every one of them is filled with fighting men."

It was my turn to nod. I had no answers for him. The time for allegiances and treaties had long passed.

"I guess what I am asking, Aunt Mel, is; do you have any bright ideas?"

I stared towards the back of the hall, hoping that Cernonnus would find another way to enlighten me with the answer. The noise in the hut blared into my ears; screaming children, groaning elderly and exhausted mothers. They each had their own mournful tune. Eventually, I shook my head. "Not a clue, I'm afraid."

I could sense his despair as he relaxed his muscles and slumped further down the furs lining the tall chair. My new scout, Senara sat on the end of a bench near to the door. She gave me a little smile before shoving a chunk of bread into her mouth and washing it down with ale. I was glad she made it through the battle unscathed. To see her among the elder families and not outside with the recruits made me inordinately happy. She deserved all the honours of a true warrior.

That gave me an idea. Hobbling back down from the top table, I wove between the old men and snivelling children to Senara's side. If anyone knew the lay of the land it was her. She jumped up from the bench and offered me her seat.

"Don't fuss, I just wanted a quick word." I said, scowling at the man sitting opposite her. He immediately vacated for me to sit down. "Thank you, very kind."

Senara wiped her greasy fingers on her tunic and sat up straight as though I was the Ruvane.

"Were any of Chief Tallack's boats still in the estuary?"

"Only a couple of the small ones." She said, intrigued by my questions.

"Any men aboard?"

"Not that I saw. I assumed they were manning the foreign ship or the larger of his boats out to sea."

I picked at my nails thinking. She waited patiently for me with her hands folded in her lap.

"You said that there was a big beacon on the headland ready to light, didn't you?" I waited for her to nod before continuing. "Were there any more, perhaps smaller fires laid out to chart their course into the estuary?"

She thought for a moment, as if she was following her route inside her mind. "There were traces of a fire at one spot on the headland, but none that were of new wood set out and ready to light. Do you want me to ride out for a more thorough look?"

The burned beacon could have been Faolan's signal for Ealar to appear during the fight at the estuary. No one was keeping an eye on the Novantae warriors' comings and goings about camp. The old wolf could have sent one of his men to light it while he rode out to discuss terms with our enemies.

I looked at the shield maiden on the bench before me. She had more gumption in her little finger than all the women of my family put together. "No, that's alright," I replied. "But have plenty to eat and keep your horse in a state of readiness. I might need you later." I wasn't sure what it was I wanted her to do, but the germ of an idea seeded in my mind. I strolled back the way I came, ruminating on the problem.

Senara had turned fire into our best weapon, rolling flaming balls of withies into the Duros camp. In return, I had ensured that we were well prepared to counter its use against us. Could fire be the solution to our current crisis too?

I pondered on this notion as I clambered back into the Ruvane chair next to Tallack. He toyed with the god sword, rolling the hilt between his palms and watching the light catch the blade at different angles. He was transfixed by its power. I'd seen that look before on his father. He was just as complacent to danger as Tallack. Barring ill health, the old fool thought he was untouchable, and chosen by the gods to lead the tribe for all time. No one lives forever.

Tallack scanned all those in the hut before him. "I suppose I ought to say something about how brave everyone was and how we all pulled together, but it feels like a hollow victory."

I could see his point. "It also might be a bit too soon to rejoice, considering Blydh's state and the fleet of enemies waiting to strike." Before I could discuss the basis of my idea, Cryda came running into the hut looking for me.

"He's a lot worse, Meliora. The willow hasn't lowered the fever at all. You must come and help him." She shouted above the clamour.

"Go back and cool him with a wet cloth. I'll go out and see if I can find some holly leaves to boil." She ran outside, leaving me to rustle up a torch that had not yet sputtered out. Crossing the wet grass to the eastern woods, I'd hoped to find a fresh torch with the watchman in the tower, but it was dark and no one was on duty. I assumed that we'd lost the person whose turn it was to watch in the battle.

In the absence of firelight, my eyes began to strengthen under the weak moon. I stepped into the undergrowth of the woodland at the western edge, squinting in the darkness for the spiked shrub. It was hard to stay upright; the roots of the trees were hidden by brambles which snagged my legs drawing blood. The more I fought against the vegetation, the more it seemed to attack me. With a stinging rash and raised welts on my ankles, I pushed through towards the smaller tributary which crossed from the horse pen right over to the eastern watchtower.

Like all the other places where the boundary wall lay over a stream, thick poles were sunk into the water course. As I neared the edge, I could see someone standing in the channel. His silhouette was slight, narrow at the hips and shoulders. No more than a tall boy. Just as I had decided to call out to him, the figure reached out and dragged a larger object into the water by his legs. From the way it rolled down the bank and splashed into the stream, I deduced that it was a dead body.

Was it a fallen Duro that was missed during the clean up? I shuffled closer, keen to see who was going to such lengths to move a dead person. The limp arms were slender and elegant like that of a woman. The boy crouched down, twisting the corpse onto its side before pushing her through the narrow gaps in the poles. He was going to float her down the river. I knew that if the woman got through, the small frame of the lad would have no trouble following, and then I would never find out who either of them were.

Making as little noise as possible, I hurried close to the wall as the boy ducked through and out into the river the other side. Cursing under my breath, I had to slip into the tributary after them to see through the gap. The water was perishing, I almost froze to the spot. I may be all skin and bone, but I was too wide to squeeze through the gaps. The best I could do was watch and wait to see if the moonlight would catch his face.

Shivering and aching from every joint in my body, I held still in the water and stuck my head as far as possible between the poles. It was deeper on the other side. The full strength of the river currents almost swept the body away downstream, but the boy held on, pushing it towards the bank on the opposite side.

Considering his size, the boy showed remarkable strength. Resting the head of the woman on the bank as an anchor, he heaved himself onto dry land and began tugging the body from the water.

That was when I first caught a glimpse of the bird's feather necklace around her neck. This was why I had not seen Kerensa during the battle or at any point since. The girl was dead. I had to cover my mouth with my sleeve to stop me from gasping.

Who was this low-life rat who thought nothing of dragging our tribal members away in the middle of the night? I couldn't tear my eyes away. I had to put a face to a silhouette, but he kept his back to the moonlight at all times. The other side of the river had a narrow path and then an expanse of marshland. The boy left the body on the track while he searched in the shrubs and bushes for something.

By now, my legs were numb with the cold and my back hurt from the bent position I'd held for too long. I contemplated what might happen if I yelled out. Would he turnabout into the lunar light, showing me his face, or run and hide? If only there was a guard on duty whom I could call on for help. Fearing that he might escape before I could identify him, I risked staying longer in the frigid stream.

I soon discovered the object of his search. He reappeared in full view on the path and straddled the body, holding a rock twice the size of his fist. With one careful swipe, he cracked Kerensa's skull open, before lobbing the rock into the river. Everyone would assume that she'd either fallen, or been attacked by the Duros. This boy was cunning. All the more reason to uncover him to the Chiefs. He reached down and grabbed at the necklace, wrenching it from her throat. As he did this, the top row of quills ruptured, showering him and Kerensa in glittering flakes of gold.

It clearly surprised him as much as it did me. He inspected the rest of the quills, shaking them and pinching the wooden stoppers from their ends. I suspect that the entire necklace was an elaborate storage of her gold. He slipped the remaining quills into his soaked pockets and scraped the spilled precious metal up from the track and her clothes. If he did not know its value, it could not have been the motive for her death. This puzzled me for some time as I watched him lift her arms and continue to drag her into the marsh beyond.

For a long while I lost sight of him, the shrubs and shadows masking his trail. I was about to give up and return to report all I had seen to Tallack, when the boy reappeared on the path. He no longer had a reason to climb back into the water. He could stroll around to the broken south gates and let himself into the compound unchallenged. For a fleeting moment before he walked from my view, he turned his face to the moonlight. Young Treeve was not aboard the Phoenician ship alongside my friend Renowden. He was disposing of Kerensa's body.

CHAPTER TWENTY-FOUR

How in the name of Cernonnus was I going to tell my nephew that his young lover was spotted staving in the skull of his brother's woman with a rock? Not only had he killed her, the kyjyan had robbed and dumped her body too.

I crawled out of the water and sat on the bank side, reeling from what I saw. In my mind, I couldn't reconcile his actions. It was Sorcha who Treeve had threatened to kill, not Kerensa. What could he have gained from her death, supposing that he knew nothing about the wealth hanging about her person?

The longer I stayed on the bank, the greater the likelihood of me succumbing to the cold. The grass was already turning white from the growing hoarfrost. My teeth chattered and my nose ran with humours, but I made it back to my hut in one piece. Cryda stood with folded arms and hurled a string of abuse at me for not getting there sooner.

Only Kewri noticed my saturated state. His brow pinched with curiosity as he draped my bed furs over my shoulders and heated a bronze rod in the fire to warm some ale. There was no time to explain anything to him, especially with Blydh fretting and sweating and fidgeting in the bunk. The last thing I wanted to do was for him to dislodge the sun disc in his head again. He certainly wouldn't survive a third procedure. That would be stretching our luck way beyond endurance.

"I couldn't find any holly to lower his fever. That's where I've been." I picked up my healing bag and emptied it onto my bed, looking for herbs to break the sweat.

"There's a big holly bush not far into the forest past the north gate. Shall I go and cut off a branch or two?" Kewri smiled. Bless that sweet giant, whatever his true name might be.

"Thank you, Kewri. You'll need one of my sharpest blades and a fresh torch to light your way."

He nodded, selected the largest knife I had left to me and disappeared into the night. I dried myself off and put on an old tunic and then rested the back of my hand to Blydh's forehead. He was hot, but then my hands were excessively cold. Sweat soaked his hair and trickled down his neck. Cryda did her best to keep his head still, holding him steady about the ears but I feared that it would not be enough. I mixed another tea of willow and tried to pour it into his mouth, but he wouldn't swallow. It dribbled down his chin onto his chest.

With tears trembling on the edges of her eyelids, Cryda looked up at me. "Is this the end?"

There was no way to coat this with honey. "I'm afraid it could well be. You should fetch the others. It might be the last time they get to see him."

She hadn't even cleared the door skins before her hysteria descended into loud sobbing. She was never this emotional before giving birth to Delen, but then new-borns have a way of draining every bit of character from their mothers for a time. Perhaps she'll spring back when the babe is off the teat. Either way, it's understandable that she should fear losing Blydh. He'd always been the strong and dependable one. He looked such a wretched thing now. The pus seeping from his scalp smelled foul and made the flesh raw. His muscles were fading quickly and his cheeks caved in over his bones where before they were plump. He had not the reserves to see him through for much longer.

It didn't take long for Cryda to round up Tallack, Derwa and Glaw. They each knelt by his bed and promised more offerings to the gods in return for Blydh's survival, while I boiled more water with which to steep the holly leaves when they arrived.

"I couldn't find Kerensa. Has anyone seen her?" Cryda asked, directing the question towards Tallack.

He shook his head and then held his brother's hand. "Why are they here? Glaw is not even of our blood. If he can't help to defend his wife and her family, he should go back to the mountains."

Derwa tightened her fists and reduced her eyes to slits. "He may not be blood, but I am. I have just as much right to be here as you."

"Half-blood, and that's only if Aebba was your father. We could never be sure."

"Stop fighting." I snapped. "This isn't the time for petty squabbles."

The mention of Aebba seemed to set Blydh off. He squirmed about in his bed, the fever making his speech slurred and incomprehensible for a time. Cryda shushed him and soothed his brow with a wet cloth. He murmured still, but calmed the thrashing of limbs for a time. Derwa grabbed hold of Blydh's other hand and stared down her half-brother in a contest of who could love their brother the most.

"Speak to us, Blydh." Derwa muttered softly, expecting him to wake and conduct a perfectly reasonable discussion with her.

"He can't hear you, stupid kyjyan. The fever has taken his wits." Tallack grumbled, but his deep voice was heard. Blydh became restless once again.

The mumbles grew louder until he opened his eyes wide, lifting his head from the furs. "You will die, Brea! I'm coming for you. You hear me?" His breathing laboured. He panted like a dog, raising his upper body to the limits of his bindings. "I know you killed my father, Brea. You'll pay, just you wait and see. I'll cut off your tongue, I'll rip out your heart. I'll chop you into a hundred pieces and feed you to the pigs for what you've done!" The exertion was too much. He fell back onto the bunk and closed his eyes. No one moved, thinking it might have been his last gasp, but I could see his chest rising and falling with his breaths.

Cryda was the first to speak. "Tell me that was the fever talking." She looked at me and then at Tallack. Neither of us dared to explain.

"Wait…" Derwa said, getting up from her knees. "Aunt Mel, is that true what he just said? That Brea killed father? It wasn't my mother who poisoned him?" Still I couldn't move nor say a word. She strode around the bunk to Tallack and shoved him in the chest. "Tell me that it's not true."

Tallack rocked backwards, letting her shove him a second time. "I can't."

"You're admitting that you murdered my mother at the low-tide mark, when all the time you knew that Brea killed father?" Her voice rose to a shriek.

"No, that's not… no. Neither of us knew at the time."

"I can't believe this. You killed my mother; you slaughtered my sister and grandfather, and you have my brother trussed up like a pet goat. Now I discover that Brea killed father. What will you do next? Have me flayed to make your new leather tunics?" She screeched at him at such a volume that he blinked from the flying spittle. He must have sensed that she might get violent. He scrambled up off his knees and stood towering over her while she pounded his chest with her fists. "You had no right to kill my mother. She was innocent."

Poor girl. Was it any wonder that her moods veered from one extreme to another so unpredictably? She had no stability in her life at all. Tallack had treated her with trinkets and gifts, but spent little or no time with her growing up. She was quite alone in the world. Maybe that was why she had begun to see the benefits of siding with her husband after hating him all winter.

It was Cryda's expression that I watched carefully. This was devastating news for her too. All through the cold season, she had cherished the clay pot containing Aebba's bones, content in the knowledge that his death was avenged and his spirit would finally gain entry into the Summerlands. This revelation only served to highlight that he was, in fact, still roaming the Between Worlds without his head. His skull was interred in the barrows at Stonehenge during the midsummer gathering. The tears she shed for her son were now falling for her dead husband too.

My hut was rapidly disintegrating into a battle ground with a sick person at the very heart. Derwa's arms whirled about, thumping and slapping Tallack. Glaw tried to drag her away. Cryda collapsed across Blydh's frail body weeping and moaning as though it was the end of the world.

By the time Kewri returned with the holly, my hut was a seething mass of turmoil. Under my direction, Kewri lifted Derwa up, held her at arm's length, and marched her outside. Glaw trotted along after her, leaving Cryda and Tallack inside with Blydh. Kewri blocked the doorway with his considerable bulk, preventing the demonic girl from re-entering.

I quickly chopped the holly leaves, avoiding the prickles where I could and steeped them in the hot water. It really needed half a day or more to stew, but time was critical. If we couldn't reduce his fever, the humours would grow inside and most likely carry him away.

All the time I nursed him, the sight of Treeve pulling Kerensa's body into the marshland plagued my thoughts. What had she done to provoke his ire? How could I tell Tallack of what I'd seen? It was beginning to feel a lot like keeping Brea's murderous tendencies a secret, but I couldn't say anything while Blydh was in such a state. What if he heard me tell his brother that she was dead?

Then there was her father to think about. Kenver was the leader of the Alchemist Clan. They held great knowledge and power within the mining communities. Without their friendship and allegiance, we would lose the source of our wealth. None of us knew how they managed to convert rocks into ingots of tin. They kept it a closely guarded secret so that Chieftain's like Tallack continued to show them respect. How would Kenver react to his daughter's death?

I poured more holly broth into Blydh's mouth, hoping that at least some would trickle down his throat. Kewri gathered ivy tendrils and wove them about Blydh's bunk to ward off the evil spirits that might come to drag him into the Underworld. He is a good lad. When I had done all I could, I noticed Cryda glaring at me.

"How dare you not tell me about Brea. We shared a hut for all that time in Bentewyn, and it didn't cross your mind to inform me that the low-life mountain girl had poisoned my Aebba."

"In my defence, Cryda, she did try to kill me twice too. She made it very clear that I would be next for the pyre if I said anything."

"That's not an excuse. You could have told me privately."

"And what would you have done about it? Blabbed to anyone who would hear and then you, me and little Delen would have all been for the chop. It was not a decision I made lightly." I picked up my medicine kit and hurried from the hut before she could bark at me anymore.

I grew tired of complaint. Kewri tried to follow me, but I pushed him back. When Cryda couldn't hear me, I whispered. "I'm not leaving camp. I just need to be out of her way." That seemed to satisfy him that I was not off on another one of my travels across the moors.

Tallack caught up with me shortly afterwards. "As much as I would like to stay by my brother's side, I need to speak with the elders." He raced past me heading for the Long Hut. It was my only chance to tell him what I'd learned.

"Wait a moment, if you will." I shouted after him.

He stopped and turned in the dirt. "What is it, Aunt. I have much to discuss."

"I know, and with your permission, I should like to sit in and listen too, but this can't wait. I have learned my lesson about keeping secrets, and this is another that you will not thank me for confessing."

His expression crumpled into hopelessness. "This had better not be about Brea again. I've had more than I can take of that woman to last me a lifetime."

"No Nephew, it's about young Treeve." It was a difficult conversation to begin. I tried to sweeten the gristle, choosing my words with care, but nothing could make my news palatable. We stood together under the dim light of the guard's torches outside the Long Hut.

For a while he stared at the ground, calming his breath. I waited, wondering if he would dismiss what I'd seen as a mistake of some sort, that there would be a rational explanation for Treeve's actions, but he said nothing. When the flush subsided from his face, he inhaled deeply, turned about and strode into the Chieftain's Hut.

Most of the elders and their families were still there, even though the moon had crested the sky. Despite the yawns of exhaustion all about me, people preferred to stay close to each other. With our southern gate busted and fewer guards on duty, it was understandable.

While Tallack mounted the platform at the top table, I took my time to see who was within the hut. Derwa and Glaw sat in their places in front of the Chief's tall chairs, the senior warriors filled the benches on both sides of the hall, and the elders and their families spanned the central space right to the back of the hut. Treeve was not in the room.

None of the musicians played. The grief from our losses was too near. People spoke quietly together until the jitters from fright and terror were soothed into calm. Tallack called out to a few of his men and three of the most senior elders to step forward. I moved closer to hear what he had decided to do about Faolan and his kin.

"But Chief," One of the elders said. "Other than your foreign vessel, there are but two boats left in the fleet. We cannot hope to take on the might of the Novantae. By all accounts, they have an impressive number of ships, with a strong and well rested crew."

The other elders murmured their support. Tallack glanced about at his warriors, none of them had anything to contribute. They had no solutions for our young Metern of the Dumnonii. None could see a way out of our situation.

I shifted forwards and cleared my throat. "May I speak, Chief Tallack?" He beckoned me closer and in front of all his warriors and the elders, I laid out what I considered to be our only course of action. When I had concluded all I had to say, they stared at me.

Tallack fondled the fluff growing on his chin, ruminating on my plan. "There is only one flaw that I can foresee, and that is that there are too few of us to make it happen." More murmurs came from the useless old men, who had nothing helpful to say and were not sound enough in body to fight.

"I agree, Nephew, if we only consider your crewmen and Blydh's warriors, but I am able in body and sound of mind, as are the wives of the men standing before you. If we all hasten and work together, we make better use of those who have a skill with bow or blade. Rally the whole tribe, Tallack and we will prevail."

The elders were not pleased with my suggestion at all.

"Chief Tallack, I don't think we should put our women folk in anymore danger than they have already endured," one said.

Another chimed in with; "Especially when you think about how many have already lost sons or husbands in the raids thus far."

There were other complaints too, mostly rehashing what had already been said. Tallack looked lost in thought. His sight drifted to the back of the hall. I followed his train of vision, but only caught the foot of someone who'd just left without recognising them. His head was not fit for such decisions after all I had told him regarding his young lover.

At the risk of further censure, I clambered up to the top table and stood in front of Blydh's chair. Clapping my hands together, I called out until I had the attention of every man, woman and child in the room.

"Hear me, friends. We have all suffered at the hands of the Duros this day, but it will be nothing compared to the losses we face against the Novantae. You will all have heard that despite our hospitality, the Skotek visitors have betrayed us. They wait in the next bay to seize our lands and kill our children." Those who knew this already hung their heads. It was as though they expected failure.

Many of the women had no idea of the extent of our danger. They gasped, then shrieked at the thought of the Novantae enslaving our young and killing our elderly. Some thumped their partners for having not told them about the dire situation. It was as I had hoped. Stirring the emotions of the women folk girded them into action.

"There is a way to defeat the marauders before they can even make it to our shores, but it will need everyone in the compound to take action." Senara set off the foot stamping. A few more joined in, pounding their fists on the tables and benches until the whole hut was one rowdy horde of angry women. “Are you all prepared to fight?”

CHAPTER TWENTY-FIVE

The bellows of the women folk drowned out that of our men. They would each protect their young to their dying breath. Tallack had his warriors, I had my shield maidens, weavers, dye makers, bakers and leather crafters. All were mothers, daughters, sisters or wives, and all were just as fierce as the men and not afraid of blood.

I turned around to face my nephew. “You have your army, Chief. Best make tracks before the day comes.”

It was a mad scramble, but the womenfolk were fast and efficient and used to taking orders. Senara led a team of her own, taking them across the marshes and along the eastern side of the estuary on horseback to build new beacons and position strong shooters. Tallack instructed his men to hide at the northern end of the channel, while he, Kewri and I took more of our tribe out along the western bank.

Kewri built a small fire from our supplies of juniper wood, shielding the flames with rock and stone. It burned with barely a trace of smoke. Further along the bank, our men and women did the same, crouching low in the sandbanks and dune grass.

We were almost set. With most of the arrows fired during the Duros raid patched up and reused, all our shooters were well armed. The waters were almost at low tide, the current winding around the shingle spit of the river mouth. Vast mud and sand banks protruded from the brine, like whales that lost their way and got stranded. I tucked my hands under my arm pits and wriggled my toes. The tiny fire was no help in keeping warm on such a bitter night as this.

Hunkered down in the frozen salt marshes, Tallack began to have doubts. "You think this will work?" He asked me.

"I don't see why not. It's practically the same plan you had when the Ivernii attacked. This time, we are rooted on dry land." His jitters started to affect me. Perhaps he was right. We only prevailed in the last instance because Ealar sailed into the estuary with a greater number of boats and chased them away.

I couldn't let Tallack know that I was not sure if my plan would work. He might have called it all off and made us run for our lives. "We have the advantage here. Ealar and Greum think that our boats were lost. If they have any sense about them at all, they would have watched Renowden and your men sail the Phoenician ship way out to sea. They will think that we are defeated both at sea and on land by the Duros."

"You'd better be right, Aunt, or the ambush will be on us instead of the other way around."

"Ealar would never think that his sister would give away their plot or their agreed signal. This should work, provided that both the brothers sail straight into the river mouth." I ran through the order of events in my mind all over again, trying to spot any fatal flaws.

We had the tide on our side this time, and no boats in which to sink. All our warriors and shield maidens could attack from dry land, providing they kept well out of sight until the time came. One misplaced flame or sighting of men on horseback and we'd be done for.

The waiting was unbearable. My innards trembled with the cold and with nerves. So many people's lives were at stake, and all I could think about was Kerensa and Treeve. Why hadn't Tallack said or done anything about him? Maybe he was waiting until this crisis was over before he dealt with such things.

When the moon was near the horizon, I saw the beacon flare up into the sky. Senara and her team of brave women had built and lit the first signal on the tip of the headland. Would it be enough to trick both of Faolan's sons to steer into the river?

I imagined that all of our tribe stationed along the banks were holding their breath at the same time, hoping to see the first of the Skotek ships chart the twisting water course around the shingle spit.

"How long would it take them?" I asked Tallack, lying in the frosted grasses on the bank side.

He shrugged his response. "How should I know? I have no idea if they have oarsmen, or relying on sails. If it's the latter, then it could take all kyjyan day." He lifted his hand into the air. "No wind. I don't know if they are waiting just outside our bay or further towards the Duros border. You do ask ridiculous questions, Aunt Mel." I tried not to take offence.

A short time later, the first boat caught the tidal push into the river mouth. I guess that answered my question. At least one of the ships was in our bay. All my muscles tensed. I should have visited Cernonnus with more grain before leaving camp. He'd seen us right so far. Was it too late to send a word or too up to the Summerlands to ask for his help once again?

Rolling over onto my knees, I peeked over the grassy ridge and squinted into the darkness. "Come on Senara. Light the second one." I muttered, wondering whether something had happened to the young shield maiden. Surely, she had left instructions with her group to set fire to another beacon closer to our camp as soon as the first was sighted?

My neck clicked and my back was painful, but still I craned to see across the estuary. There was only the one boat. It cast a shadow across the moonlit ripples as it moved rapidly through the water. When it veered closer to us on the west bank, I counted just four men aboard, rowing. Had they sent a scouting party to see if there was trouble ahead?

That was something for which I had not planned. If we fired on the four men now, the rest of the fleet would be alerted to us and our ambush would be ruined. If we waited for them to make it all the way into camp, they would discover that we were holding Faolan and Sorcha captive.

Tallack's brow furrowed. I surmised that he too was thinking the same. We had underestimated the quick minds of the Novantae. We needed to make a decision and fast. The small boat was closing in on the narrowest end of the estuary where Tallack's warriors waited with axes and blades.

A second beacon flickered into life further inland. Senara was true to her word, but I was not relieved. The plan would only come to fruition provided all the Novantae could be trapped at the turn of the tide. My heart thumped so hard I thought it might tear right through my chest. I found myself breathing so quickly, a dizziness took hold of me.

What if Faolan's sons were still in communication with Brea? They would know by now that she and her new tribe had failed to overthrow us. Bile erupted in my gullet. How do great Chieftains keep their courage when the lives of all their warriors rested on their decisions? It was not something I ever wanted to do again. The responsibility weighed too heavily. I vowed there and then to be more tolerant of my young nephews. They were doing the best they could.

"This is going to fail." Tallack groaned. "Those scouts will make it all the way upstream to the island if we don't stop them. Either way, we're done for. The Skotek warriors outnumber all our people. If they…"

I jogged his shoulder. "Look." Pointing at the furthest reaches of the river, there was just enough light to discern the fleet of boats heading inland. "They're coming." The second beacon must have done the trick. I could just make out the larger ship of Faolan's leading the procession of smaller boats. I assumed that by now Greum, the elder of his two sons, was in command. A nice enough lad, but in my opinion, he had more brawn than brain. We were lucky in that during my time spent with that family at the top of the world, I realised that the clever one was in fact, Sorcha, and she liked ale more than basket weaving.

The pain in my chest eased as the ships sailed closer. Everyone was in their place and awaiting the same signal Tallack had given before. A single flaming arrow arching across the night sky. Kewri fanned the shielded embers of our small juniper wood fire until he could light the greased strip of material fastened to the end of the arrow. Within moments, Tallack had it nocked and aimed ready to fire.

"Come on, you Skotek kyjyans." He growled, as the boats rowed upstream to the narrowest point. As soon as the final vessel passed our position, Tallack let his arrow fly. It swooped high and for such a distance that it almost reached the sand bank on the opposite side of the wide river. That was all it took to trigger our whole tribe into action.

I could hear the rumble of the horse's hooves from further south, as they galloped down onto the sand flats and crossed the shallows to trap the boats. Each man held a shield and carried a woman behind them armed with bows. From the eastern shore more rode onto the tidal banks to swell their number. Their calls and squeals were terrifying, as the women lined the narrow stretches and sent arrow after arrow into the Novantae men.

The moment they realised that they were hemmed in they attempted to turn the boats, sculling only from the port side and steering towards the open ocean. They were too late. The sheer number of arrows thudding into their vessels, ripped them apart. The more the wood splintered, the more the river poured into their hulls. Some of our sharpest shooters had direct hits, killing the men instantly while setting their clothing ablaze. Terrorised, a few jumped into the water, swimming through the deepest sections towards the sandbanks. They were picked off before they could make it to shore.

Tallack's mouth hung open. "You were right to gird the strength of our women folk, Aunt. They're deadly." His grin spread from ear to ear.

The largest of their vessels remained virtually unscathed. It was showered with flaming bolts but took on no water. The sides were sufficiently high for Greum, Ealar and their men to duck beneath for cover. While their tribesmen were being brutally cut down, they drifted to the northern point unharmed. This was a vessel we knew well, for Tallack and I had travelled from the top of the world all the way to our own lands on the very same craft. It was built for endurance and distance. It would take more than a few burning arrows to make it sink.

Tallack could see that the change in tidal flow would push them to our line of warriors waiting for them at the northern tip of the estuary. “I need to be there, Aunt.” Dashing to his horse, he slung his leg over its back and cantered along the coastal path towards the island. Kewri and I watched as the group of mounted warriors picked between the soft sand and drier banks, closing any opportunity for them to escape.

The central stretch of the river altered from murky brown to patchy red. Great pools of blood eddied and bubbled with the wash from the changing tide. The scent carried on the air, a mixture of salt and offal, shit and fear.

Some of the bravest shield maidens jumped off the back of the warrior’s horses and ran across the flats to reach those swimming ashore. It was quite a sight, their long hair flowing behind them, a crazed look of the Morrighan in their eyes. They had little trouble dispatching the stragglers, exhausted from their fight against the vicious currents.

Kewri stamped out our fire and together we mounted our steeds and galloped after Tallack. Most of our warriors did the same, squeezing the Novantae into the smallest section of the river.

I don't know how we were all able to stay focused and awake. My whole body was weary, but my thinking was clear and fast. There were no more than thirty of the Novantae left alive. All of them were within Faolan's prized ship, floating towards our fittest warriors. A few arrows flew out from the boat, but they were easily dodged.

Pulling up on my pony's reins, I saw the strength of our forces and knew what the Ivernii were up against. It was certain death. I almost pitied them. These were people whom I had grown fond of, who showed me kindness and hospitality when I was at my lowest. They were exactly like us in many respects, just trying to forge a better life for their tribe.

How could Faolan have concocted such a devious plan against us? It was sheer luck that they were found out. If that scout had not seen the old man riding off towards the Duros bearing a white banner, then we would be precisely in their shoes, fighting for our lives.

Now they faced the wrath of all our tribe; those who'd lost friends, mothers who wept for their sons, fathers who had burned their daughters on the pyre. We would all lay down our lives to prevent our remaining children from becoming Novantae slaves.

Would Tallack spare the heirs to their tribe, or send them into the Summerlands without their heads? I sat high on the river bank, struggling with my decision to go closer. I liked Greum. I was fond of Ealar. I didn't want to see them cut down with their entrails spilling over the silt and sand.

Kewri drew level with my horse, looking to me for direction. Below us, at the sides of the river, all our bowmen and woman lined up together and took aim.

The warriors at the northern fringes bore spears and shields. Our mounted fighters brought up the rear.

Tallack stood on the sand bank closest to the ship. "Surrender, Greum, and I will make your journey to Cernonnus quick and painless." He shouted so that all may hear. After a few moments, he grew impatient. "If you drag this out until we reach a bitter and bloody conclusion, I will flay your sister and have your father's eyes plucked out by the gulls at low tide."

Still the Novantae men stayed beneath safe cover. Were they hoping that they could out wait us and let the tide carry them back out to sea? We had them surrounded. Daylight peeped over the headland. They could not hold out much longer.

Ealar stood up from behind the port side and fired a single shot directly at Tallack, before flattening himself against the hull. A defiant act of one who had never seen battle. Greum must have known that their prospects were grim, even if his little brother still had hope. Everyone watched Tallack step to his left by one pace to avoid the arrow.

"I haven't got all day, boys." Tallack yelled. "I have to get back to see to your little sister. By all accounts, she's quite the ride, or so my men tell me."

Ealar bobbed up once again, fuming and indignant, but his wiser brother tugged him down by his arms. One of our bowmen took his chance and sent a bolt into the ship. It skimmed the port side and embedded in Ealar's chest. The deep grunt and wheeze told us that it found its mark. Wood creaked, boots scraped frantically as Greum cried out and scrambled to catch his kin.

"We'll take you down one at a time if we have to." Tallack yawned, inspecting his fingernails.

A moment later, a howl that tore at my heart rent the dawn in two. Ealar was dead. Was our Chief going to wipe out this whole tribe for the sin of betraying us?

One of Tallack's warriors shouted to him. "We should burn them. Set the ship ablaze. One flaming arrow to the sail, a few more to the men." His growl challenged Tallack's leadership. The men were beginning to think him weak. I knew why he delayed. It was a swift and sturdy vessel. Not quite the beauty of his own foreign ship but worthy nonetheless. A prize for any fleet. Tallack needed to replace those boats he lost. It was a decision of which old Aebba would have approved, but then he had already earned his reputation as the Wild One.

Tallack was practically untested. If it came down to a single fight between Greum and Tallack, as it had done with the leader of the Duros, I was not sure my nephew would win. I'd seen Greum in action before. He was a grisly and tough warrior, with many summers of experience more than Tallack. Mystical sword or not, I could imagine us losing our Chieftain, just at a time when Blydh was unable to take over. It was a tense moment. Our men grew restless, smacking their spears and axes against their shields in a rhythmic beat for an answer.

What would our untried Metern decide?

CHAPTER TWENTY-SIX

The longer the warriors clattered their weapons against shields, the more flustered Tallack became. Would he choose to massacre all those aboard the ship in a gory blaze, or call out Greum to face him in single combat? Our men were spoiling for a fight. They'd tasted victory over the Duros and were desperate for more, particularly when we outnumbered those remaining Novantae. I was proud of what our tribe had achieved, especially our women folk, standing tall with courage and determination. Would they still be keen on killing the boys of Skotek mothers even when they had no hope of winning?

Our men kept up the noisy racket, demanding retribution. The women held firm with their arrows nocked and well-aimed, but stayed silent and poised. Would compassion win out over a display of strength? Tallack stole a glance towards me. I was too far away to whisper my opinion. This was his decision to make alone.

Digging the Sword of Cernonnus into the wet sand, he rested both his hands on the hilt. "Burn them down, boys." He yelled. The men cheered. The women looked at one another and then back at the boat. I knew what they were feeling. A surge of shame. Those men carrying torches, walked along the row of bowmen and women, lighting their bolts.

"They can have a floating pyre." Tallack smirked to his trusted crewmen. I wondered if he would have made the same choice if Renowden had been at his side. At a time when he could have shown mercy, my nephew chose malice. Faolan's wife would suffer the loss of her entire family, at the hands of their former guests.

On my nephew's command, all the arrows were set loose at the exact same time. Those fired by the women, were aimed at the Novantae men, giving them a swift ride to the Summerlands. Our men aimed high, catching the bundled fabric of the sails and storage lockers in the stern. A few of the Novantae scuttled about stamping on flames and plucking out the arrows, but there were too many to extinguish. The fire caught hold fast, spreading from dead men to rope, from beards to hair until all we could hear were their screams. Flesh singed, fat melted, eyes exploded before their spirits could leave their bodies. It was a cruel way to send them to their forefathers.

Black smoke billowed across the estuary. Burning embers danced across the water and settled on the mud flats. Our warriors and shield maidens retreated from the rising tide and climbed up to the river banks. There we stood, until the last cries of terror were silenced. I should have been glad. Our enemies were defeated. The danger was over.

As I stared out at the charred remains of my cherished friends, a tear escaped from my eyes. It couldn't be stopped. I tugged on my pony's reins and cantered along the coastal track before my nephew could see me. He would want me to be proud of his achievements, but my heart was as blackened as Faolan's ship. If this was how he treated cornered enemies, what had he planned for Faolan and Sorcha?

There was also Tallack's half-brother to consider. He too was bound and gagged and under guard. Keen to fill my mind with purposeful work, I hurried back to camp to check up on Blydh. I had no time for feasting and singing in the Long Hut to fuel our warriors' blood lust.

What hurt the most, was that it was my twist on Tallack's original plan that had resulted in so much death, but I knew that if we hadn't prevailed, I would most likely have been killed alongside my family. As distasteful as it was to me, it was a necessary course of action that could not be avoided.

When Kewri and I got back to the compound, Treeve was taking his turn to guard the prisoners. How could Tallack trust him after all I had told him? He was in full view of all the warriors returning from the estuary, so I didn't make a fuss. It was up to our Metern how he chose to deal with him. I let Kewri take the ponies to the pen, while I carried a few logs inside my hut for the fire.

Cryda was at Blydh's side, much as we'd left her during the night.

"How is his fever?" I asked her. It was important that we reconciled. She was the twin's mother. She had to know that I had justifiable reasons for keeping Brea's duplicity a secret. At least she had a peaceful winter, thinking that her husband's murder was avenged.

"No better." She snapped at me. I thought about her predicament for a time. She hated both of Aebba's other wives. I couldn't imagine that Cryda was annoyed at me for pointing the finger of blame towards the wrong one. Her animosity could have only been the result of Aebba's final resting place. She had begun elaborate arrangements to have the rest of his bones interred on a tor on the moors. It was to have a massive quoit erected above to demarcate the boundary between our land and that of the Durotriges. Cryda had already waited for almost a full cycle to lay him to rest. I could understand her not wanting any further delay.

Every joint in my body cried out for rest. My mind spun with weariness, yet I knew that I had to crush more holly leaves and brew another broth for Blydh's fever. I dragged myself over to the bunk and touched my hand to his forehead. For all her moaning, Blydh did not seem to be quite so bad. There was still hope that my medications would work.

Kewri came in and fell onto his new bed, rolling into the furs. I envied him. Sleep was something I wanted more than food, more than ale, more than anything. As soon as I had chopped the leaves, I scooped them up with the knife and tipped them into a cup.

"Can you boil some water and pour it to half full over the holly? I have to sleep." I asked her.

"I've been awake all night too, you know, and I have a young baby to tend to as well." I'd forgotten about this side of her, the spoiled privileged daughter of a Chieftain, and former Ruvane. I was too tired to argue with her. Putting the cup on the bed before her, I turned around and fell onto my own bunk fully clothed.

That was all I remembered. I must have fell from consciousness the moment I lay my head down. When I awoke, it was to the sound of chopping wood and men shouting in the compound. From the position of the sun, I judged it to be midday or thereabouts. Kewri was up and seeing to the goats, Cryda was asleep at the side of her son, who still made no sound nor movement. His skin was cooler, but his scalp was angry with vile humours and pus. I managed to clean him up without waking Cryda and then left the hut before she could tear into me again.

A different guard was watching over the prisoner shelter. I wondered if anyone had been inside to inform the occupants about their kin. Tallack was wandering about the Long Hut in just his leggings when I walked inside. There were people all over the place. Some were bunked down on the rushes, wrapped in their furs and cradling their young tightly in their arms. Others surrounded Tallack near to the top table.

He displayed his battle-axes and the mystical sword for his warriors and crewmen to envy. "See how the bronze is notched from hitting the blades of others. Both will need to be washed to remove the Duros woad and blood, and straightened out before my brother and I can use them again, but then I probably won't need mine. It bears no comparison to my Sword of Cernonnus. I gave it quite the battering, severing the heads of so many Duros at our gates, yet look how unmarked it is…" He lifted it for the men to see. Tallack had cleaned off the stains, buffing the silvery metal to a sheen. "I think I will have the axes mounted over the tall chairs on the wall here. What do you all say? They would be a fine tribute to the gods when our time came."

Tallack almost choked on his own words. None of us knew whether Blydh would pull round from his current state. His careless mutterings made him realise that those tributes to the gods, might be needed sooner than everyone thought.

More stew and bread were brought in by Tallack's slaves through the back door. The rich smells and meat juices woke many of the overnight guests. All within camp were ravenous, except for me. I couldn't face eating a thing. There were more unpleasant tasks to address, and the quicker they were sorted out the better.

I was pleased to see that repairs to the south gates were underway. It proved that our people were resilient under duress. As much as I wanted to relax and put the whole episode behind us, there was still the question of how to deal with our prisoners. Kerensa's death also gnawed at my mind and irritated me beyond belief.

I looked in every corner and under every bench and table in the Long Hut, but Treeve was not there. Tallack was too busy bragging to his men to think of the loose ends that could unravel at any moment. Ducking back outside, I hovered close to the hostage tent. My nephew Paega, was bound alongside the Novantae.

He was a pitiful thing, but still my kin and the brother to Derwa. She too was nowhere to be found. Neither she nor her husband had played any part in the battle with the Duros or the ambushes at the Exe Estuary. She was equally as vocal as her mother had been, and yet she chose now to be silent. Something did not feel right. Her behaviour at any other time was loud and commanding. She was descended from a long line of priests, who by their very nature craved attention and respect. When it was not bestowed freely, they were prone to achieve their aims with staged performances, claiming that they had the ear of the gods.

There had to be an explanation for her absence, and I was determined to uncover what it was. Still aching from the previous days of exertion, I rushed towards the hut she and Glaw had taken over as their own. Calling out, I pushed through the door skins but found no one at home. A quick spin around, told me that none of her possessions were laid out like they usually were, trinkets from Tallack's travels, jewels from her father, furs from the bunk. The place was almost bare.

I couldn't believe that she would leave without pleading to Tallack to spare her brother's life. They may not have been close as children, but he was her true blood after all. A thought struck me then. What if she had no intention of pleading for Paega's life? What if she was planning on securing his freedom another way?

Retracing my steps, I returned to the shelter and cleared the guard aside. "Have you checked that all is well in there of late?" I asked the man, who in turn shrugged. Scoffing at his incompetence, I bobbed through the entrance and saw Faolan, who was beaten with his head lolling on his chest, and Sorcha, who looked equally abused. Where was Paega? I called out to the guard, who poked his spear through first and then his head.

"You have let one escape you kyjyan fool! Run and tell the Chief!" He did as I commanded, but after he'd gone, I wondered if Paega's escape was during this man's watch or Treeve's. One may be incompetent, but Treeve I would not trust as far as I could throw him. I took a moment to think about where Derwa might have led him, which was long enough for Sorcha to notice my presence.

"Why would you do this to us? What did we ever do to you?" She croaked up at me. It was obvious that she had no memory of how I addled her mind with resin and ale to extract Faolan's devious plan. More to the point, she was unaware of her brothers' deaths. I couldn't face being the one to put her in the picture. Call me a coward, but it was Tallack's place to decide her fate. It didn't make me feel any less shame for my part in the whole affair.

Outside the tent, the warriors were mobilising a search party. They couldn't have got far, even if they were on horseback. That notion gave me an idea. Derwa was always fond of horses. Her particular favourite was the pale tan pony belonging to Tallack. I couldn't see her leaving without taking it with her, at least to carry their belongings. Hurrying to the horse pen, there was my beautiful stag among the ponies, looking quite content with his lot. The antlers were already showing signs of growth. I wished that I could stop them altogether, for the longer they protruded, the closer he came to sacrifice at the hands of my nephew.

Inside the enclosure, I scanned all the horses that I could see. There was my old pony, ever the faithful. He trotted over and nudged me for a handful of grain but I had none to give. Behind him stood the bay mare. She was still in the pen with all the others. In fact, I couldn't see that any of our usual horses were missing. If Derwa and Glaw were on foot, they would still be close by. Perhaps they were within the forest to the north. I grabbed my pony's rein and led him outside the gate. It wouldn't take long to grab a few things and go out and look for her.

By the time I had walked him up to my hut, I heard such a commotion on the eastern side of the island. The noises came from the wooded area, close to where I'd spotted Treeve disposing of Kerensa's body. The men had already located them. They hadn't even made it beyond our walls. I closed my eyes in despair. It was understandable that Derwa would want to see her brother free, but to defy the Chief in doing so was crazy. He would have to make her punishment an example to all, or risk losing his fearsome reputation.

When I opened my eyes again, Tallack's men were prodding Derwa and Glaw with the tips of their spears, forcing them into the Long Hut to hear the sentence for their crimes. Paega was bound at the ankles and wrists, laying on the sodden grass. The warriors slid a pole through his bindings and carried him like a dead animal ready for skinning.

More than anything I wanted to turn and flee. There was nothing so stomach wrenching as seeing your kin turn on each other. Leaving my horse tied to the goat pen, I ambled over to hear their fate. Tallack would have to pronounce guilt there and then, to show the men his leadership qualities.

The crowds parted inside, allowing the warriors to carry the trussed up Paega right to the end. They dropped him on his back in front of Tallack, on the table where I normally sat. Someone had shoved a ball of grass into his mouth to quieten his cries. Derwa hissed at the men prodding her forwards. Her husband dawdled, as though he was untouchable, and to a certain extent, he was.

We couldn't afford to anger the whole of the Ordoviches by killing their heir. Especially after we'd spent so much time securing a truce. One thing that was still in our favour, was the discovery of copper on our land. We no longer needed the Ordo supplies to keep us in bronze weapons and trade goods. We were wholly self-sufficient.

Tallack balanced his sword across his lap. He couldn't tear his gaze from the thing. Now that he had tasted victory, he begun to believe that he was more than favoured by Cernonnus. That was a dangerous state for us all. His complacence had filtered down to his men, who were reluctant to perform their duties, favouring drinking and telling stories in their stead.

"Tut, tut, tut." Tallack shook his head at his sister. "It's come to this, has it? Of all the people in this land, Derwa, I thought that you and I would remain steadfast." In this respect, I agreed with him. He'd been nothing but loyal to the girl, making sure that she always had what she needed and caring for her when she was sick during the winter. He had been attentive and loving, even if he spent little time listening to her childish prattle.

"What did you expect? You think I was going to leave my sole surviving kin for you to carve up honouring Cernonnus. You have plenty of Novantae scum for sacrifice. You shan't have Paega."

"Dear little sister. We'll do as we wish with Paega. His life was forfeit the moment he sided with our enemies." Tallack shouted across to his men. "Build him a cage. If he wants to act like an animal, we'll treat him like one, until Blydh is well enough to take his life from him in whichever way he sees fit." The warriors lifted the ends of the poles and carried the moaning beast from the hut.

"Now then, little sister. What should I do with you?"

CHAPTER TWENTY-SEVEN

Tallack took a great gulp of ale from his cup, all the while squinting at his half-sister and her husband from the mountains.

Derwa sighed. "Are you trying to suggest that you wouldn't have done the exact same thing if Blydh was bound up by your enemies? All I did was burrow under the shelter skins from the back and cut his ties. You can't kill me for that."

"No? Maybe not, but I can banish you for all time. We were not enemies, you and I, but from this day onward we shall be. If you or any of the Ordos set foot on our lands without permission and a respectable tribute, you shall be hunted down and beheaded for your crimes. We have plenty of trade partners for our tin. We no longer need to appease you stinking mountain people."

Glaw looked shaken for the first time since I'd met him. Without realising it, his actions had secured our new copper supplies and ruined the agreement his father had made with us for our tin. His disgrace would spread far and wide, bringing shame on all his family.

Tallack leaned to his left and spoke quietly to one of his crewmen. "Ride out as far as the northern coast and give them nothing for their crossing. Derwa has plenty of metal jewellery to pay their passage. Make sure they leave before you return."

I had mixed feelings about Tallack's sentence, but it was a lighter punishment than if Blydh were sitting at the top table. I was sad to see her being marched from the Long Hut and out of my life for good. It could have been far worse, with her sacrifice adding to those of the Novantae captives.

There were times when Derwa reminded me of her stubborn father, but more often she resembled her mother. From that perspective she would be of more use to us alive and in the Ordoviches camp, stirring up discord wherever she went. I went to the doorway and watched the men shove her belongings into her arms and continue their prodding with spears. She would have to leave the bay mare behind. They had a long walk ahead of them and our horses belonged to the tribe.

Paega hung from that pole for most of the day while the men built him his own cage. It had no roof nor walls, just bars of timber that were too thick to break. Each pole was hammered some distance into the ground so that he could not dig his way out. Women and children threw their waste at him as they passed by, tittering at how far he'd fallen.

As soon as the southern gates were repaired, the men started to build the second pyre, and third fire, in a quarter moon. The mood about camp was sombre, not just in mourning for our fallen, but in fear for their Chieftain Blydh. Cryda had left him with Kewri while she returned to her own hut to suckle little Delen.

"Any change?" I asked. There were few enough of my kin left, without us losing another. Kewri shook his head and gestured towards the door. I was starting to understand the great lump's non-spoken language, after a fashion. He needed to stretch his legs and do something practical, instead of sitting and watching a man slowly fade away. That was best left to women. We had the patience to hope for the best, instead of expecting the worst.

Blydh's skin was cool. His fever had broken. The holly leaf broth had done its job at last, but would he awake from the trauma to his head? All I could do was wait. There was plenty to keep me busy. Blydh was a mess. Thankfully, I had slipped some waxed cloth beneath him to protect the furs from the worst. I piled wood on the fire to keep him warm and heat some water for washing. I feared that if he didn't regain consciousness soon, his insides would dry up from lack of food and drink.

When he was washed and covered again, I kept busy with my tonics and tinctures, herbal preparations and grinding grain for flour until Tallack came to visit. I could tell from his face that banishing his little sister weighed heavily in his thoughts. He was fonder of her than he would admit. Her betrayal hurt him more than anything Faolan or Paega had done. To him, it had been a personal attack. I could see both sides of the argument, and chose to keep them to myself.

"Is there any change to his condition, Aunt Mel?" He said, pulling off his cloak and settling by the fire.

"He is as you see. I found some dried mistletoe in my kit to reduce the swelling, but it's not as good as fresh." My ale jugs were almost empty from all the visitors, but I poured out what remained for him into a cup. He took it from me but didn't drink. I could tell that something was at the front of his mind, trying to find a way out. I sat next to him and waited patiently. He would open up to me when he was ready.

After a few moments of fidgeting and scratching, he said; "The men think me feeble for not giving Derwa a harsher sentence. They think that Glaw will return to the Ordoviches with tales about my weaknesses."

"Is that so? And did you say that killing the heir to their tribe would have given us even more enemies to contend with? Haven't we enough problems with Brea and the Duros, plus the Ivernii? Cernonnus knows where they have got to. For all we know, they are waiting down the coast to try again."

Tallack shook his head. "Renowden would have sent word. His orders were to patrol the shoreline for trouble and make port if there was any news to give. I gave him plenty of tin and a couple of reliable men. Anyone of them could have bought a horse from a homesteader and ridden straight here."

"Well that's a relief. Old Dathi must have decided that it wasn't worth risking his men or fleet in support of the Duros."

Tallack sniffed, smiling. "He's as changeable as the wind. I expect that he wasn't interested in the deal they had on the table. Maybe our tin was more appealing to him than maintaining his hatred for us."

"When all is said and done, any Chieftain will swap sides if it benefits their tribe. It's something you must remember for the next time you cross swords with one."

He nodded slowly, his grin fading. "What am I to do with Faolan and Sorcha? I don't want to dishonour the memory of our fallen by slinging them on the pyre."

It seemed an odd thing to ask me. His father was highly inventive when it came to dispatching our enemies. Perhaps Tallack was less like old Aebba than I thought. "What would you like to do with them?"

He pondered my question for a while, sipping at the ale. "I should like to give an offering to Cernonnus. I truly believe that you played a huge part in garnering the support of the gods for us. It would be right to give something back in return for his continued favour, especially with Blydh the way he is."

"I think Faolan would be a perfect offering to our gods. We could take him to the Nine Maidens on the moor and ask the priestess to preside over the sacrifice. She's Dumnonii born and bred. Lived here at the old compound. It would be all the more potent for her involvement."

That brought his smile back. "We could have the feast there. Blydh would love that." He glanced over his shoulder at his brother laying in the bunk and sucked in his lips.

"He won't be up to the travelling. Cryda and I should stay with him, in case..." I couldn't bring myself to finish the statement. Tallack knew what I failed to say.

"But I should like you to be with me, Aunt. If it wasn't for your advice, we would be overrun with Duros and stabbed between the shoulder blades by Novantae. You know the priestess as well. She will readily give her blessing if you are with us."

His plea was so earnest, I couldn't refuse. As it was, there was little I could do for Blydh's recovery except watch and wait. Cryda could do that, especially if I left her with plenty of willow and more holly should the fever return. "As you wish, Nephew, but there is one request I would make of you, while we are alone."

His brow furrowed in concern. Considering his latest confidence, it was a lot to ask of him.

"It is in regard to Sorcha." I began.

He rolled his eyes and gave me a great exasperated sigh. "You are too soft by half. If you think I am going to pardon her, you can think again. The men already think me weak. That would confirm it as fact."

"Hear me out first. In killing both Novantae heirs, plus Faolan and Sorcha, we risk them appointing a new leader from their family who will make it a priority to avenge their deaths. We have no idea whether Faolan has brothers or nephews who could be worthy warriors in their own right. By keeping Sorcha alive, they would be less likely to attack. She would be our living hostage. We can also use her for information about their tribe; who has ships, which tribes are their allies and what numbers and weapons are in their arsenal. That kind of thing."

He squinted at me for a moment, contemplating my idea.

I needed to give him a better reason for keeping her alive. "You could make her your slave. Not to prepare your food or anything risky like that, but she could prove useful."

I could tell from his features that he liked that idea a lot. I suspected that it had more to do with how she could service him under his furs than pour his ale.

"You are a shrewd old bird, aren't you?" He said. "But I want her to see her father's sacrifice, just as a warning to her should she fail to please me."

I stand corrected. He is exactly like his father. The matter seemed to be resolved. He walked over to Blydh and touched his forehead with affection. "Come back to us, brother. We need your strong will and courage." With that, he emptied his cup and left my hut to arrange all that we'd decided. After he'd gone, I had a pang of guilt erupt inside my chest, manifesting as heart burn. I wasn't sure whether I'd done the right thing by Sorcha after all. Would she have preferred a sacrificial death rather than a long life as a Chieftain's slave? I wasn't so sure. As brutal as her death might have been, it would have only lasted a few moments at best. By sailing south, she was aware that her father intended to bind her to one of my nephews. She would have prepared herself for the possibility of sharing at least one of their beds. Time will tell if I made the right decision.

When Cryda returned from feeding Delen, I gave her the news about Tallack's trip to the Nine Maidens and explained why it was necessary for her to stay behind. She didn't seem at all bothered to be missing the festivities. It looked to me that she needed the rest. While she watched over her son, I went to the pony pen to see the white hart.

As I went to open the gate, I saw him waiting for me. It was becoming as much a ritual for me as the daily feast of grain was for him. I muttered my thanks to Cernonnus and related my news about the forthcoming offerings in appreciation for his support. I didn't expect him to move from the safety of the trees, but as I started to empty my pockets of the wheat and oats I'd brought for him, he moved towards me.

I stood almost in a trance as he gradually approached. He was so beautiful. Those huge dark eyes against the white of his fur, the new buds of growth between his alert ears, I was in total awe of his majesty. My Jago would have called him a King of all beasts. A creature worthy of ruling enormous cities on the other side of the world. More than anything, I wished my slave could've seen this stag. He would think me truly blessed.

The more I thought of Jago, the closer the hart drew, until he was almost close enough to eat from my hand.

I stayed there for a time, not daring to move until he'd eaten all the grain from the ground. I lifted my hand and displayed the last of my offering in my palm, but he was too timid to take it from me. Letting it fall to the grass, I turned and quietly gave my thanks, before leaving the pen.

On the way back to my hut, I passed Paega in his cage. He called out to me, asking for assistance, but I scurried away pretending not to hear him. It was cowardly, I know, but there was nothing I could do to help him. I was pushing my luck as it was. If I asked Tallack for any more leniency, we would both feel the wrath of the tribe. Our family had been the cause of too many deaths. Families were struggling to come to terms with their losses, and Paega was directly accountable for many.

That evening, the whole compound turned out in respect for the lighting of the pyre. Tallack spoke eloquently, praising their valour and courage in fighting the Duros. Four tribal elders lit the kindling, sending the flames up the greased stakes to the bodies laid above. The air was as still and crisp as it had been the night before, with every bright hole in the sky open and ready to receive their spirits. As their flesh burned, tiny embers floated up with the smoke, carrying them to the Summerlands. It was a fitting tribute to such noble warriors and shield maidens.

The food in the Long Hut afterwards was humble but plentiful. Stews, boiled grains and bread to soak up the juices. All those present were invited to accompany Tallack and I to the Nine Maidens for the sacrifice of the Novantae Chieftain, and the celebration feast prepared and loaded on the cart for transportation in the morning.

When I got back to my hut late into the night, Cryda was less angry. She told me that Blydh had a few moments where he was almost conscious. During that time, she was able to get a little goat's milk into him. That was a good sign. She returned to her own hut to sleep, leaving Kewri and I to watch him overnight. I admit that I expected to wake the next morning with him sitting up in bed and demanding porridge and bacon, but there was no change in his condition. If anything, his skin looked greyer than ever, even if the wound in his scalp appeared to be healing.

With nothing more to be done for him I gathered my things and when Cryda arrived, I mounted my horse to join the processional walk to the Nine Maidens stone circle. Tallack chose his best warriors to stay on guard at the compound, just in case Brea had scouts monitoring our activities, looking for when we were most vulnerable. When everyone was ready to leave, Faolan and Sorcha were led out from the shelter and attached to ropes.

Sorcha was stripped of her shoes and outer garments, leaving her bare foot and wearing nothing more than a thin tunic. Faolan was stripped entirely. His naked flesh was sagging from hunger and he was uncommonly filthy. It saddened me to see such a great man reduced in mockery. He was too weak to fight against his treatment. Their ropes were hooked to the back of warrior horses, forcing them to run or be dragged on their faces all the way to the moors.

I knew that I would not be permitted to help either of them. This was part of the punishment; a ritual humiliation ending in death. No one had told Sorcha that she would not be killed alongside her father. Tallack intended it to seem like a mercy, thus assuring her cooperation as a slave. I wasn't sure that it was a sensible plan, but for once, I kept my mouth shut.

The Novantae are beyond tough. I doubted that Sorcha would see enslavement as a preferable option to death, but then I was glad that she wouldn't be given in sacrifice. She was so young. There was always a chance that she could be redeemed in Tallack's eyes and go on to live a happy life. Stranger things have happened.

Our journey was not swift. Although I knew the trail like the back of my hand, our prisoners slowed the pace significantly. For each settlement we passed, the people wanted to hurl rotted kawgh and spit at them as a gesture of support. We rested in the same place by the river, before beginning the climb up the long hill. From there it was mainly downhill, through the woodland at the crossing of the River Taw and up on to the plateau marking the start of the moor.

Tallack agreed to allow Sorcha and her father a brief moment or two at the river to drink and wash themselves down. It seemed appropriate that they should be clean for the ceremony. The gods would not be pleased with a stinking offering.

When we reached the circle, it was utterly deserted.

CHAPTER TWENTY-EIGHT

There were no fires, no shelters nor any of the usual cattle and goat pens associated with the maidens. The priestess and her collection of men and young girls were nowhere to be seen. Worried that I had dragged everyone from the safety of our compound for nothing, I rode back down the hillside towards the settlement further along the river. Kewri insisted on coming with me, while Tallack ordered his men to make camp and set about gathering firewood. The days were lengthening, but the nights were still bitterly cold.

Making our way along the river at dusk, we spotted light from a fire in a secluded dell ahead of us. Kewri went ahead on his sturdy cart horse armed with a spear and blade. By the time I caught up with him, he was warming himself around the flames. Endelyn and her companions were all sitting beneath hurdle shelters.

She gave me the most beguiling smile. I dismounted and she rushed towards me, touching her forehead to mine as though we were related. It was a tender moment.

"Why are you all down here in the valley?" I asked her, nodding my greetings to her maidens and priests.

"This is our last night together. From here, the maidens have decided to move on to the midsummer circle at Stonehenge. The priests will scatter, some to their homelands, others I know not."

"Really? You surprise me. I thought that this was your chosen life and that you were content to remain here."

She sat back down and offered me bread and warm milk. "After that terrible incident with those Duros when you visited, we all realised just how vulnerable we are up here. Now we don't feel safe isolated from other communities. Any one of us could have been killed if it hadn't been for Kewri." She gave him the benefit of her cheeky smile and winked at him. He blushed.

"Where will you go?"

"Actually, I was hoping that I could come back to the compound on the Exe. You said it was rebuilt and stronger than ever. I left after my family were taken by the winter ague because I thought there was no place for me. The Lady Eseld and her Priest Sect provided all the spiritual nourishment the tribe could ever need. When you told me that she was dead and the priests banished, I thought perhaps that you might be in need of my services." She looked at me with a coyness that I thought was well rehearsed. All that aside, I was happy for her to settle with us.

"As it happens, we are in need of your services right now. If you are willing to spend one more night at the circle, we can pay you well and provide more food than you can eat in one sitting."

I explained all that had happened since my last visit. Every one of the priests and maidens agreed to assist with the ceremony. Kewri and I led them back to the moor, using our horses to carry their belongings and hasten their return. Our people had the fires lit, the meats roasting and the shelters erected by the time we got back. Night had fallen, but the frost had not yet descended to chill us through.

Endelyn and her companions withdrew to prepare themselves for the ritual, while Kewri and I set out our own bedding and saw to the ponies. Tallack had already broken out the ale and was drinking far faster than he ought, given the ceremony to come. What irked me the most, was that Treeve sat in pride of place next to my nephew around the largest fire. He could not have looked smugger if he tried.

Our people were rowdy and relatively boisterous considering the high number of our losses. They danced and sang and filled up on flat bread long before the meats were cooked. When Endelyn and her companions had completed their circle preparations, she called to Tallack. I assumed that she needed to ask him for any additional instructions or requests, but when he returned to where we were sitting, he wore a smile that would not be dimmed. Endelyn had undeniable charm. She'd clearly won him over. I guessed that she'd secured her place at our compound with his blessing. She will need careful watching that one. She might charm us into ruin.

When the moon was full and fat, the drummers signalled the start of the ceremony. Those of us not involved, gathered around the circle with enough room for the maidens and priests to perform their tasks. Tallack stood at the far end of the avenue of stones, clutching the prisoner's ropes. Sorcha shivered in her thin and wet tunic behind him. Her father, still naked, had collapsed to his knees.

The maidens skipped along the avenue and entered the sacred space, sitting on their allotted stones around the circle. The priests hovered behind them, some holding onto holly wreaths while others carried blades and axes. None of us were in any doubt how it might end.

As the pipers began a baleful tune, Endelyn nodded to Tallack to walk the offerings slowly forward. Sorcha wailed and shook, until the rope was pulled taut about her hands, tugging her along. Faolan was dragged on his face for a short distance under the force, until Sorcha scrambled to help him to his feet.

I expected jeering and shouts from our warriors as the pitiful Novantae passed by, but none did. All our tribe were hushed and reverent. Too much blood had already been spilled during the last half moon. I for one, hoped that this offering would mark the last. Despite having all his dignity stripped bare, Faolan found the strength to walk at his daughter's side into the centre. He even voluntarily laid on the low altar stone at Endelyn's feet. That almost had me undone.

Endelyn took the rope ends from Tallack. "Our most honoured Chieftain of the Dumnonii. What fate lies before these traitors and false fellows?"

Tallack held his hands out to each side and spun slowly around until all eyes were focused on him. "This wretch at your feet reneged on a binding deal made between our two tribes. We were allies and friends. We welcomed Faolan and his family into our hearts and the warmth of our homes. In return, he schemed with our enemies and plotted to take over our lands."

"And what punishment will you lay down?" She said in a loud but clear voice.

"As a mark of respect, and consideration for the kindness his wife showed to my aunt and I, Sorcha will enter my household as my slave." Tallack said, looking down at Faolan on the altar. The old man closed his eyes and I swear I saw a tear fall at the side of his face. Whether this was in relief or fear for her future, I could not say.

"And for this other creature?" Endelyn lowered the intonation of her voice to a deep and foreboding growl.

"I offer Faolan of the Novantae to the God of Death, Cernonnus, in gratitude for his favour during our recent trials, and in hope that he will bestow his mercy on my brother in his time of need."

"So, it shall be." Endelyn signalled her priests, who stepped closer to drag Sorcha away and prepare Faolan for his death. Though the flat altar was mounted on short stones, there was sufficient room to place a bowl at the head end alongside a series of grooves carved into the rock. Faolan had no trouble stretching out his legs, for it was large enough to accommodate animals as hefty as a bull. He neither struggled, nor complained, just laid there accepting that his moment had come.

Endelyn tucked her cloak around her legs and then knelt on the floor. She took off his bindings and leaned in close to his head. "Do you offer yourself freely to the gods?"

I always thought this a peculiar part of any sacrificial ceremony. Why priests always insist that the offering must consent to their fate is beyond me. As though a goat dipping its head to eat grain laid down for him proves that permission to kill them is granted. No one wants to die for the gods, just as no animal would allow you to slice open its neck if it knew what was coming. Nevertheless, the old man gave her a definitive nod. After the beating, starvation and long drag across land, I was sure that he preferred death to any more dishonour.

Sorcha sobbed and cried out for him as Endelyn slipped a noose over his head and tucked the end of the rope under her knees. She expected him to buck and writhe. I knew that he would not. Priests moved in to assist her should he prove difficult, but as she raised the pointed knife, Faolan closed his eyes to the world and waited for the end.

Tilting his head to one side, she located the thick tube in his neck and pushed the tip of the blade in until the blood gushed out. Faolan could not keep himself still. He twitched and shook. With each beat of the heart, his life force spilled out along the grooves in the rock and collected in the small bowl beneath. When it was half full, she picked it up and rose to her feet.

"You must drink it now, while the life within it is still potent." Tallack grabbed the bowl, and without a moment's hesitation tipped it into his mouth. Some of it leaked over his chin but not much was lost.

"Take in the strength of a great warrior along with the power from all his ancestors before him. You will absorb all that was given from the gods, and pass it to your children, and your kin down the ages." We all watched as the steaming blood trickled down his fingers and cheeks until the last drop disappeared into his belly.

Faolan was still alive, just. Endelyn took two paces backwards and looked at each of the priests holding an axe. There were four of them. She stood firmly on the taut blood-soaked rope about his neck and gestured to the first of the men. They were slick in their procedures, making me wonder how many times they had conducted human sacrifice at this isolated spot.

Each priest stepped forwards in turn, lifted the axe high above their heads and slammed the blades down. The legs were the first to be severed; taken off at the groin and slung to the southern and western stones. The arms were sliced at the shoulders and delivered to the rocks at the eastern and northern points.

Miraculously, Faolan whimpered. He lived still, despite the brutality. The priestess removed the noose, now that he had no way of moving, and gave the last axe to Tallack. I hoped that he would be as swift as the priests and put an end to the old man's suffering, but he didn't. He walked around the stones, exhibiting the axe to his men. "This is not fit for sacrifice, no offence priestess." He said, throwing it to the ground. When he unsheathed his mystical blade, it rang with a shrill note. The faces of his men were rapt. "This is the Sword of Cernonnus. With it, I shall take on all the Novantae wisdom, their strength and their cunning. I will never be deceived again."

Our whole tribe roared. They yelled and cheered and whistled, stamping their feet on the barren soils, and concealing Sorcha's cries with their noise. The drumming and pipers stopped playing. The crowd hushed once again.

Tallack rounded the altar stone and lifted the sword. "I send you to the Underworld, to be trodden on by the God of Gods for all eternity." With one mighty swing, he cut through bone and sinew until Faolan's head rolled from the rock onto the grass. The moment was over. Tallack had his victory and Faolan's life was at an end.

There was a short time, while Tallack basked in the attention and admiration. He jabbed the sword into the thin top soil and dug out his tin pouch to pay the priestess and her companions for their service. All in all, the messy affair was over, and our Chief had regained the respect of his men.

While the warriors and elders returned to the fireside and roasting hog, the priests mounted Faolan's head on a spike at the centre of the circle. I still don't know why the maidens needed to be present. Perhaps they simply enjoyed the spectacle, or ensured that they would receive payment for the ceremony. Either way, they were first to abandon their posts and dive into the food we'd brought along.

The men were beyond jubilant, guzzling ale and chasing the maidens who were more than happy to be caught. I sat close to Tallack, wishing that he would wash off the drying blood from his face. Its smell put me off my food. It wasn't that it made me squeamish, it was that it seemed like he wore it as a badge of honour.

From across the fireside, I could see Kewri fill a bowl with bread and a few slices of meat. I thought he might be helping himself to another serving, but when he picked up one of his bed furs, I knew his heart had melted. For such an adept fighter, he was softer than snow inside. He approached Sorcha, still bound near the stones, and gave her the dish. His fur he wrapped about her shoulders before leaving her in peace with her grief.

Treeve was in fine spirits on the other side of Tallack. He gambled with the crewmen and drank more ale than I thought his slender body could hold. When I knew he could not hear me, I leaned in and whispered to my nephew. "What will you do about Treeve and him hiding Kerensa's body?"

"Nothing." Came his immediate reply. I was dumbfounded. This was the daughter of a clan leader, the favoured woman of his brother. How could he do nothing about her death?

"I don't understand?" I muttered in total confusion.

"You do know that she was feeding the Duro scouts with information about the Novantae?"

My mouth sagged open but no sound came out.

"Treeve and Renowden saw her a couple of times, meeting with a man wearing the Duro's neck tattoo. Ren carried onto the ship, while Treeve hopped out and backtracked along the coastal path to follow her."

"And you believe him?" I managed to squeak, although could not think of another plausible explanation for her murder.

"Why wouldn't I?"

I wanted to say that she had the potential to become the next Ruvane, a situation Treeve would be keen to prevent, but I said nothing. If what Treeve claimed was the truth, Renowden would back up his side of the story when I next saw him. "But then, if she was a known spy in the camp, why did he go to such lengths to smuggle her body out into the marshes? Why not just confront her and carry out her punishment in front of the whole tribe?"

"What, with Blydh at his weakest? He loved the girl. That would have killed him off. It was my decision to keep it all hushed."

Tallack may trust the little kyjyan, but I didn't. That made at least two people he'd killed without remorse and it wouldn't be the last. I made a vow to myself to keep my eyes peeled for his antics. He had cleared the path for his own tribal elevation to the top table. May the gods help anyone else who might get in his way.

My doubt cast a pall over the evening of entertainment. What was meant to be a grand celebration was tinged with too much sadness. The young may be able to shake off the deaths of so many, but us elders are closer to the grave than they. Every life lost is a reminder of our own mortality.

While I thank the gods that they have blessed me with so many summers, I fear for the ease with which these youngsters dismiss the pain suffered by others. Of course, youthful Chieftains like Tallack have to prove their worth as fierce warriors, but compassion shouldn't be reserved for the giants among us, who care not what others think of them.

I slept poorly under my tent that night. The sight of Faolan's dismembered body flashed before my eyes whenever I closed my lids. There was no room for error in this changing world. Now his traumatised daughter would wash Tallack's clothes and build his fires, take his piss pot to the dye hut and weavers, and run his messages about camp. Perhaps that was my mistake. It might have been kinder to let her perish alongside the rest of her family.

On the ride back in the morning, Sorcha and a few of the walking elders were granted permission to ride in the cart. It made the journey less bothersome. Tallack was in a talkative mood, riding the bay mare next to my old pony. For the first time since we'd left camp, his concerns centred on his brother. Mine too, for although Blydh's fever had dropped, he was still beyond waking when last I saw him.

CHAPTER TWENTY-NINE

The kind weather did not last. Before we were half way home to the island, the wind picked up and delivered black clouds filled with rain. My cloak and tunic were saturated. All around me, people grumbled and whined, adding to the general bad temper of the ale addled tribe. Tallack's crewmen and warriors seemed especially keen to get back to the compound.

I deduced that this could be because some of Endelyn's maidens had altered their plans and decided to join our party with a view to settling on the island. There were few enough unwed women among our number, and Tallack was in an amenable mood when they asked permission. It would be nice to have some cheery faces around the place after a winter of ill health and tragedy. Perhaps this spring marked a change in all our fortunes.

For myself, I urged my horse to trot faster since I wanted to see whether Blydh had made it through the night. The reduced numbers of guards at the towers had given rise to the decision to close the northern gate and lift the moving bridge upright to prevent entry. We followed the bend in the tributary around the western edge of the compound near to the charred debris from burning the bodies of the Duros. The rain washed what was left in little black rivulets, staining the water course downstream.

As I glanced to the south, I saw a single row boat sculling in our direction. The joyous grin upon seeing us was a welcome sight. Renowden had brought the Phoenician ship back to the estuary, along with a sizable catch of fish. We dismounted, and I let Kewri sort out our horses.

Tying off the row boat at the jetty, Renowden caught hold of the largest cod fish by its gills and jogged over towards us. "Ho there! It's good to see you." He gushed. "I've been out of my wits with worry. All I could see from further along the bay was the glow from massive pyres. I didn't know whether you were alive or dead." He grappled Tallack's forearm and then Treeve's, but was not sure what to do with me. In the end, he bowed his forehead to mine. "Am so happy that all is well."

"Well as can be expected." I said, patting his back with affection. "All things considered; the gods protected us."

We walked together as a group through the western gates, Ren dragging the tail fin of the fish along the grass.

"I saw Faolan's ship, or what was left of it. I take it they perished on board in the fire?" He said, keen to discover more. I told him the gist of the ambush and how it played out. As Tallack and Treeve walked ahead, it gave me a chance to ask him about Kerensa.

"Oh yes. Hard to believe isn't it? She must have made friends with Brea while we were all in the mining camp during the winter. What was she thinking? Surely everyone knew that Brea could never keep her promises. The moment she decided to spy for her, she sealed her fate." He looked at me as though he was assessing my feelings for the girl. I had formed an attachment to her and I was sad that she was dead, but there was nothing I could do to bring her back.

"I'm sorry to have missed the gathering at the Nine Maidens though." He said. "It sounds like it was quite a celebration."

I nodded slowly in response. It didn't seem fitting to explain how harrowing the entire evening had been.

Ren seemed to pick up on my reluctance to talk about the sacrifice. "Tallack had no other option, Fur Benyn. It had to be that way. Word will spread that he's as formidable as his father, and that should go a long way to protect us from further attacks, especially while Blydh is laid low." We'd almost reached my hut. "How is he by the way?"

"I honestly have no idea. That's where I'm heading now."

"Here." He said, lifting the cod into my arms. "I was just coming to hang this in your eaves, but you may as well take it now."

I blinked repeatedly, processing what he'd just said. "Wait… it was you all along? You have been leaving me food, the ducks and rabbits and such?"

His grin spread across his kind old face. "Whenever I was able to. I thought you could use the help." He shrugged. I almost cried. This hardened sailor of more summers than he could remember, had filled my larder for all this time without so much as a thank you. I am indeed blessed. After I'd expressed my deepest gratitude to him, I stood in the doorway of my hut, hoping that some of my good fortunes had spread to my nephew.

My relief was profound when I entered to find him awake and sitting up in his bunk. I wanted to throw my arms about him and squeeze the air from his lungs, but he batted me away. I suppose that was understandable. His head must have given him much pain and it looked most tender.

Blydh spoke little and smiled even less, as Tallack and I tried to update him on all that'd happened since his collapse. The list of developments was long and complex. The only thing that seem to cheer him was the thought of Paega trapped in a cage until he could decide what to do with him.

"Derwa tried to rescue him and escape with her rat-faced husband, so I banished her for all time to live with the Ordoviches." Tallack regaled, sitting on the end of the bunk.

"Good riddance too." Cryda smirked. "Little kyjyan was forever stealing my trinkets and jewels from my hut. Maybe now I can hang on to my things long enough to wear them"

"Do you know, I've had some of my things go missing too. All this time I assumed that it was Brea." Thinking about it, mentioning her name was not the wisest move.

Blydh began snorting, his nose puckered and his lip curled. The more Cryda tried to shush him and settle him down, the more agitated he became. He threw off the furs and tried to swing his legs to the floor. "Get my axe." He yelled to Tallack. "That kyjyan must die. Do you hear me?" His voice rose to a shrill pitch. "Brea must die!"

***

If you enjoyed this novel, and have a moment spare to express your opinion, **a review on any of the distribution sites would be greatly appreciated**.

For more information on the rest of the series, please go to: www.carantocpublishing.com

The next book in the series is entitled **Pagan Rage**

JOIN MY READERS' GROUP AND RECEIVE THE EXCLUSIVE EBOOK NOVELLA,

PAGAN FURY

Three unsuitable lovers.
Two valuable metals.
One critical mission.

The Dumnonii have no copper for their forges. Without a new supply, there will be no more bronze weapons for the inevitable battle ahead.

Joint Chieftain, Tallack, must cross the western ocean to negotiate an alliance with the obstinate Dathi of the Ivernii and complete an impossible task to gain his trust.

Can he succeed where once his father failed?

Join the young warrior and his crew in a lust fuelled, intense quest on the shores of Iwerdon and find out for yourself.

This story takes place between book one, Pagan Death, and book two, Pagan Curse. Please be aware that there will be spoilers that might ruin the enjoyment if they are read out of order.

Sign up here:

www.carantocpublishing.com

About the Author

Sam Taw is the pen name for fiction author Sam Nash. Sam is committed to delivering novels in two distinct genres, historical thrillers and a unique blend of science fiction and international espionage stories.

She lives in a small market town in the south of Leicestershire, in the UK but dreams of one day owning a woodland on the Cornish coast.

For information regarding the work of Sam Taw, please visit:

www.carantocpublishing.com

For information regarding the work of Sam Nash, please visit:

www.samnash.org

Printed in Great Britain
by Amazon

52779441R00180